CONSTABLE & TOOP

AMULET BOOKS
NEW YORK

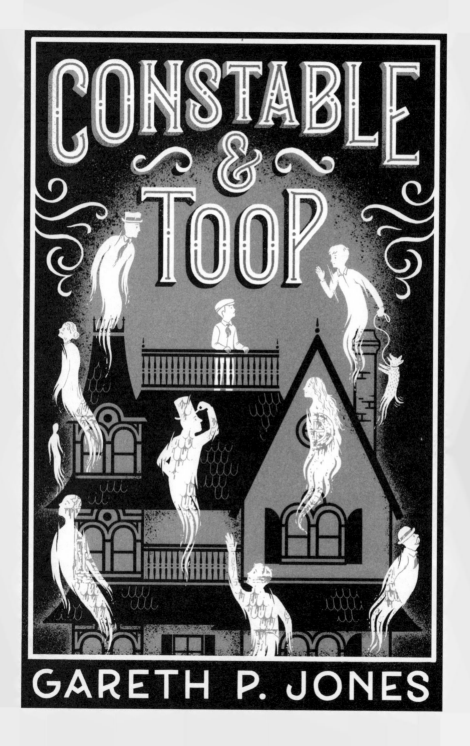

PUBLISHER'S NOTE: This is a work of fiction. Names, characters, places, and incidents are either the product of the author's imagination or are used fictitiously, and any resemblance to actual persons, living or dead, business establishments, events, or locales is entirely coincidental.

Library of Congress Cataloging-in-Publication Data

Jones, Gareth (Gareth P.)
Constable & Toop / by Gareth P. Jones.
pages cm
Originally published in London by Hot Key Books, 2012.
Summary: In Victorian London, an undertaker's son who can see ghosts and is haunted by their constant demands for attention must decide whether to help when a horrible disease imprisons ghosts in empty houses in the world of the living.
ISBN 978-1-4197-0782-7 (alk. paper)
[1. Ghosts—Fiction. 2. Future life—Fiction. 3. London (England)—History—
19th century—Fiction. 4. Great Britain—History—Victoria, 1837–1901—Fiction.]
I. Title. II. Title: Constable and Toop.
PZ7.J712Co 2013
[Fic]—dc23
2012047785

Text copyright © 2013 Gareth P. Jones
Illustrations copyright © 2013 Jim Tierney
Book design by Maria T. Middleton

First published in Great Britain by Hot Key Books in 2012.

Printed and bound in U.S.A.
10 9 8 7 6 5 4 3 2 1

Amulet Books are available at special discounts when purchased in quantity for premiums and promotions as well as fundraising or educational use. Special editions can also be created to specification. For details, contact specialsales@abramsbooks.com or the address below.

ABRAMS
THE ART OF BOOKS SINCE 1949
115 West 18th Street
New York, NY 10011
www.amuletbooks.com

PRAISE FOR

CONSTABLE & TOOP

A GHOST STORY EXTRAORDINAIRE

"An extraordinarily witty story that accurately depicts the lives of the dead and compellingly describes the death of the living." —**The Ghost of Oscar Wilde**

"As with its London setting, this book contains all that life can afford and all that death will allow. I thoroughly recommend it to all readers, the living and the dead alike." —**The Ghost of Dr. Johnson**

"There were many moments during my reading of Mr. Jones's thrilling tale that I undoubtedly would have held my breath with excitement, had there been any breath in my lungs to hold." —**The Ghost of Mary Shelley**

"I wish I had written this story." —**The Ghost of Charles Dickens**

"An intriguingly constructed story with an inventive young hero and an intricate mystery that had me gripped right up to the final page."
—The Ghost of Sir Arthur Conan Doyle

"I very much enjoyed the melancholy and tragedy contained within these pages. The humor was less to my taste." **—The Ghost of Emily Brontë**

"Most ghost stories are written for the living. Here, finally, a story has been penned that will, in equal measure, appeal to the dead."
—The Ghost of Henry James

"A singular literary joy from a most fanciful writer with a vivid imagination." **—The Ghost of Jane Austen**

"Unputdownable." **—The Ghost of Samuel Pepys**

"*Constable & Toop* is a book full of life and crammed with death. All in all, a splendidly macabre and amusing tale."
—The Ghost of Edgar Allan Poe

FOR MADI & LAUREN BLISS

PROLOGUE

THE BIRTH OF A GHOST

IN HER LAST FEW MOMENTS OF LIFE, AS THE BLOOD gushed from the knife wound in her neck, Emily Wilkins found her thoughts drifting to her mother's death. Mrs. Wilkins had lain on her deathbed for weeks without uttering a word until finally, one day, she sat up, fixed her eyes upon Emily, and spoke.

"You're a good girl, ain't you, Em?"

"I try to be, Mum," she replied.

"You deserve more than I've ever been able to get for you."

"I've never wanted for anything," said Emily.

Her mother shook her head. "You never had no schooling, but you're a bright girl. I only wish I had done better by you."

"I just want you to get well," Emily pleaded.

"There's no chance of that now, my love," said her mother. "I can hear them knocking for me."

"Who?" Emily looked up. "There's no one knocking."

Mrs. Wilkins smiled weakly. "Soon I'll have no choice but to answer. But promise me this, Em. You need to make the most of this life, because who knows what lies on the other side of that door."

"What door, Mum?"

Her mother pointed at the blank wall beside her bed. Her smile was so full of sadness and regret that it drew yet more tears from Emily's eyes. She wiped her face with the cloth she was using to mop her mother's forehead.

Her mother coughed—a dry, throaty cough that sent a splatter of bloody phlegm into the palm of her hand— before she fell back and died, leaving Emily alone and orphaned.

At the time, Emily had childishly believed that this final cough was her mother's body ejecting all its blood before dying.

She realized how very wrong she had been as the red liquid now gushed from her own throat. The human body contained much more than a handful of dusky blood. The murdering hands that were taking Emily's life were covered in it.

The hands had appeared out of nowhere.

The right had closed around her throat. The left, around her mouth. Emily tasted the salty sweat of her attacker as she struggled and kicked, but the hands were strong, and this clearly wasn't the first time they had been put to such use.

The blade slid across her neck so smoothly, she barely felt it cut the skin. The blood gushed out like water breaking through a dam until the murderer's right hand closed around the wound, stopping the flow.

"Can't 'ave you dyin' in the street like a dog, can we, girl?" snarled a gravelly voice. "That would never do."

The hands dragged her up the dark, cobbled alleyway. She could hear knocking.

"Don't you heed that, girl," said the gruff voice. "We ain't far now. Hang on."

1

LAPSEWOOD'S PAPERWORK

LAPSEWOOD DIPPED HIS PEN INTO THE POT OF BLACK ink, licked his fingers, and pulled a piece of paper from the pile on his desk. In the top right-hand corner he wrote the date: 16 January 1884. His in-box was stacked higher than ever, and today's Dispatch documents had not been delivered yet. It concerned him greatly.

He didn't mind the work. Quite the contrary. In life, Lapsewood had lived to work. In death, he was no different. Work was orderly. It was structured. It was safe. It meant arriving early, sitting down at his desk, and working his way through the paperwork to be completed by the end of the day.

Work was satisfying.

Except, recently, there had been an unsettling amount of paperwork still left in the in-box when the final bell tolled.

He tried staying late to get on top of it, but if old Mr. Turnbull, the night watchman, found him at his desk, he would take the opportunity to recount the tale of his bloody Crimean death, while idly scratching the gaping bayonet wound through his heart.

Lapsewood tried working on Sundays, but still the paperwork grew and grew. Perhaps he was being too conscientious about his processing, taking too long over each document, but he couldn't bear the thought of speeding up at the expense of doing a good job. The Bureau was all that stood between an orderly afterlife and utter chaos, and Lapsewood's Dispatch documents were a vital cog in that great machine.

The office door opened. "Morning, Lapsewood," said Grunt.

"Morning," Lapsewood responded. He didn't look up. Grunt was new. He had been hanged at Newgate for the murder of his wife and wore a silk scarf around his neck to hide the red marks from the rope. But the soft skin around his throat had been broken during the hanging, meaning that now, with no blood left in his veins, gray fluid seeped out, collecting at the top of the scarf. Every so often Grunt would wipe it away with a spotted kerchief from his waistcoat pocket. Lapsewood found this habit utterly unacceptable. In his less charitable moments he secretly wished that Grunt had been guilty of his crime, thus making him ineligible for Official Ghost Status and unable to work at the Bureau.

Grunt, however, was innocent. He had been hanged for another man's crime.

"Penhaligan wants to see you," said Grunt.

Lapsewood felt one of his headaches coming on. This was not good news. Not good news at all. It had to be the paper-work. He knew what would happen. He would be called into Colonel Penhaligan's office, given a dressing down, then escorted to the Vault, where he would reside until he was tried and convicted of professional incompetence.

"Did he say what it was about?" he asked.

"Nah," said Grunt. "He just told me to tell you to come up and see him urgently."

"'Urgently'? He used the word *urgently*?"

"I think so. Might've been *immediately*. Or just *now*. It was something like that, anyway."

"Grunt, this is important. Exactly what did he say?"

"He didn't *say* anything," replied Grunt. "He more bellowed . . ." Grunt's smile suggested that this was supposed to be funny.

"'Bellowed'?" exclaimed Lapsewood.

"I'd say it was a bellow, yes. He bellowed, '*DAMN IT. DAMN IT. DAMN IT. GRUNT, GET LAPSEWOOD UP HERE IMMEDI-ATELY.*'" The ghost looked pleased with himself for remembering this. "Yes, I think that was it."

"Did he sound angry?"

"I ain't never heard a bellow that didn't sound angry. It's

the nature of a bellow, isn't it? Shouting, now, that's different. My wife used to shout at me all the time, but that was on account of the deafness I got in one ear. Funny thing—since being dead, I can hear perfectly well in both. It's as though the hangman's rope dislodged the wax when it snapped my neck." He chuckled.

Lapsewood had no interest in Grunt's post-death hearing improvements. His mind was as busy as a beehive, bustling with questions, concerns, theories, and fears.

Colonel Penhaligan was angry with him. It had to be the paperwork, but what did he expect Lapsewood to do? He was working as fast as he could. The Bureau needed to employ more clerks to help clear the backlog. That's what he would say. He would demand help. He refused to be forced to do a second-rate job for the sake of speed. Hadn't it been Colonel Penhaligan himself who had praised Lapsewood's exemplary work ethic and attention to detail last Christmas? Admittedly, the colonel had consumed a substantial quantity of spirit punch that night, so who knew whether he had really meant what he said?

"Do you think I have time to walk?" asked Lapsewood.

"You'd better not," said Grunt. "In my experience, *immediately* means as close to now as possible. Best use the Paternoster Pipe. I would if I were you."

Lapsewood glanced with dread at the small tube in the wall that led to the Paternoster Pipe Network. While all spirits had the ability to turn into the gray smokelike substance known as Ether Dust, Lapsewood found the whole business thoroughly dehumanizing. To quite literally disappear into a puff of smoke was another blatant reminder of his own deadness. He preferred to walk one step at a time like a man rather than whoosh about like burned tobacco on a breezy day.

However, on this occasion he had no choice. He had wasted enough time already. If he stood any chance of persuading Colonel Penhaligan not to dispatch him, he needed to move quickly.

Lapsewood shook Grunt's hand solemnly. It was damp. "Mr. Grunt, it's been a pleasure working with you," he lied.

Grunt laughed. "You look like I did when I stepped up onto those gallows."

"That's precisely how I feel."

More laughter. "Didn't no one tell you? You can only die once, Lapsewood."

2

THE BODY IN THE COFFIN

SAM TOOP WAS AWAKENED BY A HAMMERING ON THE door and a voice crying out, "Let me in! Charlie, I know you're there. Let me in!"

Charlie? he thought, half asleep. Charles was his father's name, but he had never heard anyone call him Charlie.

Rain pelted against the window. Wind rattled the frame.

"For God's sake, let me in, Charlie . . ."

Sam slipped out of bed and went to the window. Bare feet on the cold floorboards. It was the middle of the night and blowing a terrible storm outside. Who would be out in such weather? Customers never came at night. The business of funerals rarely called for urgency. The funerals of

Constable & Toop were arranged as they were conducted: gracefully and calmly.

"Charlie!" yelled the voice.

Definitely not a customer. Customers only ever spoke in hushed, respectful tones. It was as though they feared waking the corpses that were occasionally kept in the coffins in the back room.

The shadowy figure Sam saw outside banged on the door. It occurred to Sam that maybe he was one of *Them*. But, no, they didn't bang on doors. Why would they, when they could easily pass through them? Sam placed his hand over his right eye to be sure. Yes, he could still see the figure.

Lightning snaked across the black sky, illuminating the man's face. His eyes looked wild and desperate. Rain dripped off his crooked, broken nose. The realization that this man was alive was of little comfort. Sam feared the living far more than the dead. Ghosts were powerless to hurt him. Their threats were empty. It was the living who could inflict pain.

A floorboard creaked, and a light appeared at the base of his door. His father was up and crossing the landing, heading down the stairs and through the shop front. Sam watched the light of his lamp through the slits in the floorboards.

He could not hear what was said, but he heard the door open and the man step inside, accompanied by a gust of wind that rushed through the building. A feeling in the pit of Sam's stomach kept him rooted to the spot. From the back room he soon heard the sound of banging. Hammer on nail. A familiar enough sound, except never before in the middle of the night. He waited until his father's footsteps came back up the stairs and had passed his room before he went back to his bed, curling up and gripping his toes to warm them.

He must have eventually fallen asleep, because when he opened his eyes, the sky was light blue and there were voices downstairs. He could hear his father saying, "I'm afraid I haven't seen a thing. It's just me and my boy here."

"Then I'd like to speak to the boy, too," said a man's voice.

"Sam!" shouted Mr. Toop. "Please come down."

Sam climbed out of bed, dressed quickly, and went downstairs. A man clad in black with gray pockmarked skin stood in the doorway. His suit had the look of clothing that had been smart when first put on but was now bedraggled and damp.

"Sam, this gentleman is the law," said Mr. Toop.

"Savage," said the man. "Detective Inspector Savage. Some of your neighbors said they heard a lot of hollering here last night. Did you hear anything, young man?"

"I fell asleep early last night and woke up just now," said Sam. "I don't know of anything in between."

Sam neither knew where the lie came from nor how it was that it sprang so readily to his lips, but he sensed his father's relief upon hearing it.

"May I ask who you're looking for?" asked Sam's father.

"A villain by the name of Jack Toop. I noticed the name on your shop sign. There's a coincidence, I thought. You wouldn't have a relation by the name of Jack, would you, Mr. Toop?"

"None that I know of," he replied. "But Toop is not such an uncommon surname."

"Nor such a common one neither. You have no brother nor uncle by that name?"

"I was born an only child and orphaned as an infant, sir," said Sam's father.

"Then you've done well for yourself, Mr. Toop. A shop with your name on it."

"I have been fortunate."

"Tell me about this fortune," said Inspector Savage.

"When I was a lad, a carpenter took me under his wing and taught me the ways of his noble trade. Then, as an adult, I had the great honor of making the acquaintance of the man who would become my business partner: Mr. Constable. A finer and more upstanding gentleman you will never meet. He made me a partner and gave me and my boy a roof above our heads. He has been as good as a second father to Sam."

Inspector Savage glanced around the undertaking shop at the solemn paintings that hung on the wall, the items of funeral paraphernalia on display in the glass cabinet, and the statues of angels carefully arranged on the shelves. These were decorations placed to set the right tone in the shop, while subtly suggesting items that could be purchased and incorporated into each funeral. To an outsider they were, no doubt, gloomy and morbid. To Sam they had the familiarity of any ordinary domestic ornaments.

"This Mr. Constable lives here, too?" asked Inspector Savage.

"He has his own house not far from here," replied Mr. Toop.

"You won't mind if I take a look around," said the inspector. It was more statement than question.

"I won't stand in the way of the law," said Mr. Toop.

"You're a wise man. Your living quarters are up there?" Inspector Savage pointed to the staircase at one side of the shop. Mr. Toop nodded, and the inspector climbed the stairs up to the landing. Sam and his father listened to his heavy footsteps on the floorboards above.

"Father . . ." Sam began.

Mr. Toop raised a finger to his lips, silencing Sam.

When Inspector Savage came back, he pointed at the door that led to the back room. "What's through there?"

"That's my workshop," said Mr. Toop. "We keep the bodies there sometimes."

"And have you a stiff in there now?"

"One. He's to be buried this afternoon."

Without invitation, Inspector Savage opened the door and entered. Sam and his father followed. Sam glanced at his father and saw the slight discoloration of fear in his eyes. There had been no body in the back room yesterday, and there was no burial planned for this afternoon—and yet, as they entered the room, there was indeed a coffin resting on the table, its lid nailed down.

"Nice carpentry," said Inspector Savage. "You make this yourself, then?"

"Yes. My partner deals with most other aspects of the business."

"Other aspects?"

"The money, the mourners, and what have you. We always say Mr. Constable is better with the living, whereas my strength is the dead." Mr. Toop smiled at his usual joke.

Inspector Savage made no effort to return the smile. He turned to Sam. "Pretty gloomy place for a lad to grow up."

"I've never known any different," said Sam.

Inspector Savage shrugged, then gestured to the coffin. "Who's in there, then?"

"Mr. Grant," said Sam's father.

Sam lowered his gaze. Mr. Grant had been buried two days ago.

"What kind of man was he?" asked Inspector Savage.

"He was the butcher."

That, at least, was true. Sam felt Savage's eyes upon him.

"Open it up," ordered the inspector.

Sam looked at his father.

"Now, really," argued Mr. Toop. "I know you have a job to do, but so do we. When people place their dearly departed in our care, they do so knowing that they are in good, capable hands."

"I just want to look at him."

"This man you're looking for," said Mr. Toop. "Tell me, what does he look like?"

"Like a rogue," said Inspector Savage sharply.

"Have you no more detailed a description?"

"I've never seen him up close," he admitted. "All I have is the name."

"And what crime is he charged with, this other Toop?"

"The worst there is. He murdered a copper, a good man by the name of Heale. Now, bid your son get a hammer and open it up."

Mr. Toop nodded his consent. Sam took a hammer from the shelf and began pulling out the nails one by one.

"Be careful now, son," said Mr. Toop. "Try not to damage the wood."

When the last nail was out, Sam stood back, and his father took the hammer from his hand.

Inspector Savage lifted the lid and leaned it against the table. Lying in the coffin was the man Sam had seen from his window last night. He recognized his broken nose, his weather-worn skin, and his lank hair, thinning in places and revealing an uneven skull. He was dressed in one of the cheap suits they kept for the deceased who had nothing smart enough to be buried in. The man, whoever he was, lay as still as a corpse, his eyes shut. Unmoving.

"Ugly-looking fella," said the inspector, eyeing him carefully.

"Now, please," said Mr. Toop. "I will not stand by and have you insult the dead."

Inspector Savage picked up one of the man's hands. "He feels cold enough to be dead. Mind you, this criminal we're looking for is also a cold man." He turned to Sam. "Boy, fetch me some pepper. Let us see how dead this man is."

Sam looked at his father uncertainly.

"Do as you're told now," said Mr. Toop calmly.

Sam went upstairs to the pantry and picked up a small tin of ground peppercorns. He returned with the pepper and handed the tin to Inspector Savage, who took a handful and sprinkled it liberally over the man's face.

"Please, Detective Inspector," said Mr. Toop. "Not satisfied with insulting this poor dead man, you are now seasoning him."

Sam noticed how tightly his father clutched the hammer. Was he contemplating attacking Savage? Or perhaps it was the man in the coffin who would receive the blow.

Inspector Savage stared at the body. There was no movement. Nothing. He grunted and said, "My condolences to this butcher's family." He turned around and marched out of the room and back through the shop to the door.

"At Constable and Toop we believe in the dignity of death," said Mr. Toop, returning the hammer to its place on the shelf and following the inspector out.

"And I believe in the sanctity of life, Mr. Toop," replied Inspector Savage, without turning. "A good day to you." The shop bell rang as he left.

Sam looked back at the man in the coffin. The man opened his eyes, making Sam jump.

"He gone?" the man asked in a low, gruff voice.

Silenced by fear, Sam nodded.

"Thank God for that," said the man. "I . . . ah . . . ah . . . ah . . ."

The sneeze that rang out was loud enough to wake the dead themselves, and Sam only hoped that Inspector Savage was far enough away not to hear it.

3
THE BEAUTY OF ALICE BIGGINS

FIRST THING IN THE MORNING WAS THE WORST TIME to be using the Paternoster Pipe Network. The pipes were clogged with the Ether Dust of clerks, scribes, dogsbodies, secretaries, and all the other working spirits running late for work or heading off to their morning appointments.

Approaching the twenty-fifth floor where Colonel Penhaligan's office was situated, Lapsewood experienced a dread similar to that he used to feel when his old schoolmaster, Mr. Thornton, summoned him to his office. Mr. Thornton had been a cruel and strict disciplinarian who deployed a heavy wooden ruler on the backsides of his pupils, hitting them in time with each remonstrating syllable he uttered.

"You . . ." *Thwack.* "Shall . . ." *Thwack.* "Learn . . ." *Thwack.* "Your Latin verbs." *Thwack, thwack-thwack, thwack.*

Having spent his formative years in abject fear of this ogre of a man, Lapsewood was pleased when Mr. Thornton's Dispatch document had arrived on his desk. Lapsewood had taken his time over that document, savoring the pleasure and smiling to learn Mr. Thornton's Christian name. If only he had known at the time that the man he feared above any other was called Hilary.

Lapsewood's eyes rematerialized first, so he could maximize the time he spent gazing at the only good thing about being summoned to his superior's office: Colonel Penhaligan's secretary and the most beautiful girl he had ever seen.

Alice Biggins.

"Hello there," she said, smiling.

Short, plump, with perfect porcelain skin and auburn hair that fell in ringlets, Alice was everything Lapsewood looked for in a girl and everything he had failed to find in life. He had never had the courage to ask what she had died of, but whatever it was didn't show from the outside. Quite the opposite. Whenever they were in the same room, Lapsewood found himself unable to tear his eyes from her. As a consequence, he could barely utter a word in her presence.

"You'll have to wait," she said. "There's someone already in with him."

Lapsewood tried to think of something to say, something

clever, something witty, something wry. Anything. Nothing came to mind.

"He's in a terrible mood," continued Alice, oblivious as usual to the inner turmoil endured by Lapsewood as a consequence of being in her company. "He's already had two clerks and the office boy carted off to the Vault, and it's not even nine o'clock. They all come out with faces like thunder, but I tell them it's not so bad. At least they won't have to hang around this miserable place anymore. Honestly, if I'd known I was going to end up working for that old sinner, I'd have thought twice about accepting a job here at all."

"You don't mean that," said Lapsewood, with more desperation in his voice than he had intended.

Alice pushed her hair away from her face and looked at him. For a moment he panicked that he had given himself away. If there was anything more unbearable than the agony of Alice not knowing how he felt, it was the dread of her finding out. Lapsewood had never been able to cope with rejection. Better, he thought, to grasp moments like this, when he could gaze upon Alice's perfect face, than attempt to reveal his true feelings and risk humiliation.

Besides, what could he possibly hope for, anyway? The dead didn't fall in love. The dead didn't marry. The dead simply trudged on, endlessly, hopelessly, inevitably, until the day they heard the Knocking and stepped through the Unseen Door.

It was so unfair. Alice deserved more. She should have had a real life in a real house with a garden and flowers. The best Lapsewood could offer her was a squalid, windowless room down the Endless Corridor, where all employees of the Bureau spent their sleepless nights, a room, no doubt, identical to her own.

"There's a Prowler in there right now," she said, a twinge of excitement in her voice. "A new one . . . French fella. I heard he worked as a detective before he came here."

"A detective?"

The door to Penhaligan's office opened, and a tall, slim man stepped out, carrying himself with easy elegance. He was immaculately dressed, with piercing blue eyes, angular cheekbones, and a thin mustache adorning his upper lip.

"*A* is the incorrect article," the man said in a smooth French accent. "You should use the definite article, *the,* as in Monsieur Eugène François Vidocq, *the* great detective."

"So you worked for the police?" said Lapsewood.

"The police are mindless brutes," replied the Frenchman. "A detective is a gentleman of superior intellect who can detect that which goes unnoticed by the common man."

Lapsewood didn't like the way Vidocq looked at him when he said *common*. He was even less keen on the way Alice gazed at Monsieur Vidocq, as though she were a pat of butter and he a piece of hot toast.

"Ah, Mademoiselle Biggins, is it possible you have grown even more beautiful since I last saw you?"

"Don't be daft. That was only five minutes ago."

"And yet, I think your beauty has increased even more in that small amount of time."

Alice giggled.

"But *beautiful* doesn't quite say it . . ." continued the Frenchman. "*Radiant*, perhaps. *Exquisite . . . desirable*. How *très difficile* it is to find the word for such beauty in this barbaric language of yours."

"Oh, Mr. Vidocq, really."

"You may call me Eugène."

With no blood in her body, blushing was a physical impossibility, but Alice came as close to it as any ghost could. Lapsewood felt miserable.

"LAPSEWOOD!" bellowed Penhaligan. "Are you out there?"

He would have done anything to avoid leaving Alice alone with the charming Frenchman, but he could no more avoid going through that door than any man can prevent the wheels of fate from turning.

"Good luck, *mon ami*," said Monsieur Vidocq, grabbing Lapsewood's hand and firmly shaking it. "I very much hope you are not . . . *pour la Voûte*."

Lapsewood didn't like Prowlers. They thought they were so superior because they got to go on missions to the physical world, walking among the living, haunting and scaring in the name of the Bureau. Of course, he understood that they were necessary, just as Enforcers were needed to bring Rogue ghosts into line. But where would any of them be without the paperwork, supplied, completed, and diligently duplicated, by the clerks?

"LAPSEWOOD, GET IN HERE NOW, OR I'LL HAVE

YOU WHISKED TO THE VAULT SO FAST, YOUR FEET WON'T TOUCH THE GROUND," bellowed Penhaligan.

A last glance at Alice's pretty face, and Lapsewood stepped inside the office.

4
UNCLE JACK

SAM HAD HATED HIS TIME AT SCHOOL, WHERE THE other boys relished taunting him every day. They would push him into walls to see whether he would pass through, failing to understand that being able to see ghosts was not the same as being one.

"You must learn to ignore Them," his father had said.

"How can I ignore them when they push me into walls?" Sam had responded.

"I mean the spirits, son. You must learn to look through Them; try not to let others know you can see Them."

Easy for him to say. He wasn't plagued by this disease. Once, Sam had even tried wearing a patch over his right eye to hide the visions, but that drew yet more ridicule from the other children. It was a relief when, at age thirteen, he had been able to stop going to school altogether. It was easier to avoid the existence of the living than ignore the presence of the dead.

Sam sprinkled a pinch more pepper into the soup and gave it another stir. He lifted the ladle and tasted it. It definitely still needed something.

"Your son cooks like a woman, Charlie," said Jack. "All tastin' and no dishin'. Come on now, enough of your delayin', boy. This ain't no royal banquet. Give your Uncle Jack some of that."

"It's not ready yet," said Sam.

"It's ready enough for me. I don't like my cooking too fussy, and I don't trust all them little jars you keep going to. I like to know what's in my food. It's too easy to drop in something that wouldn't agree with me, something along the arsenic line."

"Strangely, we don't keep arsenic in the kitchen," replied Sam. He slammed a bowl down in front of his uncle and dished a spoonful of soup into it, carelessly splashing it onto the table.

"Mind what you're doing now, lad," said Jack. "There's no point wastin' it, is there?"

Sam grabbed a cloth and sullenly wiped up the spilled liquid.

Uncle Jack tasted a spoonful. "Tastes like warm pond water," he said, gulping it down. "Ain't you got no meat?"

"The butcher shop has been shut since Mr. Grant died," said Sam.

Uncle Jack shrugged. "He looks like 'is mother, Charlie," he said. "Where is she? Not upped and left you, I hope."

Mr. Toop turned to Sam. "Sam, you can go. Your Uncle Jack will be leaving after his soup."

"Stay where you are," ordered Jack, a little fire burning in his eyes. "I only asked after Liza."

"My mother's dead," said Sam.

"That's a pity. She was a sweet girl," said Jack. "What took 'er?"

"Liza died of a fever," said Mr. Toop. "Sam was still an infant."

"I'm sorry to hear that," said Jack.

"I think you should leave, Jack," said Mr. Toop.

"Charlie," moaned Jack. "We're still blood, ain't we? You're all I've got."

"Blood is one thing you never seem short of," snapped Mr. Toop.

"You don't want to go believin' everything they say. These official types, 'alf of them are more corrupt than the criminals they're after." Uncle Jack shoveled another spoonful of soup into his mouth.

"Murdering a policeman is what he said," said Sam's father. "I'd be relieved to hear you say you played no part in that, Jack."

Jack smiled. "Oh, it's so black-and-white for you, ain't it? Livin' up here in the hills, away from the smoke. With

26

your clerks and your gentry takin' the train into London by day, then back 'ere before the city comes to life. The true London is lit by gas, not by sunlight. Down there, nothing's black nor white. It's all just gray."

"Murder's murder," said Mr. Toop.

"Some people don't deserve life," said Jack, spitting soup across the table.

"I don't want my son subjected to any more of this. You'll leave now if you know what's good for you."

Sam had never heard his father speak so sternly.

"Please, Charlie," whined Jack. "They'll string me up if they catch me. You know they will. So I've done wrong. I admit it. But I 'ad my reasons. And someone's done me over. I know they 'ave."

"I'm glad to hear you had a good reason to take another man's life," said Mr. Toop angrily.

"Things 'ave changed since we were lads," said Jack.

"You'll speak no more of that," interrupted Mr. Toop.

"No, I suppose you've forgotten, ain't you?" replied his brother. "You listening to this?" said Jack, addressing Sam. "Your father would throw his own flesh and blood to the wolves. His own flesh and blood."

Sam said nothing.

"If they found you here, we'd all hang for harboring a criminal," said Mr. Toop.

"As it is, you'd rather it was just me that felt the squeeze of the 'angman's rope, wouldn't you?" replied his brother.

"Two nights, Jack," conceded Mr. Toop.

"A week. It'll give time for the heat to die down," said Jack. "After all, as I see it, you still owe me."

Mr. Toop glowered at his brother. "I'll have to ask Mr. Constable, and you won't take one step outside. You don't even come downstairs. You're as silent as a mouse; then you leave, and you never come back. After that, we're no longer brothers. And you'll leave the boy alone, as well."

The shop bell rang, and Jack shot up from his seat like a startled rabbit.

"That will be Mr. Constable now," said Mr. Toop. "Stay here."

"You were working for 'im when I last saw you," said Jack. "How did you wheedle your way into 'is business, then?"

"He made me partner."

"He'll turn me in if he knows about me."

"No, he won't."

"It'll be in 'is interest not to." Jack spoke in a threatening whisper.

Sam's father left the room, leaving Sam alone with his uncle.

"Any more of that soup, boy?" Jack held his bowl up.

"I thought you didn't like it."

"Sensitive soul, ain't you? Funny you should act so much like a woman when you've been brought up entirely by men."

As Sam took the bowl, he saw the ghost of a young woman in a nightgown step through the wall and fall to her knees, sobbing loudly. "Oh, I've found you. Please, you must help me. How could he do it? How could he? With my own sister, too? He said he'd be mine forever, and now he's with her," she wailed.

Sam glanced at his uncle. He had no desire to reveal his gift to him. He tried to ignore the ghost, but she continued to go on. "They say you're a Talker. You can hear and see us. They say you'll help us. Please help me. I must tell my Tom not to marry her."

Sam disliked the maudlers and the mopers most of all, always coming to him, begging for help. At least this one was pretty. A few years older than Sam—twenty, perhaps—but even in death he could see she had been a beauty.

He shifted his eyes to indicate that he would speak with her outside, then poured a ladleful of soup into the bowl and placed it back in front of his uncle.

"You shouldn't listen to your old man," said Uncle Jack. "We used to be as thick as thieves, me and 'im. I don't know what he's said about me, but every story has two sides. Most have more."

"He's never mentioned you," replied Sam honestly.

Jack swallowed a mouthful of soup. "This tastes better now, lad. You'll make someone a good wife someday." He laughed. "Oh, there you go again with your sulky looks. It was a joke."

The lady in the nightdress sniffed.

"And pay no attention to her, neither," added Jack in a hushed voice. "I'll bet 'er chap's better off with the sister than with that moaning old trout."

5

PENHALIGAN'S PROBLEM

COLONEL PENHALIGAN WAS SITTING, AS USUAL, BE-
hind his desk. For a man who took every opportunity available to talk about how he had died fighting for his country,
he had always been strangely silent about his lack of legs. He
wore a plush red army jacket with shiny gold buttons and
ornate epaulets on his broad shoulders. Thick black side-
burns framed his permanently frowning face.

On the wall behind his desk was a large painting of him,
wearing exactly the same clothes while sitting on a horse,
looking every bit as stern and serious as he looked now as
Lapsewood entered the room.

"Take a seat," he barked.

Lapsewood sat down in front of the huge desk. Like everything in the Bureau, it had been finished to look as real as a fine oak desk from the physical world. The only difference was that Colonel Penhaligan was able to lean his elbows on it without their passing straight through.

"How long have you been with us, Lapsewood?"

"At the Bureau? Twenty years this December, sir. I started as a clerk in the Central Records Library, then was transferred to the Dispatch Department ten years ago."

"So you were ghost-born in 1864," said Colonel Penhaligan. He jotted down the date, then said, "1792."

"I'm sorry?" Lapsewood felt unsure how to respond to this.

"That's my date. I'll be celebrating my centenary in a few years' time. Started as a Prowler, then worked my way up to the head of the department. Few ghosts make it that long, and do you know why that is?"

"No, sir."

"They date themselves. They lose touch. They become irrelevant. As ghosts, we don't age, but as time goes on, many find it difficult to deal with the changing nature of the world. Take the steam train."

"I'm sorry, sir. I'm not following. You want me to take a steam train?"

"No, of course I don't want you to take a steam train. You think I've asked you to come up to my office in order to ask you to take a steam train? What's wrong with you, man? I'm talking about myself. The idea of being propelled across the country on a huge metal beast on tracks at unnatural speeds would have filled me with wonder and delight as a child, like being told that I could fly like a bird through the sky. It would have been a fancy. But now? I have managed to adjust to the idea. With new technologies come new ways for the living to die, and, here in the Dispatch Department, we need to adapt to these changes.

"It's not just keeping our records up to date, you know. The world is full of Rogue ghosts who seem to think they don't need Polter-licenses to mess about with things in the physical world or Opacity Permission forms to be seen. It's a real problem, Lapsewood."

"I thought Enforcement dealt with the Rogues," said Lapsewood.

"Hardknuckle's bunch of half-baked Enforcers can no more deal with the Rogue problem than a horse can knit."

"No, sir," replied Lapsewood, trying to keep up.

"It's my Prowlers who gather the intelligence that allows us to keep on top of the problem. Like that man Vidocq. Excellent Prowler. Shame about his being, you know . . ." Colonel Penhaligan lowered his voice and said, "French. But I haven't asked you here to talk about him. We're here to look at the options ahead of you."

"Options, sir?"

Colonel Penhaligan sighed, clearly annoyed at having to spell it out. "You're behind in your paperwork, Lapsewood. Woefully behind."

"I know, but—"

"Save it," said the colonel, raising a hand. "I'm afraid I've heard it all before. Tell me, Lapsewood, how did you die?"

"I don't know, sir. I fell ill and never recovered."

"Age?"

"Thirty-two, sir."

"I see. And you never heard the Knocking?"

"Of course not," said Lapsewood, shocked to be asked such a thing. "Only Rogue ghosts hear the Knocking and ignore it."

"So you have unfinished business?"

"Yes, but I don't know what."

"Perhaps you should consider applying for a research license, venture to the physical world, and finish that business of yours."

Lapsewood's head was spinning. "But, sir, I don't want to. I like my job here at the Bureau. I like my work."

"And yet you're getting behind. Why is that, Lapsewood? There's no plague at the moment, no exceptionally bloody wars. Granted, mortality rates are on the rise due to the ever-increasing population, but this has been happening for years. You have fallen behind because that's what happens. You did well to last so long. But it's time for someone new. I was thinking it might be a good opportunity to give Mr. Grunt a chance. He seems ever so eager to please, and he's rather young—in ghost terms, of course."

"Grunt, in my office, sir?" Lapsewood was sickened by the idea.

"Exactly." Colonel Penhaligan rapped his knuckles on the desk.

"But please, I'm not ready," Lapsewood protested. "I want to be like you and work here as long as possible."

"Yes, but I've got breeding. Good stock. It's the same as horses. Breed two thoroughbreds and you'll have a thoroughbred; breed donkeys and guess what you'll get?"

"I'm not a donkey, sir."

"What were your parents, Lapsewood?"

"My father was a shopkeeper, and my mother was a maid, sir."

"Exactly, Lapsewood. Donkeys, the both of them."

"Please, sir, I'm begging you. I'll do anything."

Colonel Penhaligan sighed. "I like you, Lapsewood. You've got ambition. You've got gumption. You want to prove me wrong about this whole donkey business, don't you?"

"Yes, sir."

"Very well. I'll give you a chance to prove yourself."

"You mean, I can go back to my office, sir?"

"Good grief, man, no. I don't want you in my department. Luckily for you, General Colt from Housing has been badgering me for someone to go help him out with some sort of problem he's got."

"Housing, sir?" Lapsewood had never even heard of a Housing Department.

"Haunted houses. It's one of the smaller departments," said Penhaligan. "I don't know the ins and outs of it, and I

34

have no interest in finding out. If you ask me, General Colt is about as useful as a blunt bayonet. I'd have him replaced if I had my way, but I did say I'd send him someone."

"To do what?"

"I don't know," said Colonel Penhaligan, with an exasperated sigh. "Dispatch has plenty enough to keep me occupied without any need to meddle in other people's business. Run along now before I change my mind."

"Yes, sir. Thank you, sir."

On the other side of the door, Lapsewood was relieved to find Monsieur Vidocq gone. Yet, even in his absence, the suave Frenchman was clearly holding a greater percentage of Alice's attention than Lapsewood could manage while he was present.

"How was it, then?" she asked.

"I'm being transferred to Housing," replied Lapsewood gloomily.

"Oh, General Colt's department." She leaned forward conspiratorially. "He's a lazy one, by all accounts. I know I grumble about old Colonel Grumps in there, but at least he takes an interest in the work. As I hear it, Mrs. Pringle has to do everything, while old Colt spends all his time on the golf course. I wonder what Colt wants *you* for."

Lapsewood didn't like the way she said that, as though she could never imagine anyone in his right mind ever wanting him for anything.

"At least you won't have to come up here and see Grumps anymore," said Alice.

Lapsewood hadn't thought of that. There would be no more excuses to come see Alice. He searched her face for some sign of sadness but found none.

"Oh, listen to me," she said. "Prattling on, wasting your time, when you need me to tell you where to go." She pulled out a large book from her desk drawer that listed all the departments in the Bureau. "Housing . . . ah, here we are," she said. "Room 412 on the fortieth floor."

"Thank you," said Lapsewood, cursing his cowardly heart more than ever. He walked solemnly to the door.

"Are you really going to leave like that?" asked Alice.

The words stopped Lapsewood in his tracks. He felt as though his dead heart had started beating again. Alice couldn't bear the thought of him walking out any more than he could. There was more to be said. There were feelings to reveal, sonnets to be penned, songs to be sung, declarations to be made. Finally he could admit his feelings, and Alice Biggins would reveal hers.

"No, Alice," he said, his newfound confidence deepening his voice. "I'm not going to leave like that."

She laughed. Such a beautiful laugh. As light and carefree as the song of a lark.

"I did wonder," she said. "The Paternoster Pipe will be much quicker."

All the joy vanished. All Lapsewood's dreams, all his hopes, seeped away like water down a drain.

"I prefer to walk," he said.

He opened the door and left.

6
MR. CONSTABLE'S
GOOD NATURE

So well did Mr. Constable know his old friend
and business partner, Mr. Toop, and such a kind and intuitive man was he, that he could tell something was troubling Toop from the heaviness of his footfalls descending
the stairs. However, such was Constable's tact that he spoke
no word of his suspicions. Instead, the two men exchanged
polite pleasantries and discussed matters of their working
day before Mr. Toop finally brought up what was so obviously on his mind.

"In all the years I have known you, I've never asked for a
favor, have I?" said Mr. Toop.

"None," conceded Mr. Constable.

"And yet you have bestowed many upon me. You made available these lodgings for me and my boy when we needed a home, you gave me work when none would employ me, and you made me your business partner when you could have easily kept me as an employee."

Mr. Constable raised his palm so that Mr. Toop might stop. "I do not consider these favors," he said, "but, rather, rational business decisions made for sound and wholly selfish reasons. Giving you lodging above your place of work was merely a way to ensure your punctuality. I employed you because you are a first-rate carpenter. And, as for making you a business partner, is there any better way to give someone an incentive to work hard than to give him an interest in the business he works for?"

Mr. Toop smiled at this modesty. "If not toward me, then will you at least concede that your benevolence toward my boy has no motive but philanthropy?"

"I will *not* concede that point," countered Mr. Constable. "What you call benevolence I would label the selfish indulgence of a childless old man given the great opportunity to play some small part in the upbringing of a brilliant and inspiring boy."

"You are impossible, Mr. Constable."

"And with these words you seek to butter me up for this impending favor, I suppose," said Mr. Constable with an impish grin.

Mr. Toop's face, however, remained resolutely solemn.

"Do you remember my brother, Jack?"

"Of course. Such a colorful character will leave an indelible imprint upon the mind of any who encounter him."

"He appeared at the door late last night."

"Ah, I am relieved."

"Relieved?" exclaimed Mr. Toop.

"Yes, for I feared my inability to raise a smile from you was due to my having lost my touch. Now that I can see there are extraneous factors for your determined sobriety, I am filled with relief."

"My brother is upstairs with Sam. He came here to seek refuge."

"Well, it was a horrendous night," said Mr. Constable. "I thought I would lose my chimney again in the storm."

"Refuge from the law," said Mr. Toop.

"And because of your familial loyalty, you want to help him in spite of the history between you," surmised Mr. Constable.

"It is only a week. I feel I owe him that much. He has promised never to return. But as this property belongs to you, I wouldn't feel right in keeping it secret from you."

"And yet you would rather it be kept secret from everyone else," said Mr. Constable. "Of course."

"Oh, I can see we're going to get on splendidly, all four of us," said a third voice. Jack appeared on the stairs. He walked down to the shop and offered Mr. Constable his hand. "Mr. Constable."

Mr. Constable shook it. "Jack," he said.

"What marvelous company you keep, Charlie," Jack said

to his brother. "Your own name on a shop and this excellent fellow as a partner. It seems the business of death has done you well. And that boy of yours, what a cook he is. I swear, that soup would enliven even a dead man's taste buds." Jack laughed and lifted a small black pipe to his mouth.

"If you are to stay here and remain unseen, you must also avoid arousing any of the other senses," said Mr. Toop.

"I don't follow," replied Jack, his grubby fingers packing the pipe with tobacco from the pocket of his waistcoat.

"Neither one of us smokes, so it would seem strange for customers to enter and smell tobacco." Mr. Toop snatched the pipe from Jack's mouth.

"You always did look out for me, didn't you, Charlie?" said Jack with a sneer.

"And you always found ways to embroil me in your troubles."

"As I recall, I played no small part in solving some of them."

"That's enough," Mr. Toop barked. "Get back upstairs."

"Sending me to bed with no supper, is it?" said Jack.

Mr. Constable stepped between the two brothers and said, "I believe Charles is only looking out for you. We have appointments all morning. It would be better for you to go back into hiding if you are to remain unseen."

Jack looked Mr. Constable up and down, grunted, then turned and headed back up the stairs.

7

GENERAL COLT

THE DOORS, FLOORS, AND WALLS OF THE BUREAU were constructed in a way that made them impossible to pass through. Lapsewood didn't know how it was done, but it was one of the things he liked about the place. Apart from the obvious advantage of preventing anyone from wandering into private meetings, it helped sustain the pretense that the Bureau was as real as any other place of work. Lapsewood felt the satisfaction of knuckle against solid wood as he knocked on the door with HOUSING DEPARTMENT engraved on its golden plaque.

"Enter," called Mrs. Pringle.

Lapsewood stepped inside. Alice's face was still at the

forefront of his mind, but General Colt's secretary could not have been less like her. She was old and haggard. She had been ghost-born in the late seventeenth century, judging by her clothes, and had the look of one who had not so much died as rotted away.

"Yes?" she said. She looked up from the novel she was reading and peered at Lapsewood over the top of her glasses.

"*The Mystery of Edwin Drood*," said Lapsewood, reading the title. "Dickens's unfinished novel."

"Actually, Mr. Dickens was kind enough to supply me with the final chapters posthumously," she replied, unsmiling. "Can I help you?"

"Mr. Lapsewood, transfer from Dispatch," he announced.

She looked him up and down. "Oh, really? Oh, dear. Well, go on in."

Lapsewood went through toward the main office. He could see that its walls were lined with large dusty books, hundreds of volumes detailing every rule, law, bylaw, edict, clause, and guideline that made up the complex Bureaucratic Procedure. General Colt was sitting with his feet on the desk, eyes shut, his enormous walrus mustache moving in time to the sound of his heavy breathing. The rest of his face was covered by a wide-brimmed hat.

Lapsewood paused before entering the room and turned back to Mrs. Pringle. "He appears to be asleep," he said.

"Yes," she replied.

"But that's impossible. Ghosts can't sleep."

Mrs. Pringle placed a finger at the point she was up to in her book and looked up. "You'd be surprised by the lengths some people will go to avoid signing a batch of New Resident Allocation documents." In spite of the fact that she shouted this, her words apparently went unheard by the general.

"Should I come back later?" asked Lapsewood.

"I'd give him a nudge if I were you."

Lapsewood stepped inside the room.

"And close the door," added Mrs. Pringle.

Lapsewood pulled the door shut, hoping the sound would rouse him, but the general continued to snore. He coughed. Nothing. "Ahem," he said. Still no movement.

Lapsewood went around the back of the desk and, ever so slowly, nudged one of the general's supporting elbows and then quickly darted back to the other side.

The general sat up with a start. "What? Why the . . . Who are you?"

"Lapsewood, sir," he said. "Dispatch. Colonel Penhaligan sent me."

"Pen-hal-igan?" he repeated, in a pronounced accent that Lapsewood vaguely placed as coming from somewhere in the southern states of America. "Oh, yes. Penhaligan." He looked at Lapsewood. "Are you quite sure he sent you?"

"Positive, sir."

"Well, you won't do at all. Not at all, son."

"Penhaligan never had any complaints about my work, sir."

"Why did he send you here, then?"

Lapsewood didn't respond.

"What we have here," continued General Colt, "if I'm not very much mistaken, is a fob-off, and I don't care for being fobbed off. You trying to fob me off, boy?"

"No, sir."

General Colt stood up, walked around in a small circle, and sat back down.

"Perhaps if you could let me know the nature of the work, I might be able to assist," said Lapsewood.

"The nature of the work, as you put it, is that I need someone with haunting experience, someone with a brain, someone with legitimate contacts in the living world and a current Polter-license."

"You mean a Prowler, sir?"

"Exactly, and just looking at you, I'd be willing to bet that you haven't so much as stepped out of this building since the day you died. Am I right? Don't answer that. I know I'm right."

"My work has been mostly office-bound till now, but—"

"Don't give me any flannel," interrupted the furious general. "You're about as useful as a three-legged horse."

Lapsewood wondered whether a three-legged horse was better or worse than a donkey.

General Colt pulled out a large silver gun from his holster. "I'd put you down if you weren't already dead."

Worse, thought Lapsewood. Definitely worse.

General Colt aimed at the ceiling and pulled the trigger. There was a loud *bang*.

"No firearms!" screamed Mrs. Pringle from the other side of the door.

"Old witch," muttered General Colt.

Lapsewood wondered whether the general really would have shot him if he thought it would do any harm. He feared the man would have. Perhaps he should have taken Colonel Penhaligan's first offer to resolve his unfinished business.

But, quite aside from the fear of stepping through the Unseen Door into whatever lay on the other side, Lapsewood hadn't the faintest idea what could be left unfinished in his wholly unremarkable life.

"I can do it," he said in a shaky voice.

"What was that, boy?" demanded General Colt.

"I can do it, whatever it is you need doing. I'm sure I can do it. What I lack in experience I make up for in determination and initiative."

General Colt laughed and holstered his gun. "You got guts, boy. I'll give you that." He removed his hat, placing it on the table, and Lapsewood's eyes were drawn to the perfectly round hole in the general's temple revealing the gray matter inside his skull. General Colt noticed him looking. "Ah, I see you've spotted my old death wound. I tell you, if my own gun hadn't jammed on me, I'd have hit that son of a gun first. Still, the man who gave me this brain ventilation swung for his crime. I was there. I watched his ghost rise up from his limp, hanging body and go straight through to the other side. Whereas I ended up with a job here. So who's laughing now, eh? Don't answer that."

"What do you need me for, sir?" asked Lapsewood.

"What do you know about haunted houses?"

"They're houses with ghosts in them?" ventured Lapsewood.

"I'm beginning to see why Penhaligan was willing to let you go." General Colt raised his eyebrows. "Yes, houses with ghosts in them. Do you know why this happens?" he asked, as though addressing a child, and a simple one, at that.

"It's something to do with . . . or it's because of . . . Actually, no. I don't think I do know."

"Let me enlighten you," said General Colt. "Houses are made of physical materials—wood, brick, stone, and so on— but even inanimate objects can retain the imprint of a life that comes into regular contact with them."

"You mean like how a medium can use an object such as a ring to contact a spirit?" said Lapsewood.

"Don't interrupt. But yes. A building has much more contact with life than a ring, though. It *contains* life. Think of it like the shell of a hermit crab. You've heard of hermit crabs, I suppose? Don't answer that. The fact is that structures that contain life for a very long time get used to it. They come to require it. Over time, they come to need life. Are you following me?"

"Houses need life, sir."

"It's not just houses, Lapsewood. All buildings. Theaters, churches, pubs . . . barns, even. Anything with four walls and a roof. And if a house that has become accustomed to a great deal of life suddenly finds itself empty, it latches on to a soul and holds the ghost back. It becomes a prison for that spirit, even after new tenants move in."

"So if someone dies in an empty old house . . . or theater or whatever it is, then the building hangs on to the ghost?"

"Exactly. The force of that sudden departure turns the house into a prison, holding back the ghost of the newly departed soul. This is why haunted houses are all old and have been, at some point, empty."

"Are you telling me that houses are . . . well, alive, sir?"

"Alive? Of course not. Structures have no thoughts or feelings. You can't have a meaningful conversation with a cowshed. People would think you had gone mad. No, the spirit's life force seeps into the inanimate materials of the building. The spirit and the building become inseparable. Think of it this way: when you were still alive, did you ever walk into a place that appeared to have a character of its own, something beyond the furnishings and wallpaper?"

"Yes, my Aunt Maud's place was like that. It was always really cold and—"

"Don't interrupt," barked General Colt. "I don't give a feathered fig about your Aunt Maud's place. I'm talking about the special relationship between a house and a ghost. If a ghost becomes bound to a home, the ghost and the home become reliant on each other. Do you follow me? Don't answer that. Anyway, here at the Housing Department we act as a point of liaison for housebound spirits, dealing with their requests for Polter-licenses, Opacity

Permission applications, correspondence, and so on. Our small team of Outreach Workers spends their time visiting each Resident. It can be a lonely life, stuck in an attic for eternity. And then there are all the problems they have when new, living tenants move in, changing the wallpaper, throwing out furniture—you know the kind of thing."

"And why, exactly, do you need me?"

"One of my Outreach Workers has gone missing." He looked down at a piece of paper in front of him. "Doris McNally's her name."

"Missing?" said Lapsewood nervously.

"Yep, disappeared without a trace. She covers the London area. Lots of haunted houses there, but she stopped reporting in a couple of weeks ago. Probably got fed up and went Rogue. So, you see, what I really need is a Prowler. Tracking down ghosts is no task for a pen pusher."

"I can do it," said Lapsewood, with what he hoped would sound like confidence.

"I seriously doubt that, boy, but since I'm not exactly drowning in options here . . ."

The general reached under the desk, and, for a moment, Lapsewood thought he was going for his gun again. To his relief, Colt opened a drawer and pulled out a file. "This is a copy of the London Tenancy List. It itemizes every haunted house in London in the right-hand column. The left has its Resident and the date of their ghost-birth. Doris has the other copy. I need you to go to London and find her. It involved enough paperwork getting you here in the first place. Assigning a new Outreach Worker will take months."

Lapsewood picked up the list. "I'll do it, sir."

"Confidence," said General Colt, grinning. "That's what I like to see. Have I misjudged you, boy? Don't answer that. Mrs. Pringle will issue you all the licenses and permissions you'll need. Now, unless you've got any more questions, I've an important appointment with Mr. Wingrave. Good luck, Lackwood."

"Lapsewood, sir."

General Colt stood up and walked out of the room. "Mrs. Pringle, I'll be out for the rest of the day," he announced. "Get my caddie to meet me on the fairway."

8
THE NEW TENANTS OF AYSGARTH HOUSE

LADY AYSGARTH DETESTED BREAKFASTING WITH THE Tiltmans. She only did it because she considered it the polite thing to do. Her new tenants, however, were unaware of her benevolent sacrifice. In fact, they were utterly unaware of her existence at all, due to what she tended to think of as her *condition*. It had been sixteen years since the Tiltmans chose the house in a quiet courtyard off Fleet Street as their new home, and yet Her Ladyship still considered them new tenants. She had watched their daughter, Clara, grow into an unruly fifteen-year-old girl who, in Lady Aysgarth's opinion, needed taking in hand.

The Tiltmans, with their money, garish wallpaper, and

modern ideas, were a daily reminder that Lady Aysgarth's death had signified the end of her own, much nobler blood-line. The enormous chandelier that hung in the hall was just about the only original feature that remained after Mrs. Tiltman got to work demonstrating what she laughingly referred to as her "flair for interior design."

How Lady Aysgarth longed to hear the Knocking. How frustrating it was that her application was routinely refused by that awful McNally woman on the basis that *"the house needs a spirit."* To which Lady Aysgarth always responded with another question: *"Yes, but why mine?"* When Mrs. Tiltman's mother had moved in, sick and clearly on the way out, Lady Aysgarth had suggested that the old lady's ghost take her place. Doris McNally had explained that it didn't work that way, and Lady Aysgarth had been forced to watch the old lady die and her spirit disappear through the Unseen Door.

Lady Aysgarth sat miserably watching the Tiltmans eat.

"I shall be back late this evening, darling," said Mr. Tiltman. "It's to be one of those days at the exchange, I fear."

After all these years, Lady Aysgarth still had no idea what it was that Mr. Tiltman did for a living, beyond its having something to do with money. But then, as far as she could tell, neither did Mrs. Tiltman, who was content to spend his earnings while glossing over the exactitudes of how he came by it. Occasionally Lady Aysgarth wondered whether even Mr. Tiltman himself knew precisely what it was he did.

"I hope you have remembered we're having guests this evening," said Mrs. Tiltman.

"Oh, we aren't, are we?" replied her husband.

"I reminded you yesterday and twice on Monday."

"I do hate guests," he said, winking at his daughter mischievously.

Clara sniggered.

"George, you shouldn't speak in such a way in front of Clara," scolded Mrs. Tiltman. "Besides, my sister is bringing one of her people."

Mr. Tiltman groaned. "Oh, spare us from Hetty's people."

"She says this one is completely unique. She says we're in for the most amusing evening."

"She said the same about the one-eyed dwarf."

"Well, he *was* amusing."

"He stole our cutlery."

"You don't know that for sure. Anyway, this isn't a dwarf."

"What is it this time? A giant? A bearded lady? A Spaniard? It's sure to be some monstrous freak on loan from the circus."

"I don't know what—who—it will be, exactly, but if Hetty says it's going to be a diverting evening, I believe it will be."

"It's difficult not to be diverted when there's a diminutive cyclops making off with the silverware."

This time Mrs. Tiltman was unable to hide a smile, but that did not stop her from chastising her daughter for giggling.

"Please may I stay up and meet Hetty's person?" asked Clara.

"No," stated her mother. "Children do not attend dinner parties."

"I could write an article about it."

"You won't be writing any such thing," said Mrs. Tiltman.

"But—"

"I'll hear no more about it."

Mr. Tiltman smiled indulgently at his daughter. "If the person seems appropriate, I'll ask Hetty to bring them 'round again to meet you one day soon," he said kindly. "But we are probably doing you a great favor by keeping you out of sight. I should prefer to be upstairs hiding away, too."

Mrs. Tiltman stood up angrily. "You are each as bad as the other."

Lady Aysgarth stood, too. She remembered as a child being given in church a vivid picture of hell. Burning flames, fire and brimstone. She recalled sitting up one night reading Dante's account of each layer, filled with sinners toiling away for eternity. This was worse. Sitting at a table, listening to this family planning a dinner party of great vulgarity, spending their money on vile objects that seemed specially designed to uglify the house that bore her family name. She stepped through the wall into the hallway, turned to Ether Dust, and drifted up to the attic.

9

THE ANGER OF VIOLA TRUMP

Jack sat down heavily on the bed Sam had made for him in a corner of his room.

"So, how did you get the gift, then?" he asked.

"I've always been able to see Them," replied Sam. "Father used to think I was talking to myself, but it was always Them."

"She'd heard of you, that one in the kitchen. You don't want to be getting a reputation as a Talker. They all got things they want said to people, don't they? You wanna spend your life running errands for dead'uns?"

Sam shrugged.

"Then why 'elp her? Because she's got a pretty face? You

won't get satisfaction from a dead woman." Jack laughed crudely.

"It's not like that," snapped Sam, more angrily than he had intended. "She asked sweetly. She didn't try to scare me or anything like that. I'll help her this once."

"The dead can't be 'elped," replied Jack. "You want some female company, you'd be better off doing what your old man did and preying on grieving widows."

"Father met my mother when she came to bury her own father," said Sam.

"That right, is it?" sneered Jack. "Then I guess I stand corrected."

Sam didn't want to talk about his mother. "Have *you* always been able to see Them?" he asked.

"No." Jack unlaced his boots and pulled them off, releasing a terrible stench from within. "My first was a lad by the name of Brownin'. We were outside a pub uptown. There was a drunken quarrel over somethin'. I forget what. A girl? A bet? Somethin'. Anyway, Brownin' started saying things 'e shouldn't. Speaking out of turn. So I silenced 'im with my blade."

Jack pulled out a knife. The handle looked grubby, but the blade was as sharp and clean as Sam's best bread knife. Jack held it up admiringly. Tenderly, even.

"You killed him?" asked Sam.

"We're all on paths toward our graves," said Jack, shrugging. "Some of us are goin' faster than others, is the only difference. Brownin' was always headin' fast. My little incision just pushed him on a little. I held 'im while the life drained out of 'im to keep 'im from hollerin'. They say it's them that have been up close to death that get the gift, don't they? I suppose it's being surrounded by all these stiffs that did it for you."

"I suppose."

Jack snorted. "Anyway, so I let Brownin' fall into the gutter. Only when I look, 'e's still standin' there. He's back on his feet. I go at 'im again, but this time the knife just passes through 'im like he's nothing but air." Jack chuckled, but Sam could tell there was dread within his laughter.

"I don't know which of us looked more surprised, me or 'im. He just kept saying, '*You've done me in, Jack. You've done me in,*' over and over again. Eventually I told 'im that if I had done him in, he might as well shut up about it. Then I heard that Knockin' they all hear. That was the last I ever saw of 'im, but since then I see Them everywhere. Just with my right eye. At first I thought, maybe I could use Them in some way. After all, a man who can pass through a wall has gotta be useful, even if 'e can't unlock the door or make off with nothin'. But the thing about ghosts is, they're selfish. They don't wanna help people like us. They just want us to help Them with their petty needs."

"I'm going out," said Sam. He didn't want to listen to any more.

Jack reached into his pocket and pulled out a few coins, which he pushed into Sam's hand. "Bring your uncle a little something back, will you?" he asked.

"Like what?"

"Beer, whiskey, wine . . . I don't care. Anything to numb the boredom of this miserable place."

Sam pocketed the money and went downstairs. He asked Mr. Constable whether he could be allowed to take a short stroll.

"Of course," said Mr. Constable, winking. He always seemed to know when Sam was heading out on one of his errands.

Outside, the streets were wet underfoot, but the air was crisp and the sky was clear blue. Sam crossed the railway bridge and met the ghost in the nightdress at the bottom of the steps leading up to the church, a spot he often chose. It was secluded enough to speak without attracting attention.

"My name's Viola," she said. "Viola Trump. Thank you for helping me."

"If I do, you must never tell any of the others," said Sam. "I will not speak to you if there is any chance we can be seen by anyone else, alive or dead. So you should not speak to me either."

"I just want you to remind my Tom of what he said. That's all. He said he'd love me forever, and now he's marrying my sister."

"You want him to live his life in mourning?" asked Sam.

Viola pouted and tilted her head to one side. "Not his whole life," she said slowly. "But I've only been dead a month, and he's already engaged to her. I want him to know how that makes me feel."

Sam followed the ghost up the hill. His role as messenger for the dead had often brought him into closer contact with matters that should not have troubled a boy of fourteen. It was yet another thing that distanced him from those his own age. Sometimes he wondered whether he had more in common with the lost souls he could see with his right eye than the living ones he could see with his left.

At the top of the hill he paused to look at the rising smoke of the city in the distance. London was home to so many embittered souls. Viola led him down toward Peckham Rye. Carts and carriages rattled past them, heading in the direction of the market. Sam and Viola turned into a side road lined with newly built terraced houses. They walked in silence. Eventually Viola pointed to one and said with a huge sob, "Here. My Tom lives here."

Sam waited for her to stop crying.

When she had pulled herself together, he knocked on the door. A somber-looking man opened it. He was tall with red hair and a pale, freckled face. He wore a suit, although neither the material nor the cut suggested a wealthy man. He looked uncomfortable enough in it to lead Sam to the conclusion that it was new—to him, at least. From the wailing, moaning noise that Viola was making, Sam knew this was Tom.

"My name is Sam Toop," said Sam. "I have business with a Tom Melia?"

"That's my name. Do I know you?" said the young man.

"No. I live on the other side of the hill."

"Then you wish to sell me something?"

"I simply ask for a few minutes of your time."

"I'm afraid time is one thing I am short on right now. I'm already late." He stepped out and closed the door behind him.

"Perhaps we can talk as we walk," suggested Sam.

Tom seemed more amused than annoyed by Sam's insistence. "This business you have with me cannot wait?"

"You must tell him now," urged Viola.

"I'd be grateful to get it over and done with," said Sam.

"Very well. Although I am only walking to the church, and it isn't far."

"The church?" said Sam.

"I am getting married today."

"Today?" he exclaimed, looking over his shoulder to glare at Viola.

"That's why it couldn't wait," she said. "We have to stop it."

"You seem surprised," said Tom. "People get married all the time, you know."

"It's just . . . I wouldn't want to upset someone on his wedding day," he said, speaking to both Viola and Tom.

"I didn't realize upsetting me was your intention," said Tom, with a smile. "It makes me think twice about allowing you to accompany me."

"He promised to love me," moaned Viola.

"I'm sorry," said Sam. "You must think me most peculiar."

"Yes," replied Tom. "I do, rather."

Last night's downpour meant Tom and Sam had to jump over muddy puddles on the way to the church, which Viola walked straight through without disturbance or reflection.

"It's a lovely day to get married," said Sam. "May I ask the name of the girl you are to wed?"

"Her name is Perdita," replied Tom. "A more beautiful, honest, and kind girl you could never imagine."

"That harlot . . . That double-crossing witch!" Viola muttered.

"Then you're a lucky man," said Sam, ignoring her. "How did you find her?"

"I have known her family all my life," admitted Tom.

"What about me?" demanded Viola.

"You've been sweethearts since childhood?" asked Sam.

"I . . ." Tom faltered. "I have never wanted to marry any other girl."

"Liar," screamed the ghost. "Liar!"

"There was never any other for you?" inquired Sam.

Tom stopped walking. They were standing at a corner where they could see the steeple of the church only a couple of streets away. "Is this your urgent business with me?" he asked, the smile having fallen from his face.

"I don't mean to interrogate you," said Sam. "But I suppose when I grow up, I would like to find a love of my own. I'm intrigued to know how such unions come about."

"I was engaged to her sister," admitted Tom.

Whether it was due to Sam's youth or his disarming

manner, this was not the first time he had persuaded a total stranger to open up his heart to him in such a way.

"Ha!" proclaimed Viola triumphantly. "The truth. Finally."

"But I thought you said you always wanted to marry Perdita," said Sam. "How did you find yourself engaged to her sister?"

"It was a kindness," said Tom. "But it doesn't always seem so."

"A cruelty, more like," said Viola.

"I don't understand," said Sam.

"I proposed to Perdita three years ago to this day," said Tom. "I knew she felt the same way, but she would not marry me. She told me that her sister had confided in her that she had feelings for me also. I swear I did nothing to encourage them." Tom paused, as though awaiting further questioning. Sam said nothing, so he continued. "Her sister was never long for this world. All her childhood she was plagued by illness, and Perdita knew she had precious few years left with us. She told me that if I truly loved her, I would put her out of mind and make her sister happy in whatever time she had remaining."

"She ordered you to love her sister?" said Sam.

Tom nodded solemnly. "And so I did. For Perdita. I told Viola I loved her. I told her we would marry. I wrapped up my feelings and became an actor, playing the part of Viola's lover. Every day it broke my heart afresh, but Perdita was right. I made her sister happy. Was it right? I don't know."

Sam's eyes flickered over to Viola. She said nothing, but her eyes revealed she knew this to be true.

"If my opinion counts for anything," said Sam, "then I'd say it does sound like a kindness. You gave hope to one who had none."

"Thank you," said Tom. "A strange young man you are that you should appear like this to tell me so, and on my wedding day of all days, but for some reason, I do appreciate your opinion. It has not been easy keeping this secret. The gossips have me as a fickle, cruel, shallow man. Perdita and I will move away once we are wed. We'll start anew."

The three of them continued the slow trudge to the church. Neither Tom nor Sam spoke a word as they walked side by side. Viola walked behind them silently.

They arrived at the gate that led up to the church. "We're here," said Tom. "And you have not told me of this business of yours."

"It hardly seems important now," said Sam. "Please let me wish you the best with your marriage."

"And good luck finding your own love," said Tom.

"That is some way off yet," said Sam.

"Well, when it happens, I only hope your journey to love is less strange and heartbreaking than mine has been."

They parted with a handshake, and Tom took the path to the church door. An icy breeze picked up and rustled the leafless branches of the trees in the graveyard.

There came a knocking sound, unlike any earthly noise but one Sam had heard many times before. It was the sound ghosts heard before they stepped through the Unseen Door.

"That's for me, isn't it?" said Viola.

Sam nodded.

"I'm scared."

"Yes," said Sam.

He had no words of comfort for Viola Trump. She was about to step through a door that led somewhere beyond Sam's imagination. He expected no thank-you and received none.

The dead were rarely grateful for his help.

10

THE BOY TANNER

THE JOURNEY WAS EVEN WORSE THAN LAPSEWOOD had expected. He loathed the indignity of the Paternoster Pipe, making his smoky self intermingle with all the other commuters. Enforcers and Prowlers were heading out into the living world or returning with shackled spirits destined for the Vault. Lapsewood was relieved when he flew up and out of the chimney.

Entering the physical world was a shock. Lapsewood felt things he hadn't felt in decades, yet the elements had no effect upon him, and the cold, wind, and drizzle passed through him as though he were nothing.

Hazy lamplights and fires burned within the dense fog

that hung over London. Lapsewood drifted down with the raindrops and wondered how much his fellow spirits were responsible for the thick fog enveloping the city and how much of it was due to the winter fuel burned to battle the biting cold of the night.

He rematerialized on a cobbled backstreet. He rubbed his temples to rid himself of the spinning sensation in his head. He had picked a quiet lane, hoping to have a moment to gather his thoughts, but as he stood gazing at the brickwork that surrounded him, two men stumbled through him, giving him a brief but disturbing glimpse of the inside of one of their heads. Both men reeked of alcohol.

"Why not the Old King?" said one.

"I've not been allowed in there since that incident with the landlord's missus. What about the Trafalgar?" said the other.

"Neither of us is allowed in there."

"Then the Coach and Horses it is. Don't forget, it's your round."

"My round? I bought the last one."

The two men staggered to the end of the alley and onto the main thoroughfare. Lapsewood had gotten so used to the quiet life in the Bureau, he had forgotten what the living world was like, how full of smells and noises, sights and sounds. It was awful. He would have felt nauseated if he still had a stomach. He followed the two men out into the street.

The early-evening darkness of winter had led him to believe it was much later than it was, so he was surprised to find the Strand so alive with activity. Tradespeople were selling their goods. All manner of folk were making their way in search of food, entertainment, or one of the many other diversions provided by the city. Lapsewood felt fearful of stepping out into such a bustling street. He pulled out the London Tenancy List and looked at it, but with no map of the city, how was he to find these addresses?

General Colt was right. He was unqualified for this job. He felt sick with dread. He needed somewhere to sit down, somewhere to gather his thoughts and decide upon the best course of action. He saw the two men from the alley go into a public house and decided to follow them, if only to get away from the chaos of the street. Out of habit, he tried to open the door, but his hand went straight through, and he stepped inside.

It was even more chaotic and lively inside the pub than in the street. Everyone shouted over one another. With so many people talking, he wondered if there was anyone left to listen to what they had to say. The place was full of the thundering laughs of the men and the high, shrill shrieks of the women, all of them either drunk or on their way. In life, Lapsewood had never been one for drinking. Liquor represented everything he found unsettling about life: its unruly wildness, its loss of inhibition.

In among the throng, his attention was drawn to a small boy. For a moment he wondered whether he might be a pickpocket, but his translucence revealed him to be a ghost. The boy was standing next to the two men from the alley.

He noticed Lapsewood looking at him, winked, and nudged the smaller man's arm, sending the contents of his glass over his friend.

"What did you do that for?" demanded his friend.

"Me? You knocked my hand," shouted the first man.

"You think I wanted to douse myself in beer?"

"No, I think you're a clumsy oaf, and you owe me a fresh pint."

"I already paid for the last two, you skinflint."

The first man punched the other in the nose. The other came back at the first with a blow to the stomach. Neither noticed the small boy who had caused the argument in the first place. The fight spread like fire through a dry wooden cabin, and soon fists were flying in all directions until the entire pub had descended into a chaotic brawl.

Lapsewood watched as the boy slipped unnoticed through the crowd and straight through a brick wall. "Hey," he cried. Lapsewood followed him into a side alley. "Hey," he repeated.

"What?" replied the boy.

"Why did you do that?"

"What's it to you?"

"Let me see your Polter-license," demanded Lapsewood. "You can't cause such a ruckus in a public place without permission from your local administrative officer, plus the signature from his superior and a stamp from the Department of Polter-Activity. All of which is a considerable amount of work for the sake of a moment's havoc."

The boy laughed. "'A moment's havoc,'" he repeated. "I like that. You got a way with words, mister. I'm Tanner."

Lapsewood was unsure what was so funny. "I think I should speak to your local administrative officer," he said.

Tanner laughed. "I'm a free spirit, mate."

"Even free spirits have assigned local administrative officers. Show me your paperwork."

"I ain't got no paperwork, and you ain't no Enforcer. That's plain enough to see."

The color would have drained from Lapsewood's face, had there been any in the first place. He followed Tanner along the alleyway, down a set of steps, and onto a road by the side of the Thames. The river was dark, murky, and uninviting. He lowered his voice. "You mean, you're a Rogue ghost?"

"I didn't answer to no one in the last life, and I ain't gonna start in this one," said the boy. "I ain't ready to go through that door yet. There's too much fun to be had here."

"By 'fun' I presume you mean contraventions of the extensive regulations regarding Polter-Activity and necessary haunting?"

"I suppose I would mean that if I knew what half of it meant."

"How did you even manage to knock that gentleman's arm without a Polter-license?"

"You Bureau lot are always on about licenses, but poltering just takes concentration. You ain't gonna find a better poltergeist than me, license or no license. I've even unlocked doors. That takes real skill."

"How have you avoided capture by the Enforcers?"

"I'm too quick for them clumsy oafs," said Tanner. "What about you then, Words? What you doing down here in the grime?"

"I have a special mission."

"What mission?" asked Tanner.

"I'm working for the Housing Department. I'm looking for a ghost called Doris McNally. She's an Outreach Worker for housebound spirits."

"How do you plan on finding her, then?"

"I have a copy of the same list of haunted buildings she was working from. I plan to check each one and ask the Residents when they last saw her."

"You don't want to be messing about with haunted houses these days, mate," said Tanner.

"What do you mean?"

"The Black Rot."

"The what?"

"The Black Rot. All us Rogues know about it," said Tanner. "It don't surprise me it hasn't reached the Bureau, though. You'll all be searching for a form to fill out about it."

"What is it?" asked Lapsewood.

They were walking along the riverbank. Tanner was casually strolling without a care for the living people passing through him, while Lapsewood was leaping around, trying to avoid everyone heading toward him, constantly looking over his shoulder for people coming from behind.

"The Black Rot sets in when a house loses its ghost; then it traps the next ghost to step inside," said Tanner.

"How can a house lose its ghost?" asked Lapsewood, wondering why General Colt hadn't mentioned any of this. "And how will we find Doris if we can't risk entering the buildings?"

"'We'? I ain't helping you."

"But I need help locating these addresses."

"Not my problem, chum."

"You are a Rogue spirit, an illegal ghost, without license or authorization," said Lapsewood. "If you don't help, I'll make sure that you're tracked down and thrown into the Vault."

"Yeah, right. By an Enforcer? Good luck with that. They never caught me yet."

"By a Prowler, then."

"Prowlers wouldn't bother with a littl'un like me."

Lapsewood stopped walking, failing to see the taxicab behind, which went straight through him, giving him a fleeting, frightening glimpse of the inside of the cab and its passengers. He shuddered.

Tanner laughed. "All right. I'll help you out. Not because of your threats but 'cause I've always had a soft spot for helpless creatures. Give us that list."

Lapsewood handed it to him.

Tanner examined it closely. "Looks like the Drury Lane

Theatre is the nearest one. I'll meet you outside in ten minutes."

"But where is it?" asked Lapsewood.

Tanner threw him another pitying look. "You never been to the theater?"

"Well, no, I . . ."

Tanner laughed. "A ghost that's never even lived. If that ain't funny, I don't know what is. Drury Lane's up that alley and to the right."

"Where are you going?"

"I've had one of my ideas, ain't I? You're lucky you bumped into me, Words. Make sure you don't go inside until I get back." Tanner handed the list back to Lapsewood.

A thought struck Lapsewood. "So you can read?"

"What, I suppose you think a poor little urchin like me wouldn't have had no schooling?"

"No, but, well, yes . . ."

"As it happens, I learned to read after I died. See you in a minute."

II
MR. GLIDDON'S DYING WISH

WHEN SAM ARRIVED BACK HOME, HE FOUND MR. Gliddon, the local grocer, as well as his two sons, who were talking loudly over each other while Mr. Constable sat patiently waiting for a moment to interject. Richard Gliddon, the elder brother, was in his mid-twenties and worked with his father in the shop. Sam was less familiar with Edward, the younger brother, who had moved to London in pursuit of a career as an actor. Mr. Gliddon himself had evidently died since Sam had last seen him, for, while his sons were sitting opposite Mr. Constable, Mr. Gliddon was standing in the middle of the desk, his words going unheard by the others.

"Our father deserves a send-off suited to a man who earned much respect in his community," said Richard.

"Our father would have shuddered at the cost of what you're proposing," said Edward, who wore a flamboyantly patterned coat.

"Exactly," agreed the late Mr. Gliddon. "Why waste good money on a dead man? I've always said that, haven't I, Edward?"

"I don't know how you have the gall to sit here speaking of our father's intentions," said Richard. "You, who up and left to chase your own foolish dreams."

"My father never thought them foolish dreams," replied Edward.

"Oh, he's *your* father now, is he?"

"I meant 'our.'"

"And how would you know what he thought, since you spent all your time consorting with thieves and vagabonds?"

"I call them actors and actresses," said Edward.

"You sit here and bicker, and yet neither of you can remember my only request!" exclaimed Mr. Gliddon.

"If your profession is such a noble one, perhaps you can foot the bill for the funeral," said Richard.

"I am proposing we minimize that cost, in which case, yes, I will gladly split the bill with you," countered his brother.

"Gentlemen," said Mr. Constable, speaking quietly but firmly enough for both men to stop their quarrelling and pay attention. "The death of a loved one is a difficult time.

It is a time when many of us say things we do not mean. It is, therefore, a time when the biting of one's tongue is sometimes the wisest course of action. A little thought before each word spoken can save a great deal of hurt and upset. I am sure we can find a compromise that will keep both of you happy while remaining true to the wishes of your dear, departed father."

"Well, I don't think there will be any surprise on which side of things the undertaker will be erring," said Edward. "He'll just want to maximize his profit."

Such a mild-mannered man was Mr. Constable that Sam had never seen him actually lose his temper, but it was at moments like this when he came the closest.

"I assure you," he said unsmilingly, "here at Constable and Toop we seek only to provide the most appropriate funeral for the dearly departed. Many in my profession would see the two of you, assess the budget likely available to you, and suggest a funeral to fit. Why have two horses in the cortege when you can have four? And let each of them be adorned with black ostrich feathers. Why an elm coffin when oak is available? And let us not forget all the other trimmings on offer to the grieving. I assure you, Mr. Gliddon, we have all of those things at your disposal, but I can also assure you that when my late father started this business, he did so with an intention of bringing integrity to the business of funerals. My partner and I believe above all else that a funeral should be a moment when the grieving family can mark the passing of a life in a way suitable to that in which it was lived. I knew and respected your father. I think it may be time for the two of you to remember some of that respect he garnered and act appropriately."

Edward Gliddon looked shamefaced. "It is a difficult time for us both," he mumbled by way of apology.

"For you both?" exploded the ghost of Mr. Gliddon. "How do you think *I* feel? One minute I'm walking back home from the pub, the next, I'm dead in a puddle."

Mr. Constable turned to Sam for the first time since he had entered the shop. "I think you know my partner's son, Sam Toop," he said.

The two men nodded and offered mumbled greetings.

"I'm very sorry for your loss," said Sam.

"Oh, everyone is very sorry now, aren't they?" said the late Mr. Gliddon. "That's all I hear now that I'm dead. 'Sorry for your loss.' Never heard so many kind words when I still had breath in my body."

"Sam, we are discussing what kind of funeral Mr. Gliddon might have wanted," said Mr. Constable. "But it is difficult. Mr. Gliddon passed very suddenly. There was no opportunity for us to discuss these details."

"Honestly," sighed Mr. Gliddon, "I told them both where I wanted to be buried: the same place as my father."

"Did your father never express an interest in a particular burial place?" asked Sam.

Father and sons turned to look at Sam. If any had heard tell of Sam's abilities, they had all clearly chosen to dismiss them as rumors spread by silly schoolchildren.

"Perhaps a place of significance to your family?" Sam prompted.

"I do recall one conversation . . ." said Edward. "We were all three there."

"The night Mother died . . ." said Richard, the memory flickering behind his eyes.

Edward nodded. "That's right. You remember? We sat there drinking that bottle of whiskey."

"Brandy," said Richard.

"It was port," said Mr. Gliddon.

"He said he wanted to be buried by Grandfather's side," said Edward.

"Finally!" Mr. Gliddon clapped his hands.

"And where would that be?" asked Mr. Constable.

"St. Paul's," said Richard.

"St. Paul's?" exclaimed Mr. Constable.

"Not the cathedral," said Edward. "A small church off the High Street in Shadwell with the same name."

"Ah." Mr. Constable stroked his chin. "Still, interment in churchyards, crowded as they are, is a tall order in this day and age. And I'm guessing that your father, living and working here in Honor Oak, was not a regular attendee at his father's church."

"It was where he was baptized, but no," said Richard.

Mr. Constable turned to Sam. "Sam, perhaps you could go there and speak to the rector?"

"It would be my pleasure," said Sam.

"Thank you," said Edward.

"It is what we are here for," said Mr. Constable. "To steer you through this difficult time. It is what we take pride in. Now, gentlemen, shall we discuss the rest of the details?"

Mr. Constable's hand passed through Mr. Gliddon's stomach as he opened a large book on his desk. Mr. Gliddon stepped out of the desk and peered over Mr. Constable's shoulder, while the undertaker spoke to the Gliddon brothers regarding types of headstones, materials for a coffin, the available adornments, the number of carriages and horses, and all the other countless details that went into the business of funerals.

Sam was relieved to have an excuse to avoid going upstairs. He still had the money Jack had given him to buy alcohol. He had no desire to see Jack drunk, but neither did he want to return empty-handed and risk angering his uncle. Better, he decided, to stay out of the house altogether for as long as possible. Even if it did mean a trip to London.

12

LADY AYSGARTH'S DIARY

CLARA TILTMAN HAD FOUND THE DIARY SOME months back in an oak bureau in the attic of Aysgarth House. Her mother and father never ventured up there, and Hopkins, the butler, had stopped using the space for storage since his back started giving him trouble. Mrs. Preston, the cook, never so much as ventured upstairs, let alone as far as the attic. Clara, however, liked the chaos of the place. Aysgarth House was so orderly and every item of furniture so well chosen that the attic, with its jumble of old broken tables and chairs, felt like its guilty secret.

She also liked the way she could see all the way down to Fleet Street from the small window in the eaves. She liked to watch the journalists going in and out of the *Times* building, imagining one day she might be one of them, even though she never once saw a woman among their number.

Clara wanted to be a writer, but not of novels, plays, or poems. It was the real world that fascinated her. It was this persistent curiosity that had led to her discovery of a black book with a golden clasp tucked away in one of the drawers of the bureau.

Clara had taken the book back to her bedroom to read. The handwriting inside was exquisite and precise. It was the private diary of the house's previous owner, Lady Aysgarth, a woman whose formidable looks had been captured in a dusty old portrait that was now under a sheet in the attic. Clara had an idea about using the diary to write about the history of the house, but at first it was difficult to make sense of it at all. Every name was abbreviated, and the entries were frustratingly short, often seeming more concerned with the weather than anything of importance. A typical entry read:

H away again. J in high spirits. Morning bright, afternoon gray.

Clara did a little more research, looking through other old documents in the bureau, and learned that H was Lady Aysgarth's husband, Henry. J referred to her son, James.

Took J to watch H play cricket. Overcast.

On and on the diary went in this vein. Clara found it extremely frustrating and was on the verge of giving up with it when things took a turn for the worse in the lives of the Aysgarths.

Dr. came to see J. Inconclusive. H frustrated. Demanded a different Dr. Rain all day.

More doctors came, but none of them, it seemed, could provide any comfort. Lady Aysgarth's son grew worse until the day she wrote her final entry.

J died today. H wept, then planted a willow tree in his memory.

It was the only day Lady Aysgarth had omitted mention of the weather. Clara supposed it no longer mattered to a woman who had just witnessed the death of her only son.

From the other documents she found in the bureau, Clara pieced together what had followed. She found the death certificate of Lady Aysgarth's husband the following year. She found letters of regret from the house staff as they were all dismissed, leaving Lady Aysgarth alone in the big old house.

As sad as it was, there was no story in it, and Clara forgot about the diary until the day her father suggested they have a man come and chop down the willow tree in the garden, fearing that its roots might be interfering with the outer wall.

Suddenly the strangest thing happened. The drawing-room curtain flapped wildly, and the rod holding it fell away from the wall and crashed to the floor.

Once everyone had recovered from the shock, and a man had been called to come and make the necessary repairs, there was much discussion of what had happened. Mrs. Tiltman blamed poor workmanship in the installation of the curtain rod. Mr. Tiltman wondered whether a freak gust of wind could have blown in and unseated it. But Clara had seen perfectly clearly the two creases at the bottom of the curtains as a pair of invisible hands yanked at them.

Clara said nothing, but it was clear to her that her father's suggestion to remove the tree planted in memory of Lady Aysgarth's lost child had angered Her Ladyship so much that she had made her presence known. Clara had long held a suspicion, but now she knew it was true. Aysgarth House had a ghost.

13

THE MAN IN GRAY

LAPSEWOOD STOOD OUTSIDE THE DRURY LANE Theatre watching crowds of people enter through the double
doors between the two magnificent pillars. It was so busy
that it was impossible to avoid being walked through, but
that didn't stop him from trying. He had always had a squea-
mish disposition and had no desire to see any more of the
inner workings of people's heads than was strictly necessary.

"That some kind of new dance you're doing, love?"

He turned to see an attractive woman wearing a blouse
that hung precariously off each shoulder, with daringly few
buttons done up. She was clearly a ghost, but he had never
seen such life in a spirit's eyes.

Lapsewood's inability to speak in the presence of female beauty prevented him from uttering anything but a series of disconnected grunts and stammered half words. Unsure where to look, he held up his hands, giving the impression that he was, quite literally, dazzled by the woman's beauty.

"There something the matter with you?" she asked.

"I'm waiting for a friend," he replied, thankful that he managed to form a complete sentence, even if the remark was utterly incongruous.

She laughed. "You never seen a lady before?"

"Never, er . . . never quite so much of one," replied Lapsewood.

The woman laughed. "I don't normally get no complaints," she said, holding out her hand. "Nell. Pleased to meet you."

"Lapsewood," he replied, taking her hand and holding it, unsure whether he was supposed to shake or kiss it and compromising by waving it somewhere near his face.

More laughter from the woman.

"I wouldn't go into that theater, if that's what you're planning," said Nell.

"You mean in case it's infected with the Black Rot?" asked Lapsewood in hushed fear.

"No. It's *Hamlet* tonight, and the lead is one of those slow talkers. I heard this version is running over five hours long." She laughed and slapped him on the arm.

"I must enter. You see, I'm looking for a woman," said Lapsewood, rubbing his arm.

Nell laughed and fluttered her eyelashes flirtatiously. "What a fresh one you are," she said. "If you're after female company, then look no farther than old Nell."

Lapsewood coughed, embarrassed. "I mean to say, a woman by the name of Doris McNally."

"Never heard of her," replied Nell, sounding a little put out. "But you want to be careful which houses you step into these days. The Black Rot is infecting more every day."

"So I've heard. Do you know what could be causing it?"

Nell leaned close to Lapsewood, making him feel uncomfortable and uncertain where to look. "It's a sickness brought on by a ghost leaving its abode. Haunted houses need their ghosts, don't they? And their Residents can't exactly walk out. So it must be someone vanquishing ghosts, I reckon," she whispered.

"Vanquishing?" replied Lapsewood.

"Exorcism."

"Exorcism," scoffed Lapsewood. "Surely that's one of those myths made up by the living."

"Is it, though?" asked Nell.

"I can see you two are getting friendly," said a voice from nearby.

Lapsewood noticed Tanner standing behind Nell, grinning from ear to ear.

"Hello, Tanner," said Nell, pulling away from Lapsewood. "What you doing with all them spirit hounds?"

Tanner was holding five leads, each with the ghost of a dog on the end. In most cases, it was stomach-churningly obvious what had killed them. They all had patchy, mangy coats revealing sore pink skin underneath. Some had been beaten, others run over, run through, or shot.

"Dogs?" exclaimed Lapsewood.

"Yeah. They're sweet." Tanner picked up a three-legged Jack Russell and ruffled its head.

"They're anomalies," said Lapsewood.

"I think most of them are mongrels, actually."

"I mean, they shouldn't exist. Dogs don't have souls. The Bureau doesn't even officially recognize their existence."

"Poor things." Tanner scratched the dog under its chin. "They don't know what to do with themselves without hunger to drive them. I found this lot chasing after living cats, getting confused when the creatures slipped through their paws."

"What use are they to us?" asked Lapsewood.

"Well, as I see it, the problem we have is that you can't see the Black Rot from the outside . . ."

"You can when it gets real bad," said Nell.

"Yeah, but not always," said Tanner. "So how do we know if a house is safe to enter?"

Nell and Lapsewood looked at him, awaiting the answer.

"The dogs. That's how. A spirit hound will be no more able to escape a building with Black Rot than one of us would."

"That's true," said Nell. "But the spirit of a dog won't quench the appetite of an empty building. A haunted house needs a human spirit."

"That may be," admitted Tanner, "but the point is, if they don't come back, then we'll know it's not safe to go in."

"Is that true?" asked Lapsewood.

Nell laughed. "I can see which one's the boss out of you two."

Lapsewood felt embarrassed but could think of nothing to say to the contrary. "How do we make the dogs go into the buildings?" he asked.

"Like this. Watch." Tanner pulled out a stick tucked into his belt and held it up for a black Labrador to sniff. He then took the dog off the lead and threw the stick straight through the wall of the theater. All the dogs barked wildly trying to get it, but the freed Labrador ran after it and jumped through the wall.

"How do you know he'll come back at all?" asked Lapsewood.

"He'll come back," said Tanner. "These dogs just want caring for."

The Labrador bounded out of the wall, holding the stick in its mouth happily.

Tanner took it and patted the dog. "Good boy," he said, tying it back up. "You see?"

"Smart lad," said Nell affectionately. "Now, old Nell has somewhere she needs to be. I'll see you later, Tanner."

"See you, Nell," said Tanner.

"It was lovely to make your acquaintance, Mr. Lapsewood," said Nell. She leaned toward him and pecked him on the cheek.

Lapsewood stood, stunned, unable to move or speak until a taxicab went past and its wheel hit a puddle, spraying water straight through him.

Tanner laughed. "Come on, Romeo," he said. "We've got work to do."

The last few stragglers were trying to get to their seats before the play began as Lapsewood and Tanner stepped into the theater lobby. Lapsewood gazed up at the columns and statues as he followed Tanner up the stairs, unseen by the theater workers checking tickets.

If the lobby had been impressive, it was nothing compared to the splendor and elegance of the high-ceilinged auditorium itself, with row upon row of expectant people chatting among themselves as they waited for the curtain to rise. In the center, hanging from the ceiling, a gas chandelier gave the whole place a gentle glow that felt almost magical to Lapsewood.

"There's our fella now," said Tanner.

At first Lapsewood didn't see whom he was talking about, but then he noticed the man. He wore clothes more suited to a gentleman living some hundred years earlier, with a rather fussy shirt, yellow tights, a gray coat, and, on top of his head, a three-cornered hat. He was sharing his seat with a heavy, fidgety lady.

Seeing them approach, the Man in Gray stood up. "Greetings," he said, raising his hat and bowing flamboyantly. "Please have a seat, my friends. You're in for a treat tonight. *The Tragedy of Hamlet*, by our greatest playwright, Mr.

William Shakespeare. I have seen many performances over the years, but the talk of the theater is that tonight's lead is something very special indeed."

Tanner rolled his eyes, but Lapsewood pulled out his list and a pen from his top pocket. "Sorry to bother you, sir. I'm here from the Housing Department. I'm looking for Doris McNally."

"Ah, dear Doris, a charming lady. She prefers the comedies, you know," replied the Man in Gray. "I'm afraid I haven't seen her in some time."

"May I take your details?" asked Lapsewood. "For my records."

"Of course. Mr. David Kerby. Born into life 1771, born into death 1806. Known to the living as the Man in Gray, a title that, as you can see, fails to take into account the daring color of my legwear, but one which I have grown accustomed to over the years."

"The living can see you?"

"Occasionally. I have a license for infrequent visibility, up to sixty percent on the Opacity scale, in accordance with the rulings on the haunting of public places."

"What's that mean?" asked Tanner.

"It means he's good for the tourist trade," replied Lapsewood.

"Ah, yes, they flock here, hoping to catch a glimpse of the ghost of the man murdered in this very building," said Mr. Kerby dramatically. "The theater itself has burned down and been rebuilt since then, of course, but as my life was taken down near the very foundation, this glorious theater has remained my home."

"You were murdered?" said Lapsewood.

Mr. Kerby laughed and nodded, then pulled out a dagger and held it aloft. "By this very dagger," he said grandly. "Stabbed in the gut and left to die beneath the stage, then bricked up in these walls. A death of such drama is in keeping with our dramatic surroundings, wouldn't you say?"

"I'm guessing you were an actor yourself, with the way you talk and all," said Tanner.

"An actor?" Mr. Kerby chuckled. "No, young man. In life I was a bookkeeper."

"What were you killed for, then?" asked Tanner.

"Ah, well." Mr. Kerby emitted a small, embarrassed cough. "My fault entirely. You see, the management at the time had some pecuniary complications."

Tanner looked to Lapsewood, who translated, "Money problems."

"Why didn't he just say that, then?" asked Tanner.

"I noticed discrepancies in the books and brought them to light. I went to the then manager, who saw to it that I didn't bring any more to light. Now, hush please; the play is about to start."

The lights on the great chandelier dimmed, and Mr. Kerby turned to the stage. "Do you know the play?" he asked. "It begins with the appearance of a ghost. I've been watching rehearsals, and they've done it rather well in this production. Not too much moaning and wailing. I don't know why they always have us ghosts wailing and moaning. Most of the wailers and moaners I have known have been very much alive."

The fidgety woman leaned forward and said, "Would you please get out of my way? I can't see a thing."

"I am sorry, madam," said Mr. Kerby, stepping to one side. "She doesn't know I'm a ghost," he mouthed to the others, with a mischievous wink.

"Come on. Let's go," said Tanner, tugging Lapsewood's sleeve.

14

THE BLACKENED CHURCH

S AM CHOSE TO TAKE THE BUS TO LONDON, THEN walk the rest of the way to St. Paul's church in Shadwell. As he would charge his day's expenses to the Gliddon brothers, he could have taken the train, which would have been quicker, but he preferred the slower route. Its bumpy, winding journey emphasized the distance between Honor Oak and London.

Sam recognized the bus driver as Mr. Herring, a friendly fellow with wild whiskers and weather-beaten skin as worn and discolored as the backsides of the horses that he drove. He sometimes took work driving the hearses for Constable & Toop.

Mr. Herring insisted that Sam come and sit up front with him for company. As they traveled toward London, he reeled off an endless list of the aches, pains, discomforts, complaints, illnesses, and ailments that currently plagued him.

Up the Old Kent Road, the journey was made slower by all the other vehicles. They drove under a railway bridge just as a train rattled overhead, then on to the Elephant and Castle, where Mr. Herring stopped in order to relieve himself. The passengers in the back complained loudly at his impertinence, but he paid them no heed. Nor did he rush back, on account of the terrible blisters on the soles of his feet.

Back in the driving seat, he said, "They'd have me suffer for the sake of their precious time, that lot, but you can't argue with a man's bladder. The bladder will always 'ave the final say. And I won't go sufferin' any more for them lot than I do anyhow. Life is all sufferin', lad. My hands are cold and broken from 'olding these reins, my insides are joggled around by the ups and downs of this job, my back aches, and my eyes ain't what they were, but you don't hear me grumble."

Over the bridge, they passed the Monument at Pudding Lane, where Sam spied with his right eye three figures, unseen by the other passersby, each with blackened clothes and disfiguring burns all over their skin. They sat by the foot of the monument playing cards. They were victims of the Great Fire. Sam had encountered them before. They were a friendly enough bunch and always knew everything that was going on in the world of ghosts, but Sam found it extremely uncomfortable to look at their terrible wounds. Besides, he knew from previous encounters that a couple of them were terrific cheats at whist.

At the end of the line Sam paid Mr. Herring and got off, taking the rest of the journey on foot. He walked past the Tower of London as quickly as possible. He couldn't stand the place, with its turrets packed with dead kings and queens bickering with one another and hurling abuse at everyone. While visitors paid sixpence to walk around its grounds, its previous inhabitants screamed and hollered about the injustices that had befallen them in life. Here could be found the city's most gruesome ghouls, many of them carrying their heads separately from their bodies. Sam couldn't bear to look at the two murdered sons of Edward IV, nor the Countess of Salisbury, who had been hacked to pieces by the executioner and remained so in death.

Local guides liked to talk about London's rich history, but as far as Sam was concerned, it was a tapestry of violence and death.

Thankfully, once Sam had passed the Tower, things were much quieter. He followed the High Street, past the docks of Wapping, with its drowned sailors and swearing pirate ghosts embittered by their inability to claim the hidden treasure they had amassed in life.

St. Paul's of Shadwell was just off the High Street. By no means as magnificent as the cathedral that bore the same name, it was still an impressive bell tower that Sam spotted over the tops of the trees. As he got nearer, he realized that there was something wrong with it. A plaque on the front gave the date of its completion as 1820, and yet Sam would have taken it for much older. The edges of the brickwork were blackened and decaying. Only when he covered his left eye did he see that this was not from age or soot from the factories across the river. It was as though a supernatural substance was slowly devouring the church, eating away at it from within. It hummed with disease. He had never seen anything like it.

Sam gazed up at the church and wondered what was wrong with it. Hearing the click of a door, he turned around. Standing in the doorway of the rectory opposite the church was a red-faced man wearing a clerical collar.

"May I help you?" asked the man.

"Are you the rector?"

"Yes. Bray is my name. What business have you here?"

"I have traveled from Honor Oak on behalf of a gentleman who wishes to be buried in your churchyard."

"I take it you have traveled on behalf of this gentleman's family rather than the man himself, unless you are in the habit of running errands for the dead," said the rector. "You'd better come in."

Sam followed Rector Bray inside, where he was offered a glass of whiskey to "ward off the winter cold." Sam declined the offer but could tell from the rector's breath that he had already begun "warding" himself.

"I'm afraid it's quite impossible to accept new interments," said Rector Bray. "We have not had a new burial here in many years. We have cemeteries for that purpose these days."

"It was the man's dying wish that he be buried here, alongside his own father," said Sam.

The rector drained his glass of its contents and poured himself another. "You were looking at the church in a strange way just now," he said.

"Yes. Is there something wrong with it?" asked Sam.

The rector pushed the cork back into the bottle. "There is something very wrong with it, but I know not what. People no longer want to enter. A darkness has descended upon it. I even fear stepping inside myself."

Rector Bray's hands had started to shake so much that he had to place his glass down on the arm of his chair to avoid spilling it.

"A spirit, perhaps?" ventured Sam.

Rector Bray took a deep breath. "Our spirit was expelled."

"Expelled?"

"A reverend by the name of Fallowfield performed the exorcism."

Sam didn't believe in exorcisms. He had personally witnessed ghosts standing by, watching as priests waved their arms around dramatically and spoke in tongues. And yet, it was impossible to deny that something had happened to this church. "Tell me about the ghost," he said.

"They say his name was Sercombe," replied Rector Bray. "He was a bell ringer. A simple soul, but a man devoted to God. However, when the woman he loved ran off with a sailor, not even the bells could drown out his sorrow. He hanged himself on the rope that rings the bell."

Sam was used to hearing stories of deaths, either from those who came into the shop or from the victims themselves, but something about this story sent a shiver down his spine. "Did you ever see the ghost?"

"No, but I heard him. He would ring the bell at night when the church was empty."

"So you had him exorcised?"

"I had not intended to, but this Fallowfield turned up and offered his services to rid me of the ghost. He said a spirit had no place in the house of God."

"But it didn't help?" asked Sam.

"It is only since then that the church has grown so . . ." Rector Bray searched for the right word. "So cold," he said. "So dark."

"And the bell?"

"It no longer rings. I wonder sometimes if this exorcism didn't let something worse in. No one will enter the church. What is a church without people? What is a rector without a congregation?" Rector Bray stared at his whiskey as though hoping for a response, but his questions remained unanswered.

Sam had not set out with any intention to use his gift, but seeing the desperation in the rector's eyes, he realized he had an opportunity to strike a deal with the man. "I will go inside and find out what is wrong with your church if you will agree to this interment," he said.

Rector Bray's eyes flickered up from the glass to Sam, peering at him with intense curiosity. "You have the gift, don't you?" he said. "You can see Them."

Sam left the question unanswered, having no desire to discuss his abilities with this drunk rector. "I will enter that place and tell you what I find if you grant permission for Mr. Gliddon to be buried here," he said firmly. "But I can make no guarantees."

Rector Bray gulped down another mouthful of whiskey. "My son," he said, his eyes alight with desperation and hope, "if you can rid me of whatever demon inhabits my church, your Mr. Gliddon will be buried here even if I have to claw up the dirt with my own fingers."

15

THE DEATH OF A GHOST

LADY AYSGARTH SAT AT HER DESK IN THE GLOOMY attic. It was the only item of her furniture that hadn't been sold, broken, or thrown away when the Tiltmans made the house their own. From the sound of Mrs. Tiltman's sister, Hetty, hooting with laughter downstairs, she knew the dinner party to be in full swing.

When Lady Aysgarth was younger, she had enjoyed a good party, but she had no desire whatsoever to venture downstairs to watch this frightful freak show. Other ghosts in her position might have applied for a Polter-license and delighted in causing all sorts of amusing havoc, but the whole business of active haunting seemed excessively uncouth to

Her Ladyship. She wanted nothing to do with her new tenants. Scare them? She didn't even want to speak to them.

Approaching footsteps brought Lady Aysgarth's attention immediately back to the present. Someone was climbing the stairs. Probably Hopkins, needing an extra chair for the party, she thought. But when the door opened, it was Clara Tiltman who appeared.

"Lady Aysgarth?" she said.

"Yes?" said the ghost, inwardly chastising herself for the idiocy of replying.

"Lady Aysgarth," said Clara. "I think you're here. I think you can hear me."

"I'm sure I don't know why you would think such a thing, child."

"I think you've always been here," continued Clara. "I know I might be talking to myself, but if so, then it doesn't matter, as there's no one here to mock me, is there?"

"'Mock'? I would have you beaten for such insolence. Leave me alone," ordered Lady Aysgarth sternly.

"You see, I saw what you did when Father talked of chopping down the willow. The curtain rod coming loose. That was you, wasn't it?"

"Don't go blaming me for the inadequacy of your wall fittings." Lady Aysgarth folded her arms defiantly.

"You were angry because your husband planted that tree in memory of your son," said Clara.

Lady Aysgarth took a sharp intake of breath. "How could you possibly know such a thing?"

Clara held up a small black book.

"My diary?" said Lady Aysgarth. "How dare you read my personal thoughts? How dare you?"

"It's sad," said Clara.

"This is inappropriate . . ."

"You must have loved him so much." Clara's voice wavered. Lady Aysgarth stepped into her line of sight so that Clara was unknowingly staring straight at her. "He should have carried on the family name. He should have lived here, not us."

"Please stop," begged the ghost. She tried to knock the diary from Clara's hand to scare the impertinent girl away, but self-pity wasn't strong enough an emotion to affect the physical world.

"You must resent my family so for coming into your home and treating it like our own," continued Clara. "I'm sorry."

"Why are you doing this?" whispered Lady Aysgarth.

Clara walked to the desk, unaware that she was stepping through the ghost. "I've come because of what they're doing downstairs. I'm worried that tonight might be your last here."

"I only wish it were," said Lady Aysgarth.

"They're downstairs now," said Clara. "I've been watching them through the keyhole. You need to find somewhere to hide. Can you leave the house? I don't know how it works. But if you stay here, I think they'll send you back."

"Send me back?" snorted Lady Aysgarth. "Back where, exactly?"

"I feel as if you've watched me all these years, like a guardian angel. I don't want to lose you now."

"'Guardian angel'? Ridiculous . . ."

In all her years as a ghost, Lady Aysgarth had turned to Ether Dust many times, but only ever by choice. Now, all of a sudden, she felt a loss of control such as she had never experienced before. Her body began to lose its shape. She fought to hold herself together, but something was manipulating her like a hapless marionette being worked by an unseen puppeteer. When Lady Aysgarth saw the look on Clara's face, she realized that, for the first time since her death, she was visible. But before she could utter a word, she was dragged down through the gaps in the floorboards.

"Lady Aysgarth!" cried Clara.

But Lady Aysgarth was flowing down through the house. Down, down, until she felt particles of her body re-form and saw that she had arrived in the drawing room, suspended above the large wooden table where Mrs. Tiltman liked to play card games with her friends. Except there were no cards laid out on the table, and the people who sat around it were all holding hands, staring up at her. They included Mr. and Mrs. Tiltman, Hetty, and their friends Dr. Wyatt and his wife, sitting next to a man dressed in black. More disturbingly, the living people could see her. Mrs. Tiltman and Mrs. Wyatt screamed. Dr. Wyatt and Mr. Tiltman gasped. Hetty released the hands she was holding and clapped excitedly.

"Please do not be concerned," said the man in black.

"The spirit cannot harm us. She is in my control." He had a bald head with a three-pointed birthmark, blood-red in color, across his skull. He wore a clerical collar around his neck, and his eyes bulged like those of a strangulated frog, while his pink tongue stuck out between his teeth.

"What do you want with me?" demanded Lady Aysgarth.

"It sees us," whispered Mrs. Tiltman.

"'It'? What do you mean, 'it'?" Lady Aysgarth exclaimed. "Of course I can see you. I've always been able to see you, you terrible people."

The Tiltmans and their guests laughed nervously. Lady Aysgarth had become so accustomed to insulting the Tiltmans without being heard that she wasn't sure what to say now that they could hear her every word. She simply wanted to leave. But no matter how she struggled, it was as if there was a chain holding her in place, slowly moving her around.

"What message have you from the other side, spirit?" asked Dr. Wyatt in a tone of quiet reverence.

"You're all awful people," said Lady Aysgarth.

Again, the laughter.

"Do not ask this spirit for wisdom," said the clerical-collared man. "She is an earthbound demon. She knows no more of the afterlife than you or I." He raised his hands and wailed, "Oh, forces of the afterworld, draw unto you this spirit. Release her from this earthly prison. Rid us of her demonic presence."

"Yes, find me a door," said Lady Aysgarth. "All I want is to hear the Knocking."

But no knocking came. No door appeared. Instead, cracks appeared all around her, in the walls, the floor, the ceiling. Hairline cracks at first, but rapidly widening. From the blackness within came a crescendo of pained screams.

"Oh, cursed spirit," cried the man in black. "It is time for you to go. Let your soul split. Let your form disassemble. Leave this house, leave this earth, and never, *ever* return."

The man slammed his hands down on the desk, and Lady Aysgarth felt the agony of being torn apart. It was so much more potent than physical pain. It was the pain of a soul being shattered.

Then she was no more.

16

A TRAIL OF INFECTION

LAPSEWOOD AND TANNER MADE THEIR WAY EAST across London on foot, searching buildings on the London Tenancy List for Doris McNally. Traveling as Ether Dust would have been quicker but would have made it hard to hang on to the spirit hounds. Slowly they worked their way down the list, each time sending a dog in first, awaiting its return, then venturing in themselves to interview the Resident.

In an Aldwych residence they found a ghost by the name of Mrs. Heber, who had died in childbirth and been forced to remain in the house and watch as the daughter who had unwittingly killed her grew up, got married, and then died in the same way herself. Mrs. Heber sobbed as she explained that her daughter had heard the Knocking upon the moment of her death and stepped straight through the Unseen Door, but, imprisoned by the house, Mrs. Heber was unable to follow. Lapsewood and Tanner listened patiently to her story, then asked about Doris. Mrs. Heber hadn't seen her in several months.

Lapsewood had been greatly affected by the story and was upset when Tanner revealed that he had pilfered the stick that Mrs. Heber had clenched between her teeth during her last moments of life.

"We're gonna need a few things to throw," he said in his defense. "I mean, when we find an infected house, if the dog don't come out, nor will the stick. And it's not always that easy to find ghost objects. They've got to be something the spirit was touching at the point of death."

The next house they visited proved Tanner right. He threw the stick and sent in the Labrador as usual, but neither returned.

"Perhaps it came out another way," said Lapsewood.

"I don't think so. Look," said Tanner.

Upon closer inspection, around the edges of the building's brickwork was a very subtle discoloration.

"Black Rot," said Lapsewood.

"Certainly seems so. Must be a pretty bad case to be visible from the outside."

Lapsewood made a note of it on the list, holding the nib of the pen on the paper for a moment, allowing the ink of the dot he made to spread a little before writing *i* for *infected* next to it.

They continued on their way with the four remaining dogs in tow. As they moved down the list, Lapsewood noticed how the three-legged Jack Russell always walked at the front, but that Tanner routinely pushed it to the back whenever he was choosing the next one to go inside a property.

They lost another dog to a house in a courtyard off Fleet Street that had no visible signs of Black Rot from the outside. In a nearby public house called the Boar's Head they found the ghost of a former publican by the name of Paddy O'Twain, an extremely welcoming Irishman, as thin as a rake, who offered them both a drink as soon as they entered.

"A very good evening to you fine fellows," he said, spreading his arms wide as if they were old friends. "May I interest you in some fine, strong, freshly brewed spirit ale? Finest in the city, it is. Oh, that all ghosts should know the happiness of imprisonment in a pub."

Lapsewood refused, but Tanner happily took a glass of the dubious-looking concoction from the man. When Lapsewood pointed out that Tanner was too young for liquor, the boy brushed off the suggestion, pointing out that since he had now been ten years alive and ten dead, he was actually twenty years of age and therefore old enough to partake. However, the moment they left the establishment, Lapsewood noticed a decline in Tanner's ability to speak without giggling and how he took an extremely long time to untangle the three remaining dogs when it came to the next building. Paddy had seen Doris McNally a month ago but had heard nothing of her since and did not know in which direction she had been heading.

In an attic in Eastcheap, they met a poet who insisted they sit and appraise his latest poem before he answered their questions. Tanner had fully sobered up by the time the young man had read all thirty stanzas, but he was polite enough in his assessment of the poem. The poet said he had been visited by Doris a week ago.

"We are getting closer," said Lapsewood, stepping back into the street. "Doris must have been heading in the same direction as us."

"I wouldn't trust anything that poet said," said Tanner. "The man was a fool."

"He had some talent with words, though," said Lapsewood. "I thought his poem excellent."

"Really?"

"You said so, too."

"I was just being polite."

"You didn't like it?"

"It wasn't that I didn't like it so much as, having sat through him prattling on about the stars and the oceans and the color of his true love's eyes, I think I'd still be hard-pressed to tell you what it was about."

"Well, I suppose you had little exposure to such things in life," said Lapsewood.

"OK, if you're so poetic, then you tell me what it was about."

"It was a . . . well, it was a musing on the futility of life, I think, or perhaps on the endlessness of death . . ."

Tanner laughed triumphantly. "Just as I thought. Not a clue."

17

DORIS McNALLY'S NEW RESIDENCE

By the time Lapsewood and Tanner reached Whitechapel, the three-legged Jack Russell was the only dog left and there were four black dots on Lapsewood's list. Four infected houses.

Tanner cradled the remaining dog in his arms as they walked silently toward their next destination, St. Winifred's School.

"We can find more dogs if you don't want to send her in," said Lapsewood.

"Don't be soft," said Tanner. "She's only a dead dog. Aren't you, Li'l Mags?" He tickled the dog under her chin, and she let out a contented bark.

"We'll need more, anyway," said Lapsewood kindly. "We may as well get them now."

"We'll get more when we need more," replied Tanner. "Come on, now, let's get this done."

Lapsewood stopped outside the school. An imposing redbrick building, it was empty and deserted so late at night. They had both gotten into the habit of checking carefully for signs of Black Rot first, to avoid wasting dogs, but Tanner studied this one extra diligently.

"I told you, we can get another dog if you're worried," said Lapsewood.

"No," replied Tanner. He placed Li'l Mags down and held up a bedpost he had pinched from the poet's bed. Li'l Mags sniffed it eagerly, excited that it was finally her turn to play the game of fetch.

"Good luck, Li'l Mags," whispered Tanner, and he lobbed the bedpost in.

The Jack Russell looked up at him, and for a moment Lapsewood thought the dog wasn't going to follow it, but she turned around and bounded in, vanishing inside the building.

Lapsewood said nothing while they waited, but the look of relief on Tanner's face was plain enough to see when the dog came out with the bedpost between her teeth.

"Good girl," said Tanner, playfully trying to get the bedpost from her. "Good girl."

They stepped through the wall into a large school hall where they were instantly accosted by the ghost of a woman wearing a green dress and a blood-soaked apron, her red hair tied up on top of her head.

"Och, at last you've come," she exclaimed. "I was beginning to think I'd been forgotten about. I suppose General Colt sent you."

"Yes," said Lapsewood. They were standing among rows of wooden desks. It took Lapsewood back to his own school days. Tanner was happily patting Li'l Mags.

"Are you Doris McNally?"

"I was the last time I checked, aye. Try telling this school that, though. It thinks I'm its ghost."

Lapsewood looked down at the list. "It says that should be Janey Brown."

"You don't need to tell me that," said Doris, holding up her copy of the London Tenancy List. "I've been visiting Janey for years. Poor girl was locked in the cellar as punishment for talking out of turn. Only the schoolmaster forgot about her, didn't he? She died of starvation, her poor, frail body discovered by a teacher two weeks later. Sad story, but a lovely girl. Not one of the moaners. The ones who die in their own homes are always worse. It's always the wallpaper with that lot."

"Where did Janey go?" asked Lapsewood.

"I wish I knew. When I got here, Janey was'ne here."

"But we checked. The school is not infected," said Lapsewood.

"I guess maybe the Black Rot goes when the building gets a new Resident," replied Tanner.

"Infected? Black Rot?" exclaimed Doris. "What are you two blathering about?"

"It's happening all over London," said Lapsewood. "Residents are going missing."

"I think I'd have heard about something like that," replied Doris. "I've been an Outreach Worker since you were still breathing air into your lungs."

"Of course," said Lapsewood to Tanner. "She wouldn't have learned about it until she stepped into an infected building."

"By which time it would have been too late," agreed Tanner.

"I've no idea what you're going on about, but since you're here, this place can have one of you as its new Resident." Doris turned to Ether Dust and flew at the outside wall. But rather than flying straight through, she rematerialized as she smacked into it and fell to the ground with a thud.

Tanner laughed.

Lapsewood walked over to give her a hand. "I'm sorry," he said.

"I can'ne be stuck in this place for the rest of eternity. I did'ne die here. There are rules about these things." Doris leaned against the outside wall. "I'm a prisoner," she said with a sigh. "I'm a prisoner, stuck in here with these wee bairns repeating sums for all eternity."

"I'll go back to the Bureau and submit my findings," said Lapsewood. "I'm sure General Colt will find a way to get you out. He did send me to find you, after all."

"There's nothing to be done. Of all people, I should know that."

"Of course there is. They can probably get Extraction documents or something. You do work for the Bureau."

She shook her head sadly. "I've done this job long enough to know that all you can do for Residents is support them, because the house will never let them go. You make out as if you're helping, you listen to their complaints, but there's nothing you can actually do."

Lapsewood patted her back awkwardly and said, "I will do something about this. I promise."

"Thank you," said Doris. "But I don't think there's anything to be done. Acceptance. That's what I tell new Residents. Acceptance is the first step. Once you accept you're never getting out, then you can start to get on with things." She sighed. "It's not so easy to tell yourself that."

STEPPING OUT OF THE SCHOOL INTO THE STREET, Lapsewood allowed an easy smile to spread across his face. He had done it. He had found Doris McNally.

All he had to do now was write up his findings, return to the Bureau, and tell them what he had discovered. When they saw what a good job he had done, not only in locating Doris McNally but in discovering the Black Rot problem, he would be rewarded. Perhaps he would be given a new assignment, or maybe Colonel Penhaligan would get wind of his success and request that he come back and work for him. He had showed them all. He was Prowler material after all.

He imagined Alice's face when he returned the hero. The man who'd saved London.

"What's next?" asked Tanner.

Lapsewood held out the London Tenancy List. "I must return. But you need to carry on," he said.

"I don't 'need' to do nothing," replied Tanner.

"We'll need a proper map of infected structures if we're to deal with this problem."

"'We'?"

"The Bureau."

"I don't work for the Bureau. Remember? I was just helping you out."

"And I'm asking you to keep doing that," said Lapsewood. "Can't you see how important this is? Something is very wrong here, and it will affect all of us if we do not deal with it immediately. There's a great deal at stake. If ghosts keep going missing, the problem will grow and grow until it won't be safe to enter any building in London."

"Someone else's problem, ain't it?" replied Tanner, shrugging. "I said I'd help you find Doris, but we've done that now."

"Accepting responsibility for the problems of others is the only way to achieve a civilized, organized society. Caring for one another is what makes us human."

"You might not have noticed, but we're dead, mate. We ain't part of 'society' no more."

"We still have a responsibility."

"Not me."

"So, what will it take for you to carry on helping me?"

"You could try asking, I suppose."

"That's what I have been doing."

"Not really." Tanner shrugged. "Try dropping all this *you need to do this* and *we need to do that* stuff, and actually ask me . . . nicely."

"Will you take the list and carry on checking for infected houses?" asked Lapsewood.

"What's the word you're searching for?"

"Please," said Lapsewood.

"Yeah, all right." Tanner took the list. "Since you asked so nicely, I will continue feeding dogs to houses."

"Thank you," said Lapsewood.

"I'm getting new ones, though. I ain't risking Li'l Mags again."

Lapsewood smiled. "I thought she was just a dead dog."

"Yeah, well, sometimes dogs are more reliable than people."

Lapsewood shook Tanner's hand and said solemnly, "Thank you, Tanner. I'll be back."

Tanner laughed. "Somber sort of fella, ain't you, Lapsewood?"

Lapsewood smiled, then turned to Ether Dust and drifted up into the sky.

18
THE BELL TOWER

SAM STOOD IN THE DOORWAY OF ST. PAUL'S CHURCH and peered inside. Sunlight spilled through the stained-glass windows, but when Sam looked only with his right eye, the interior appeared as dark as night. The wooden paneling had been eaten away by the mysterious black substance that covered the outside. Sam had never seen anything like it. It filled every crack. It had sunk into every gap. It had eaten away at the walls and spread up to the rafters in the ceiling. When he stared at it, Sam almost felt as if he could see it slowly moving. Spreading.

"I'll wait here," said Rector Bray, holding the door.

"You will not come in with me?"

"I don't think I can," he replied.

Sam stepped into the church.

"The bell tower is just to your right there," said Bray. "That's where the exorcism took place."

Sam ascended the spiral staircase, each footstep echoing off the walls. He stopped when he heard the front door slam.

"Rector Bray?" he cried. "Rector Bray?"

There was no reply. Sam wanted to run back down and escape this place, but there was something compelling him forward. At the top of the staircase he stepped into the bell tower, where a long piece of white material hung down from the end of the rope used to ring the bell. A breeze blew through gaps in the brickwork, and the sheet moved.

"Hello?" said Sam. "Is there anyone here? I come to make peace."

Inside the bell tower the black substance was even thicker. It was as if it had worked its way into the brickwork of the church. He reached his hand toward it and felt only the cold brick, but as his hand passed through the substance, it caused strange, slow ripples. He withdrew his hand and clasped his fingers to warm them. Sam looked up at the bell above him, thinking of the poor, heartbroken man who had hung there listening to the bell sounding his own demise.

"Hello?" he called.

His voice reverberated around the inside of the bell. He turned to leave, but the breeze picked up, and the flapping material whipped against the back of his head. He pushed it away and felt it wrap itself around his arm, then around his neck. He tried to free himself, but it was strong and determined. Sam stumbled and fell, catching his chin on a table edge. He tore himself free from the material. He struggled to stand, but the black substance was creeping up his legs and arms and back, keeping him rooted to the spot, growing over him as it had grown over the church. He felt it sink into the pores in his skin, seep into the marrow of his bones, chilling his blood.

"Help, help, Rector Bray, help me!" Sam tried to shout. He pulled one hand free and grabbed the flapping cloth, attempting to heave himself off the floor. He felt the pull of the bell and heard the sound of it reverberate through his bones. It rang again. And again. And again. But the sound it made was not that of a bell. It was a voice. A voice such as he had never heard before. Low. Rasping. Inhuman.

TALKER, it said.

"What are you?" gasped Sam helplessly. "What are you doing here?"

TALKER!

"What do you want?" he whispered.

TO KILL. TO FEED, spoke the voice.

Sam lost consciousness.

19
THE DISAPPEARANCE OF LI'L MAGS

TANNER ROUNDED UP MORE DOGS ON CABLE STREET, then continued working his way down the list until he reached an odd little church in Shadwell. Even in the night's gloom it was possible to see that it was deeply infected. It was the worst he had seen. He put a dot and scribbled an *i* next to the name on the list, tied up the other dogs, and picked up Li'l Mags to take a closer look. As he got nearer, she barked and snarled at it.

"Don't worry. You ain't going in there," said Tanner. "I'm just having a look."

The church virtually pulsated with Black Rot. Tanner felt as if the actual building was watching.

Li'l Mags growled fearfully.

"Hush now," said Tanner, but nothing would silence her.

"Calm down, girl." He placed his hand over her mouth, but she bit down on it.

"Ouch." He loosened his grip for a moment, and she wriggled free. She ran toward the church. The other dogs were barking, too.

"No, Li'l Mags! No!" Tanner charged after her, but he wasn't quick enough to stop her from leaping straight through the door and disappearing into the blackened church.

"Li'l Mags!" he screamed, falling to his knees. "Li'l Mags!"

Why had she left him? It was his fault. He should have kept her on the leash. He cursed himself for naming her at all. The dead weren't supposed to get attached to things. And why call her Mags, of all names? Why had he named her after the mother who had abandoned him in life? *Stupid, sentimental boy,* he thought. *What were you thinking?* Tanner covered his eyes, but ghosts were not afforded the luxury of actual tears. He lowered his hands and, to his astonishment, saw that the Black Rot was receding. The substance was disappearing into the bricks. It was releasing the building from its corrosive grip. The building was healing itself. Tanner stared in amazement as the normal color returned to the church and the black sludge that had covered it vanished. A few minutes and the building was back to normal.

The other dogs barked furiously. Tanner ran back and grabbed one, a whippet with dried blood down the side of its face. He hastily released it. There was no need to throw anything for it to fetch; the freed dog followed Li'l Mags into the building.

For a moment Tanner waited anxiously; then there was a sudden barking, and the whippet returned, running straight past him and away across the road into the darkness. The building was safe. The Black Rot had gone.

"Li'l Mags," called Tanner. "I'm coming in to get you." He approached but, seeing the door rattle, stopped dead.

Something was behind it. After a moment the doors burst open, and a great cloud of black smoke rushed out, swirling around him. Tanner coughed and sputtered and covered his mouth. The smoke had an acidic, bitter taste and an unworldly stench. Tanner was used to passing through people, getting that brief glimpse into the insides of their bodies. But this was different. The smoke, whatever it was, passed through *him*, giving him a vision into the utter darkness of it. It felt like being embodied by a scream. A world of horror and torment passed through Tanner's head and then was suddenly gone. He turned and watched as the black smoke vanished.

20

THE BOY IN THE CHURCH

Sam opened his eyes, but it was too dark to see now with either eye. The thought that he might be dead was speedily expelled by the pain in his back. One thing he had learned from dealing with ghosts was that physical pain was the property of the living. But where was he? Why was he lying on this cold wooden floor in the dark?

Slowly the memory of what had happened came back to him. The church. The black substance. Feeling it tugging at him. Falling down.

He felt something brush across his face. He reached up and grabbed it. It was the piece of material that hung down from the bell pull. He used it to pull himself to his feet, creating a soft, sustained note from the bell above. He wondered what had happened to the ghost of the bell ringer. He had met enough housebound spirits to know that their houses were like prisons to them. Yet here was a prison with no prisoner.

He remembered seeing a candle on the small table when he'd clipped his chin on it. He moved slowly and cautiously toward it, feeling for it with his hands like a blind man. His fingers moved uncertainly, unable to identify objects in the dark, until he felt the candle's cold wax between his fingers. By its side was a box of matches. He struck one and lit the wick.

In the weak yellow glow of the candlelight Sam could see for sure what he already knew; the black substance that had covered the walls was gone.

"Mags! Li'l Mags!" The voice came from downstairs.

"Rector Bray? Is that you?"

"Who's there?" called the voice.

Sam fell silent, fearful, wishing he had not spoken. He crept across the creaking floorboards, the candle in his hand casting dark shadows. He followed the stairs down and stepped into the main body of the church. He held up the candle, illuminating the rows of empty seats that led up to the pulpit and the pipe organ.

"My name is Sam Toop," he said. "I mean you no harm."

The outline of a boy stepped out from behind a lectern.

It was too dark to make out his features, but the silence of his approach gave away that this was a ghost. He stepped into the candlelight, looked Sam up and down, and said, "You ain't dead."

"And you aren't the bell ringer," replied Sam. "You're a little boy."

"You ain't so old yourself."

"Why are you here?" said Sam.

"I'm looking for my dog. Her name's Li'l Mags. Mine's Tanner."

"You have a dog?"

"She's a spirit hound, but a good one nonetheless."

"You're very young for a ghost."

The boy smiled. "There's no age limit when it comes to dying," he replied. "But you're right. Most littl'uns that pop their clogs head straight through the Unseen Door. No stayin' power, most of them. Not me, though. I thought I'd hang around."

"You're very odd," said Sam.

"Oh, a real charmer you are," said Tanner. "I've never met a Talker before. They all as charmin' as you? I heard those who get the gift are the ones who rub up against death so close, they see it everywhere. What are you, then? An executioner? A grave digger? A murderer?"

"Undertaker's son," admitted Sam.

The boy laughed. "Well, you needn't look so worried. I got no business with a Talker. I got no messages to pass on. Unless you seen my dog."

"I haven't."

"I'll see you around, Talker. Hey, I just thought, you

ain't exactly talkative for a Talker." The boy laughed, then turned to Ether Dust and flew out of the building.

Sam followed him, pushing open the great doors in time to see the boy walking away into the night with four spirit hounds on leads.

"Hey," shouted Sam. "What happened here? What was wrong with this church?"

But either the boy ignored him or his words were carried away by the cold wind that drove drizzle into Sam's face.

"Tanner," Sam yelled.

Usually the ghosts he met begged him for his help, or else they wanted him to listen to their woes and sympathize with the tragedies of their deaths. This boy was different. He'd wanted nothing from Sam.

Sam looked up at the church. The black substance had gone now. He wondered if the boy had somehow gotten rid of it. It had just passed three o'clock according to the clock on the spire of the church.

Sam crossed the damp ground to the rectory window, where there was a dim, flickering light. Rector Bray was inside, asleep on a threadbare rug in front of the dwindling remains of a dying fire. Next to him on the floor lay an empty whiskey bottle.

Sam tried the door. It was open. He walked to a desk in the corner, where he found a pencil and scribbled a short note explaining that, having fulfilled his side of the bargain, he would return with Mr. Gliddon's body for burial in a couple of days' time, giving Bray opportunity enough to organize a gravedigger and to prepare for Mr. Gliddon's interment. Sam bent down and swapped the whiskey bottle for the note so that Rector Bray would see it when he awoke. He then straightened, pulled up the collar of his coat, and set off on the long walk home.

21
LAPSEWOOD'S RETURN

RETURNING TO THE FAKE SOLIDITY OF THE BUREAU, Lapsewood was struck by how unreal the place felt in comparison to the physical world. The wooden chair opposite Mrs. Pringle, outside General Colt's office, was unyielding beneath his buttocks, but when he looked at it up close, it was disappointingly lacking in the detail of real wooden items.

Mrs. Pringle was reading a posthumously penned novella by Jane Austen entitled *Spirits and Spirituality*. Lapsewood had never been one for fiction. For him, a well-maintained accounts ledger had always provided more compelling reading than any story of invention. But Mrs. Pringle was as immersed in the book as though nothing outside it existed. Or maybe she was just ignoring him.

When General Colt did finally walk into the office, he was whistling a chirpy melody while tossing and catching a golf ball in one hand.

"If there's nothing else urgent today, Mrs. Pringle, I thought I'd take the rest of the afternoon off," he said.

"Very good," replied Mrs. Pringle.

Lapsewood stood. The general and his secretary turned to look at him, apparently both suddenly being made aware of his presence.

"Who's this?" General Colt asked Mrs. Pringle.

"Mr. Lapsewood," she replied flatly.

Lapsewood offered up the kind of salute he imagined might be employed by those in military service. This attempted act of professionalism and respect was received by the general with equal measures of confusion and uncertainty.

"You assigned him the London case," said Mrs. Pringle, to clarify. "Finding Doris McNally."

"Did I?" He looked at Lapsewood critically. "Well, you'd better get on with it. No point hanging around here. Mrs. Pringle will furnish you with all the necessary documentation."

"Er . . . she already did, sir," said Lapsewood. "I mean, I've been there. I need to talk to you about some quite shocking results of my investigation . . ."

"Excellent. Write up your report, hand it in to Mrs.

Pringle, and be on your way now." General Colt continued toward his office, only to find Lapsewood standing in his way.

"I'm sorry, sir," said Lapsewood.

"Sorry is exactly what you will be if you do not step out of my way immediately," snarled the general.

Lapsewood stepped aside. "But you see, I think this might be more urgent than that. I found her, you see. I found Doris."

"Who on earth is Doris?" bellowed General Colt.

"Doris McNally," chipped in Mrs. Pringle. "She was the Outreach Worker you sent him to find." She rolled her eyes at Lapsewood in apparent despair of her superior's ineptitude.

"Doris McNally," said General Colt. "Ah yes, good old Doris. What happened to her, then? Went Rogue, did she? Got fed up with all the moaners?"

"No, sir," replied Lapsewood. "She's being held prisoner in one of the structures on the list. St. Winifred's School, to be precise."

In case his look of disdain wasn't clear enough, the general leaned forward and snorted directly into Lapsewood's face. "Why would the school take her prisoner?"

"It had lost its Resident, sir."

"Lost its Resident?" cried the general. "Where? Underneath an armchair? In a cupboard? Buildings can't lose Residents."

"With respect, they can, sir. And once they have, they get

infected with the Black Rot, which means they become prisons for the next ghost to step inside. That's what happened to Doris."

"Infected? Black Rot? What on earth are you on about, man? Mrs. Pringle, does any of this mean anything to you?"

"There may be something about it in the Compendium," she replied. "Or else in the Central Records Library."

"Yes," said Lapsewood excitedly. "There must be something about it there. I'd never heard about it either, but Tanner and Nell both knew about it."

"Tanner?" exclaimed General Colt. "Nell?"

"Rogue ghosts, sir. Tanner was helping me."

"Rogue ghosts? I gave you no permission to recruit. Don't you know there are procedures to follow?"

"Yes, but there was no time . . . You said yourself that buildings and ghosts need each other. Who knows what damage the Black Rot could do to the physical world if it isn't dealt with? I think if we don't act quickly, then—"

"Then what?" interrupted the general. "Then hell will rise up, and heaven will fall from the sky? Because it had better be something that dramatic to justify your actions. What were you doing with this Rogue ghost?"

"We were using spirit hounds, sir."

"Anomalies? Well, thank God you're back. Because now I know what a liability you are. Mrs. Pringle, call for a guard."

"Certainly," she replied.

"But, sir, you don't understand . . ." begged Lapsewood.

"I'm afraid I understand all too clearly. When Penhaligan sent me an office clerk to do the job of a Prowler, I thought it a fob-off. Now I see it for what it really is . . . sabotage," he hissed.

"Sabotage?"

"Yes, I can see how all this will play out. Rogue ghosts and dead dogs being drafted in without permissions or licenses. They'll have my head for this. Penhaligan has been gunning for me for some time, but these are low, deplorable tactics, employing spies to bring my department into disrepute. Well, I won't have it. Do you hear me, Flackwood?"

"Lapsewood, sir."

"Don't interrupt. This espionage won't work. It hasn't worked. I've seen through you. Now, hand me back my list, and begone."

"The list, sir?"

"The London Tenancy List," he replied impatiently.

"Why do you need that back?"

"Listen, you little squeak of a melon pip, there are only three copies of that list." General Colt counted them off on his fingers. "There's Doris's, the one you had, and a safety copy in the Central Records Library. And you know how long it can take getting anything from the CRL."

"I'm sorry, sir. I don't have it."

"Well, where is it?"

"With the boy I told you about. He's to continue assessing the extent of the damage. I think unless we have proper data—"

"I think I can assess the extent of the damage," interrupted General Colt. "The extent of the damage is considerable. You have placed Bureau property in the hands of an unlicensed Rogue ghost. This is even more serious than I thought. I find you in breach of so many regulations, I haven't time to go through them all, but rest assured you will now find yourself very much under arrest." General Colt pulled out his gun and pointed its muzzle between Lapsewood's eyes. "It's the Vault for you, Latchwood."

22
CHARLIE AND JACK

SAM'S WALK BACK FROM SHADWELL TOOK FOREVER.
The city was quiet in the early-morning hours, offering no
diversion from the sound of his trudging feet. It was a time
when most were in their beds, so all Sam had for company
was the constant drizzle dampening his clothes and creating
vast puddles in the uneven roads leading toward Peckham.

As he walked, he tried to remember what had happened
while he was passed out, but it was like a nightmare that retreated further into the recesses of his memory every time
he tried to recall it. He only remembered the voice. *TALKER*,
it had said. *TO KILL. TO FEED.* Had he been asleep when he
heard it, or awake? By the time he reached the top of the

hill that led down into Honor Oak, he was soaked through and shivering. His trousers were splattered with mud, and his nose was streaming.

A dim light shone from the shop window. Sam pushed the door open, and the shop bell sounded. His father and Mr. Constable were inside. They both stood upon seeing him.

"Sam?" whispered Mr. Toop hoarsely. "Where on earth have you been? We've been out of our minds with worry."

"Are you all right, Sam?" asked Mr. Constable.

"Wet is what I mostly am," replied Sam.

"Of course you are," said Mr. Constable. He handed him a piece of velvet coffin-lining with which to dry his hair.

"Have you been drinking?" demanded Mr. Toop. "Is that it? Let me smell your breath."

"I haven't been drinking anything other than rain-water," stated Sam, wrapping the material around himself like a blanket.

"He's safe, Charles," said Mr. Constable in a quiet voice that had an immediate calming effect on Mr. Toop. "Sam, did you visit the church?"

"Yes. I got locked in."

"Locked in?" said his father.

"Yes. Thankfully, the rector was so apologetic about it that he has agreed to take Mr. Gliddon's interment."

"So both good and bad luck," said Mr. Constable, attempting to bring a moment of levity to the conversation.

"I suppose," said Sam.

Mr. Constable had the power to see straight through Sam's lies as though they were constructed of the clearest glass, and yet he turned to Mr. Toop and said, "You see, Charles? I said there would be an explanation."

"You were locked in a church?" said Mr. Toop doubtfully.

"Exactly," said Mr. Constable. "He was locked in a church. Now, Sam, you must be tired. I know I am. I suggest you dry off and go straight to bed."

"Thank you for waiting up with me," said Mr. Toop to his partner.

"I wouldn't have slept a wink either," replied Mr. Constable, "knowing that Sam was out there on a night like this because of me." He picked up his hat and coat and opened the door. "I will see you both tomorrow."

Mr. Toop closed the door quietly behind him and locked it. "Your uncle is asleep," he said. "I hope his snoring doesn't disturb you."

"After that walk, I'm not sure any noise could be so loud as to keep me from sleep," replied Sam.

Father and son took the stairs up to the landing, where they parted, Mr. Toop going into his room, Sam into his.

Jack's snoring was indeed loud. He was lying on his side, his back to the door. Sam removed his wet clothes, dried himself as best he could, pulled on a nightshirt, and climbed into bed. For a moment, he lay shivering; then he heard Jack mutter, "Night on the town, eh, lad?"

. . .

THE NEXT DAY, SAM AWOKE TO THE TINKLING OF
the shop bell. He had slept late. The shop was already open.
He opened his eyes to find Jack sitting up with Sam's muddy
trousers across his knees. In his hand, Jack held the coins he
had given him the previous day.

"A queer one, you are, lad," he said. "Someone gives you
money to buy booze, and not only do you return empty-
handed, but you come back with the money. Me, in your
position I'd 'ave bought the liquor and drunk it myself. Or
else spent the money on some other entertainment."

"There was no opportunity to buy what you wanted," replied Sam.

"Opportunities ain't somethin' you get given," said Jack.
"They're somethin' you take."

"Like the opportunity to kill someone?" said Sam, feeling angry with his uncle that he would so easily look through
his pockets without any attempt to hide it.

"Don't go thinkin' you can get away with saying things
like that on account of you being family, boy."

"We won't be family after this week is done."

"You don't want to go believin' everything your old man
says," said Jack. "We've been through a lot together, me and
'im. Charlie and Jack, that was us. A right pair of lads. The
best pair of thieves in Whitechapel. He never told you about
them days, though, I guess."

"My father was never a thief," said Sam.

Jack's lips curled upward. "There's a lot you don't know

about your old man," he said. "And a thief 'e most definitely was. A good one, too."

"He was a carpenter's apprentice," said Sam.

"Ah, the carpenter, yes. Your old man knew about takin' opportunities, too. When Old Man Chester caught him red-handed, your pa saw an opportunity to leave me high and dry. He duped the carpenter into takin' 'im in, givin' 'im some sob story about his life as a poor little urchin. He left me to fend for myself. Imagine that, my big brother leavin' me to the mercy of the streets when he'd tricked some old fella into an apprenticeship. Done him all right, too, hasn't it? His own business with the name Toop on the front. I never thought I'd see the day. Almost makes me proud." Jack was leering at Sam, his dark eyes fixed on Sam's. "'Cept pride's a sin, ain't it?"

Sam grabbed a clean set of clothes and left the room.

"Fetch me a cup of tea, will you, lad?" Jack shouted after him.

23
BREAKFASTING ALONE

Clara looked sadly at the chair in which she imagined Lady Aysgarth's ghost to have sat. Breakfast felt emptier without her.

In fact, Lady Aysgarth's chair was at the opposite end of the table from the one Clara had picked out for her. It had been the chair as far as possible from the Tiltmans.

The appearance of Lady Aysgarth's ghost in the drawing room had been as sudden and fleeting as it had been violent and traumatic. Watching through the keyhole, Clara had seen a priest destroy a human soul for the sake of dinner-party entertainment. The look of horror in Lady Aysgarth's eyes had contrasted sharply with the wonder and delight worn by Clara's parents and guests. The priest's eyes, however, had revealed a different kind of pleasure, like that of the hangman relishing his work.

A polite round of applause had followed the vanquishing of Lady Aysgarth's soul. Afterward, back in her room, Clara had made copious notes about it all, spending a lot of time laboring over her comparison to Romans watching Christians being fed to lions for the sake of entertainment—an analogy that, in spite of her best endeavors, she was still struggling to make work.

"So, was Hetty's friend suitably entertaining?" she asked, finally breaking the silence that had hung over the table since she entered the dining room.

"He was most intriguing, thank you," said her mother.

Her father, hidden behind a newspaper, said nothing.

"I'd very much like to meet him," said Clara.

"I don't think that would be suitable," replied her mother, quickly.

Clara turned to her father and employed her most appealing voice. "Please could I meet him? It's for my article."

Mrs. Tiltman frowned. "I expressly told you that you would be writing no such article."

Mr. Tiltman lowered his paper. "Perhaps she should meet him," he said. "Find out how it's done."

"We saw how it was done," snapped Mrs. Tiltman.

"How it's really done. What the trick is," said Mr. Tiltman.

"Honestly, it was in our own house. There were no mirrors or conjuring equipment. You saw her with your own eyes."

"Saw whom?" asked Clara innocently. "What was he, this friend of Hetty's?"

"His name was Reverend Fallowfield," said her father, ignoring the look his wife was casting across the table. "He is a priest who performs exorcisms."

"Exorcisms," said Clara, sounding convincingly surprised.

"It was very well done," said Mr. Tiltman.

"Because it was real," added his wife.

"Oh, please. London is full of conjurors, all performing miracles, and none of them able to conjure up enough money to stop me calling them beggars. I tell you, it's all a sham—a good sham, I grant you, but a sham nonetheless."

"Reverend Fallowfield didn't charge for his services," said Mrs. Tiltman.

"Quite happily accepted donations, though, didn't he? Did you see the check that Malcolm wrote? Such extraction of money is a cunning enough trick."

Clara enjoyed it when her parents argued like this. There was a spark between them. She had friends who claimed that their mothers never contradicted their husbands, but the Tiltmans' family life was enlivened by the tos and fros of debate.

Mrs. Tiltman, uncomfortable with her daughter being exposed to such arguments, said, "You shouldn't disagree with me over breakfast. You'll give yourself indigestion."

Mr. Hopkins, the butler, refilled her teacup.

"Thank you," Mrs. Tiltman said.

"I could find out for you whether he's a trickster or not," said Clara.

"Clara Tiltman," scolded her mother. "Reverend Fallowfield is a man of God. No one is calling him a trickster."

"I am," said Mr. Tiltman.

"Let me contact Aunt Hetty and meet this man," said Clara. "I'll find out what he is."

"I do not think this hobby of yours at all suitable for a young lady," said her mother.

"I feel a wager coming on," said Mr. Tiltman. "I think it a splendid idea that Clara attempt to reveal the truth behind this Fallowfield. I'll bet you ten pounds she can discover his method."

"I do not accept your wager, and I will not encourage any of this." Mrs. Tiltman frowned.

Mr. Tiltman smiled at his wife. He reached across the table and took her hand, lifting it toward his lips as though to kiss it, then, at the last minute, shaking it instead.

"Ten pounds it is," he said. "Clara will meet Reverend Fallowfield and expose the truth behind his show."

24
THE VAULT

THE ENFORCER WHO ARRIVED TO TAKE LAPSEWOOD away was a huge-boned bear of a man. He wore a navy-blue suit and a badge with his name on it: SERGEANT BRINKS. Broad shoulders, bulging arms—Lapsewood wouldn't have been surprised to find that he had more than five fingers on each of his huge hands. The cuffs he slapped over Lapsewood's wrists were molded into the shape of a pair of metal hands connected by a chain.

"Just try turning to Ether Dust with these on," grunted Sergeant Brinks.

"Please, General Colt," Lapsewood protested as the Enforcer led him out of the office. "Send someone to find

Doris McNally. She'll explain. She's at the school in White-chapel."

"Get him out of here," barked General Colt.

The door closed behind them, and Sergeant Brinks dragged Lapsewood along the corridor and down the stair-case. "You keep on struggling like that and I'll be forced to use my Ether Beater," he said.

"There's been a mistake," said Lapsewood.

"That's good," replied Sergeant Brinks.

"It's not good. It means you're arresting an innocent man."

"I'm not arresting you."

"You're not?"

"Oh, no, your actual arrest requires a lot more paper-work. This is a simple detention prior to the application of an arrest. You'll be held in the Vault until your hearing, when you will either be formally arrested or released, once a full acquittal application has been filled in and verified."

"How long will that take?"

"Oh, not long. What've you done, then?"

"That's what I'm saying. I haven't done anything."

"The General mentioned something about consorting with Rogue ghosts."

"Yes, but only because I needed help."

Sergeant Brinks took a sharp intake of breath. "The chief don't look too kindly on that sort of thing. My cousin Dawl-ish is an Enforcer—he says the chief wants all the Rogues locked up, but they're tricky to catch, see." At the bottom of the stairs there was a huge wooden door with metal bolts adorning its edges. "Hand over your papers," said Sergeant Brinks.

"I can't," replied Lapsewood.

"You have no choice. Vault prisoners have to hand over their papers," said Sergeant Brinks.

"I mean, I can't because I'm still wearing these cuffs."

Sergeant Brinks laughed. "Oh, yes. Let's get them off, shall we?" From his belt, he pulled out a large silver ring with hundreds of keys on it. He unlocked Lapsewood's handcuffs, and the metallic fingers sprang open. Lapsewood reached into his inside pocket and handed over his papers. Sergeant Brinks took them and then pulled a large key from the key ring.

He pushed to one side the cover that hung in front of the keyhole and quickly inserted the key. "The Vault is made of impassable materials," he said. "So a keyhole would be one of the few ways out." He gripped the door handle and drew his Beater. "Now you'll see how this works," he said.

He opened the door, and a cloud of swirling Ether Dust gushed from the gap. Sergeant Brinks brought his Beater down hard on it, causing it to re-form and a man wearing a white wig, a ruffled shirt, and a finely made velvet jacket to fall to the ground.

"Nice try, Marquis," said Sergeant Brinks.

"One day, Sergeant Brinks." The man got to his feet and brushed down his jacket.

"Not on my watch. Now I'll leave you two fellas to get acquainted."

Brinks shoved both Lapsewood and the Marquis inside and slammed the door shut. The Marquis dived to his knees and put his eye to the keyhole, but the cover was back in place. He stood up and offered his hand to Lapsewood.

"Delighted to meet you," he said. "What brings you here?"

"Nothing. You see, I'm—"

"Innocent?" interrupted the Marquis.

"Yes, you see, it was just a—"

"Misunderstanding?" he interrupted again.

"Exactly, but . . . How did you know?"

"We're all innocent, my boy." He placed his hand on Lapsewood's arm. "We're all victims of misunderstandings."

"Ah, yes, but, you see, I haven't even been—"

"Arrested?"

"Yes, I'm awaiting my—"

"Your hearing, yes. Once again, ditto. And ditto on behalf of every other poor soul locked in this damnable place."

"But he said I wouldn't be here long."

"If he had said you would spend the rest of eternity awaiting a hearing that would, according to all evidence, never materialize—if he had said that—would you have walked so quietly and placidly into this cell?"

"Well, I . . . I'm not sure."

"Of course you wouldn't, dear boy. You'd have to be insane. And insanity is something I do have a little experience with. Now, why don't you tell me all about it?"

25

THE EXORCISM OF ST. WINIFRED'S SCHOOL

AUNT HETTY HAD OFFERED TO BRING REVEREND Fallowfield to Aysgarth House again, but Clara had said that since he had already exorcised their home, it would be better if they were to meet elsewhere. Mrs. Tiltman emphatically refused to allow her daughter to attend one of the dinner parties at which Reverend Fallowfield was proving so popular all over London, but, happily, Hetty told her that the Reverend had an engagement at a school in the east end of London on Sunday.

"Mr. Fallowfield is an extraordinary man," said Aunt Hetty as the taxi rattled along Commercial Road.

"Where did you find him?" asked Clara.

"He was recommended by a friend whose house he exorcised, and, knowing what I'm like for collecting interesting people, she put me on to him."

"Father thinks it's a trick."

Aunt Hetty laughed. "Your father was scared out of his wits when the Reverend revealed the ghost that had been living in your house."

"What do you think happens to the ghosts once he's exorcised Them?"

Aunt Hetty shrugged indifferently. "I suppose they go to hell. Or some such place."

St. Winifred's School was an imposing redbrick building. It being Sunday, there were no children or teachers there. Reverend Fallowfield was standing outside the front door. Seen in daylight and without the encumbrance of a keyhole, he was even more striking in appearance. The three-pointed birthmark on his head, his bulging eyes, and his hook nose made him look like a heavily made-up actor Clara had once seen playing Shakespeare's Richard III. But there was no makeup, and his shifting eyes were not part of an act.

"Ah, Hetty, my child," he said, taking her hand and kissing her on the cheek. His eyes fell upon Clara. "And you must be the niece."

"I'm Clara."

"What are you, then?" he asked.

Clara was unsure how to respond. "I'd like to be a journalist one day."

147

"I mean, are you cynic or believer?"

"I believe in ghosts, if that's what you mean."

"'Ghosts,'" hissed Reverend Fallowfield. "Such a tame word for these lingering demons. You should understand that I perform God's work. I send these evil spirits down into the underworld, where they belong."

"Why do you call Them evil?"

"They are lost souls, rejected by heaven, fearful of hell. They wander God's earth like beggars."

"Are beggars not unfortunate creatures who deserve our charity and sympathy?" asked Clara.

"Who would say such a thing?"

"I believe it is the teaching of the Bible."

He smiled, revealing his coffee-stained teeth. "Then they're like thieves," he stated.

"What do they steal?"

"Their time here is stolen."

"Well, listen to us, with our intellectual musings," said Aunt Hetty, trying to lighten the mood.

Clara scribbled down as much as she could in her notebook, grateful to her aunt for diverting Reverend Fallowfield's intense stare.

A caretaker met them outside. An elderly man with a limp and a lazy eye, he led them into the school hall.

"What kind of school is this?" asked Clara.

"A ragged school, miss," he replied. "Set up to teach those without the means to pay."

Ragged was the right word, thought Clara. There was a

marked difference to the school she had attended. The hall bore a closer resemblance to a factory than to a place of education.

"Here we are, then," said the caretaker.

"May I ask why you have no service on a Sunday, Reverend Fallowfield?" asked Clara.

"The world is my parish," he replied.

"So these exorcisms are your only source of income?" she asked.

"Now, Clara, I don't think Reverend Fallowfield wishes to discuss his finances with you," scolded Aunt Hetty.

Reverend Fallowfield smiled. "I can see you have a journalist's instinct. But, no, I do not charge for my services. As I said before, this is God's work."

"But you accept donations," said Clara.

"As I have no other income at present, yes, I do accept donations. Eating is not a sin, Miss Tiltman. Now, I must ask for your silence."

Reverend Fallowfield walked around the hall with his eyes shut and his fingers outstretched.

"How did you hear about him?" Clara whispered to the caretaker.

"He came once before," the caretaker replied. "There was a ghost of a little girl then."

"You saw her?"

"Not me, but some of the teachers used to say she would hide the chalk or write words on the board at night."

"That's why you wanted her exorcised?"

"I never did, miss . . . want her exorcised, that is. This fellow turned up one day and got rid of her. No one asked him to. Just did it."

"And now you have a new ghost?"

"So he says."

"I must have silence!" cried Reverend Fallowfield.

"Sorry," said the caretaker.

"Oh, cursed spirit," the Reverend began.

"Oh, I love this bit," whispered Hetty.

Reverend Fallowfield reached out his hands like claws and made a great show of pulling an invisible something toward him as though there was a great strain on his arms. "Draw close, come out, reveal yourself. Resist not my command." He muttered strange incantations in a tongue Clara did not recognize but knew to be neither Greek nor Latin.

A moment passed, and then another voice spoke. "No, leave me alone," said a Scottish female voice.

Clara gripped her aunt's hand. She looked to see where the voice had come from, but they were alone in the hall.

"Oh, cursed spirit," wailed Reverend Fallowfield. "Do my bidding, and recognize the higher authority of the living over the dead."

More incantations followed in the mysterious tongue. Then, slowly, gray smoke drifted down from the cracks in the ceiling and formed a human shape. The shape gained definition and color. Still transparent but now clearly that of a woman. She had untidy red hair, a green dress, and a bloodstained apron.

"You have no right to do this," she said, addressing Reverend Fallowfield.

"I have every right," he replied. "This is our realm. You are the trespasser here."

"I did'ne want to get stuck in this wretched school," she replied.

"Silence!" cried Reverend Fallowfield. "You shall be silent forevermore. For now His kingdom will come, His will be done. You shall be vanquished, no more to roam. Forces of the afterworld, open now and draw unto you this spirit."

"You're a barrel of laughs, you are," the woman started to say, but suddenly something unseen gripped her throat, and she began to struggle, writhe, and scream. She staggered backward.

Clara moved closer to watch. The woman turned to her in horror. She dropped to her knees. The gray smoke that formed her was ebbing away, removing her form, her shape.

"Help me," she uttered in a strangulated whisper.

"Stop it!" yelled Clara. "You're hurting her."

"Demons feel no pain," replied Reverend Fallowfield.

Clara stepped forward and crouched to help the poor woman and was surprised to feel a pair of ice-cold hands grab her own and thrust something into them. The woman's scream grew and grew until it was indistinguishable from the sound of wind rushing through the old school, rattling the window frames, shaking the building's very foundations.

Then she was gone. Silence followed.

"Clara, are you all right?" asked Aunt Hetty, dropping to her side.

"Yes, I'm fine," she stammered, unable to put into words her true feelings at having witnessed such horror up close.

"As I said, demons," said Reverend Fallowfield triumphantly.

Clara lifted her notebook and pen to write and found a piece of paper in her hands that had not been there before. She glanced at the list of names and addresses but did not want to draw Reverend Fallowfield's attention to it, so she folded it up and slipped it between the pages of her notebook.

26
A PARENT'S PAST

SAM DID NOT RELISH RETURNING TO THE CHURCH IN Shadwell. He felt a cold shiver whenever he thought of the strange black substance that had enveloped him in the bell tower, but life had to go on. And so did the business of death. Sam frequently acted as mute for funerals, his naturally somber appearance making him ideal for the role of walking ahead of the hearse, carrying a mourning wand with a black cloth draped over it.

There being such distance to cover for Mr. Gliddon's funeral, Mr. Constable suggested to Richard and Edward Gliddon that it would make more sense for Sam to ride up front in the hearse until the final leg of the journey.

The Gliddon boys agreed to the point. They would be in a second carriage along with the rest of the family attending the burial.

Mr. Constable sat beside Sam, holding the reins, having ordered the designated driver home and to bed when he'd arrived that morning with a stinking cold. Behind them was the late Mr. Gliddon himself, sitting on his own coffin.

"The death of a patriarch is a difficult time, but I feel it has brought the Gliddon boys closer together," said Mr. Constable. "While their father lived, they could only see their differences. In death, they have been reminded of the familial bond that holds them together."

"They're good boys," agreed Mr. Gliddon, as though the remark had been directed toward him.

"Talking of family matters," said Mr. Constable, "how are you finding Uncle Jack?"

"I'll be glad when he's gone," said Sam. "I do not like him."

"I don't think Jack means to be liked. Or at least if he does, he goes about it an extremely peculiar way."

"Why is Father protecting him?"

"Because Jack is his brother. You and I, we have no brothers. Indeed, I have precious few blood relations, except for a cousin in Rochester who only visits when in need of financial assistance. But one cannot underestimate the strength of blood. Even when there are such differences in every other respect."

"Yes, but murder . . ." protested Sam.

"Jack will be gone soon enough. And your father's conscience will be eased. He will have helped his brother in his time of need. And my guess is that, given Jack's nature, the sanctuary he finds above the shop will only delay his ultimate destination."

"You mean, you think he will hang," said Sam. Then he added, "Good."

"No man's death should be the cause of delight, no matter who he is."

Sam hated disappointing Mr. Constable. He sought his approval and respect above anyone else's, even above his own father's. He would have changed the subject, but Uncle Jack still weighed heavily on his thoughts. "Jack says they both thieved as children," said Sam.

Mr. Constable didn't respond immediately. They were on the part of the journey between Peckham and the Old Kent Road, where there were far fewer houses and, thus, fewer people to stop and stare. Sam had often felt that riding in a funeral carriage was not so different from riding in a royal carriage, the number of people who gawked or stood on tiptoe to get a better look.

"Your father didn't have the same privileges as you or I, growing up."

"So he was a thief?"

"In the district of London where your father grew up, thievery is often the only option available. But Charles Toop was like a rare flower growing in a swamp. He lifted himself out of his situation and made himself a better man.

Many have achieved great things with opportunities, but your father had none. No education, no father to provide for him and guide him, no mother to teach him right from wrong. And yet, against all the odds, he learned a skill, and a noble one, that of our Savior himself. These are no mean achievements."

The rest of the journey went smoothly enough, except for a brief drama just before London Bridge, when they got stuck behind a cart carrying a pile of apples, which had spilled across the road after a wheel had come loose and fallen off. The owner of the cart had been shouting and swearing loudly about his predicament, and Mr. Constable had been forced to intervene, sternly reminding the apple-cart owner that he was not the only one inconvenienced.

Once the cart had been lifted to the side of the road, they continued over the river.

"You'd met Jack before," said Sam.

"I had," agreed Mr. Constable.

"And when he first saw me, he said I looked like my mother," said Sam.

"He was right about that," said Mr. Constable.

"So he visited Honor Oak before."

Mr. Constable looked down at the murky waters of the Thames. "Learning that one's parent has a past all his own is hard, but your father has been the best of men for as long as I've known him. Now, I'm afraid to say that as soon as we arrive on the north bank, I must ask that you step down and take up your role on foot."

27
MRS. PRINGLE

GENERAL COLT WAS NO FOOL. HE UNDERSTOOD THAT being the head of the Housing Department sounded far more impressive than it actually was. The department basically ran itself. Occasionally an Outreach Worker would need replacing, but that was hardly enough to occupy the hours he was expected to spend in the office. Which was just as well, as far as he was concerned, as it meant that he could spend all the more time working on his golf swing. General Colt had not been one of life's hard workers, and he saw no reason to alter this in death.

Mrs. Pringle, however, had other ideas and was forever trying to make him do things.

"General Colt, I'd like a word," she said, entering his office before he had time to pretend to be asleep.

"I have a meeting," he blurted out.

"Since it is I who schedules your meetings, I'd be surprised if that were true," said the woman.

"Sharp as ever, Mrs. Pringle," conceded General Colt through gritted teeth. "Sharp like a razor."

"It's about Mr. Lapsewood," she continued.

"Who?"

"The clerk you had carted off to the Vault."

"Oh, him. Yes, what of him?"

"I rather think there may have been something in what he said."

"The man was trying to undermine me," snapped General Colt. "He was trying to bring my name into disrepute by consorting with Rogue ghosts."

"I took it upon myself to look up the Black Rot he mentioned. It turns out it does exist."

"So?"

"Have you ever heard of the Parisian Problem?"

"Garlic breath?" ventured General Colt.

"No," replied Mrs. Pringle, distinctly unamused. "Perhaps you should read this." She dropped a heavy file onto his empty desk.

"Ah, well," said the general, flicking through the pages. "Perhaps I should save this for the morning. It looks pretty hard going."

"It *is* the morning," replied Mrs. Pringle.

General Colt found his secretary to be a singularly for-midable woman, especially when she was in a mood like this. He opened the report and reluctantly began to read.

28
THE PARISIAN PROBLEM

THE VAULT WAS A VAST CAVERN OF A PRISON, DIMLY lit by meager torches that hung from the pillars stretching up to the impossibly high ceiling. The far corners were shrouded in shadow, and yet the Marquis never strayed more than a few feet from the door.

"Should we not look for another way out?" asked Lapsewood.

"Wander into the darkness, and you will become like one of those poor souls," the Marquis replied, pointing out toward the far corners of the Vault. From the gloom came distant screams, animalistic groans, and pained moans, echoing off the walls.

"Who are they?" asked Lapsewood, peering into the darkness.

"Dissipated souls," the Marquis whispered. "Hundreds—thousands—of them. Unable to escape this terrible hell-hole and driven mad by their determination to find a crack through which to slip, they have been Ether Dust for so long, they have forgotten their forms." He chuckled darkly. "Screaming dust. The stuff of nightmares even for us ghosts, wouldn't you say?"

"But you've stayed whole?"

"Exactly," cried the Marquis. "One must never lose hope in the prevailing human spirit. What are we ghosts if not prevailing human spirits?" He looked at Lapsewood, searching for some kind of acknowledgment of what he clearly considered an excellent speech.

"I must get out," said Lapsewood. "The Black Rot is eating away at London. I must do something to prevent it."

"There is Black Rot in London?" said the Marquis.

"You know of it?"

"Indeed," replied the Marquis. "Some years ago, when I was in Paris, they had a similar problem. There they called it *la Pourriture Noire*."

"Paris?"

"Yes, I was staying there. The French Bureau has a much more liberal attitude toward Rogue ghosts."

"And buildings were getting infected in the same way?"

"Yes."

"How did the buildings come to lose their ghosts?"

"There is only one way to remove a Resident from its building," replied the Marquis. "Exorcism."

"Is it really possible?" asked Lapsewood.

"It is. Of course, the vast majority of exorcists can no more exorcise a house than they can urinate marmalade, but there are a few exceptions. There was one such exception in Paris at this time, and it became briefly fashionable among the living to have their houses exorcised," replied the Marquis.

"The living dispatching the dead?" said Lapsewood.

The Marquis's look darkened. "This was not 'dispatching,'" he said. "A true exorcist is not opening a door. He is calling the other side to drag the spirit through the crack in the veil between this world and the Void."

"But with no door—"

The Marquis interrupted him. "With no door the spirit's soul is torn apart. It is split and splintered."

"What happened to the exorcist?"

"Ah, now there lies the beauty of that city. So susceptible are the Parisians to fashion and so fickle and short of attention that it didn't take long for the city's gentry to grow tired of this man's show. Exorcisms went the way of every other fashion."

"But he must have left many infected houses."

"Indeed he did. Most were filled by roaming spirits who stepped inside and found themselves trapped, but I remember one chateau in the south of the city that became so bad that the rot was visible from the outside. None would venture near it. Neither living nor dead. If a house gets that bad, it looks elsewhere for an inhabitant."

"You mean it looks among the living?"

"The living? No. The inanimate material of a house has no power over the living, no matter how badly infected it gets. They say this chateau drew something from the Void."

Lapsewood looked with disbelief at the Marquis. "But . . . surely nothing can come back from the other side."

"You speak with such certainty for one who has only just learned of these things."

"If what you say is true, we must do something."

"Certainly something must be done," agreed the Marquis, "but we can do nothing on this side of that door. We must make our escape. Come, see . . ." The Marquis beckoned him over to one of the walls.

"I can't see anything," replied Lapsewood.

"Place your hand here." He pointed out a low part of the wall.

Lapsewood ran his hand along it and felt a tiny indentation. "What is that?" he asked.

The Marquis laughed. "I have for some years now been chipping away at this wall using the nail of the large toe on my right foot."

"But these walls are thick. It would take thousands of years to actually make a hole to get through, if such a thing is even possible at all."

"That's true, but look down here."

The Marquis led him to another spot on the ground,

where he had placed several chippings from the wall in rows and scratched rough lines on the ground.

"I don't understand," said Lapsewood.

"It's a chessboard, dear boy," proclaimed the Marquis.

"A chessboard? What use is that in escaping?"

"None whatsoever. I told you, the only way of escaping is to make a break for it whenever that guard opens the door. But chess will help pass the time while we wait. Which will you be? Black or white? You have to imagine the colors, of course."

29
CLARA'S LIST

CLARA'S AUNT HETTY HAD DONE ALL THE TALKING in the taxi journey back from the school in Whitechapel. She had been full of ideas for how Reverend Fallowfield could improve his act. Clara had not spoken a word. Unlike her aunt, she felt as if she had witnessed something terrible. Try as she might, she could not rid herself of the memory of that poor woman's horrifying screams.

At home she went straight up to her room, where she sat down by her toy theater. It was a beautifully rendered version in miniature of Drury Lane, bought for her seventh birthday. With its stringed actors and moving curtains, it had provided many hours of entertainment for Clara as a child as she inflicted countless plays on her nanny. The plots mostly derived from real play titles she had heard her parents discussing but which she had not seen. Her versions of *She Stoops to Conquer, The Duchess of Malfi,* and *Love's Labour's Lost* were particular triumphs, even if they did bear little resemblance to the original works.

Clara had given up her career as theater-impresario-in-miniature some years ago, and she was not the kind of girl to cling to items of her childhood out of sentimentality. Few of her dolls had survived the great cull of 1881, when she turned twelve and decided she was no longer a child. But the theater and its puppets had remained in a corner, being too beautiful to throw away, even for as unsentimental a young lady as herself.

She sat silently moving the actors on and off the stage, thinking about Reverend Fallowfield, Lady Aysgarth, and the poor woman in the school.

Opening her notebook, she pulled out the list. She could scarcely believe it had come from the ghost, but the more she thought about it, the more she believed it to be true.

Clara unfolded it and read the title at the top.

The London Tenancy List: D. McNally's Copy

Below was a list of London addresses. There were private residences, theaters, schools, and public houses. Some were familiar, others were not. Down the right-hand column was a list of names. By Drury Lane Theatre was the name

Mr. David Kerby. The space alongside the Tower of London was crammed with long-dead kings and queens. Then she found her own address.

Aysgarth House, Three Kings Court

Clara moved her finger to the right and found the corresponding name:

Lady Aysgarth (g-b 1864)

Clara's hands trembled as the sudden realization hit her. "Ghosts," she whispered to herself. "It's a list of ghosts."

30

THE BURIAL OF MR. GLIDDON

SAM STOOD BY THE HEARSE WATCHING MR. GLID-
don's coffin being lowered into the ground. The brothers
stood next to each other, their shoulders touching, their
heads lowered. Their dead father stood silently opposite
them. Sam had attended so many funerals that he could not
remember a time when they hadn't been a part of his life.
He had grown up watching black-shrouded widows weep for
their dear, departed husbands, parents beat their chests with
pain over their lost infants, and every other manifestation
of grief. It wasn't that he was uncaring, just that the procedure and routine of funerals cloaked the raw human emotions they contained. Perhaps that was the point of them.

Sam looked at Mr. Constable. He, too, had long inhabited this world of grief, so how was it he was able to convey a veneer of pained sorrow as he stood at a respectful distance behind the family? Had Sam not known him so well, he would have considered this a remarkable act, worthy of the stage. But Sam knew that Mr. Constable was blessed with a natural empathy for every living soul and an ability to sincerely mourn the passing of each one. When so many in the profession of undertaking were considered cynical profiteers, none who met him had anything but kind words to say about Mr. Constable.

Rector Bray threw a handful of dust onto the coffin lid. There had still been a whiff of alcohol on his breath when Sam had greeted him, but the fear had gone from his eyes. Mr. Gliddon's gravestone lay against the stone wall, bearing the euphemism *Fell Asleep*. Sam stared at the words. If death was sleep, then what were ghosts? Dreams? Nightmares?

Neither the rector nor Sam had mentioned his previous visit, although it weighed heavily on Sam's mind, and he had relived the experience over and over in his dreams the previous two nights. He had looked for signs of the strange black substance in other buildings but seen none. He had wondered what role the boy ghost with the pack of dogs had played in the whole business. It was rare that Sam wanted to see a ghost again, but the boy Tanner intrigued him.

After a short eulogy from Edward Gliddon and a few words from Rector Bray, the funeral was over. When Sam heard the sound of knocking, he knew it was for Mr. Gliddon. Relief, fear, and sadness swept across the ghost's face as he turned to face the door that was only visible to him. He glanced at his sons. "Richard, take good care of the business," he said. "Edward, take good care of yourself." With these final words the ghost of Mr. Gliddon stepped through the Unseen Door and vanished from sight.

Before the funeral troupe headed home, Rector Bray came to speak to Sam by the hearse while Mr. Constable was talking to the mourners.

"My church is reborn," said Rector Bray. "Thank you. I don't know what you did, but . . ."

"I didn't do anything," replied Sam quietly.

"You're too modest," said the rector. "May I ask what method you used?"

"I don't know what you mean."

"To exorcise the church. The Lord's Prayer, words from the Gospels? I am told the Book of Revelations has much of use."

Sam could smell brandy on the rector's breath. "I did not exorcise anything," he said. "Whatever was here chose to leave."

"Really? How fascinating," said the rector. He pulled out from beneath his robes a small hip flask, which he lifted to his lips. "Communion wine," he said by way of explanation.

"Tell me," said Sam. "Are you aware of a boy ghost in these parts? A boy who has lost a dog?"

"A boy?" replied Bray. "No. There are plenty enough dying children around here. And plenty enough dogs, come to think of it, but none associated with this church as far as I know." The conversation came to an abrupt end when Mr. Constable returned and informed them that the family was ready to leave. He thanked Rector Bray once again for allowing the interment in his churchyard, and the funeral party began the long journey back to Honor Oak.

31
FLOUTING
PROCEDURE

Impromptu meetings were unheard of in the Bureau. Heads of department only ever met at the monthly General Business Cross-Departmental Meetings, which were such slavishly methodical affairs that General Colt usually went out of his way to "forget" them, no matter how many times Mrs. Pringle reminded him.

It was no wonder, then, that Alice Biggins greeted General Colt with a look of confused shock when he materialized in front of her and demanded to speak to Colonel Penhaligan at once.

"I don't have a note of a meeting scheduled," she said, looking at her appointment book.

"I just want to speak to Penhaligan," replied the general.

"I'm afraid he's in with someone right now. Perhaps if you could return to your office and have Mrs. Pringle schedule an—"

"There's no time for that," said General Colt, and, before she could stop him, he pushed open the door to find Colonel Penhaligan sitting behind his desk in discussion with a well-dressed gentleman with a thin mustache.

"General Colt," said Colonel Penhaligan, raising his eyebrows. "I think you have stumbled into the wrong room."

"I don't stumble, and I am in the right room," replied the general. "I have urgent business."

"Sorry, sir," said Alice from behind him.

"That's all right, Alice," said Colonel Penhaligan. "As it happens, Eugène and I have concluded our business." He turned to the other ghost and said, "Thank you, Monsieur Vidocq."

Monsieur Vidocq nodded and left, closing the door behind him, leaving the colonel and the general alone in the room.

"Now, General Colt, what is it that is so pressing to deserve such utter disregard for centuries of procedural processes?"

"Black Rot," said General Colt, slamming the report onto the colonel's desk.

Colonel Penhaligan didn't look at it and instead kept his eyes trained on the general. "I'm sorry, but you may have to speak in full sentences."

"Black Rot," repeated the general. "It's a phantasmago-rical wasting disease. It occurs when a haunted house loses its ghost. The last known incidence was in Paris, France."

"Ah, yes, the Parisian Problem," said Colonel Penha-ligan, resting his elbows on the report and knitting his fin-gers together. "What of it?"

"It's back. We have a Black Rot problem in London."

Colonel Penhaligan placed his chin on his hands. "I find that quite hard to believe. My man Vidocq just got back from there. He didn't mention any such thing."

"Well, my man Lapsewool found differently."

"You mean Lapsewood?" Colonel Penhaligan snorted, then let out a kind of coughing, spluttering laugh. "This has come from Lapsewood, the donkey?"

"I'll admit, at first I thought you'd sent me a real dud there, too," said General Colt. "But our boy has discovered a problem that has gone unnoticed by your Prowlers and by Admiral Hardknuckle's Enforcers."

"And where is Lapsewood now, pray?"

General Colt shifted uncomfortably. "As it happens, I sent him to the Vault," he admitted. "Accidentally, I might add."

"Accidentally?" guffawed Colonel Penhaligan.

"Yeah, well, some of his methods were a little unortho-dox."

"As unorthodox as marching into a senior head of de-partment's office unannounced, would you say?"

"Listen here," said General Colt, wagging a finger in

Colonel Penhaligan's face. "This business requires an unorthodox approach. You know what happened in Paris. We have to keep that from happening here."

Colonel Penhaligan sighed. "General Colt, as you'll recall, it was I who recommended you for your current position, and with equal ease I can call for a review of your competence, so I'll ask you not to wave your fingers in my face. I know very well what happened in Paris, and I have no intention of letting the same thing happen on our own soil. But we have procedures for a reason. First we need proof that such a problem exists in London. I take these things very seriously, but the testimony of a donkey like Lapsewood won't cut it. In spite of the unacceptable way you have gone about this, I am willing to personally ensure that a motion is made at the next monthly General Business Cross-Departmental Meeting and that everything is then done to investigate this matter."

"But that's not for weeks . . ." began General Colt.

"I'm surprised you know the date at all." Colonel Penhaligan smiled and spoke calmly. "But don't worry yourself. When you've been in this job as long as I, you'll understand that procedures and process exist for a reason. Indeed, they are the foundations upon which this great establishment was built."

"It could be too late by the time that bunch of fusty old duffers decides to do anything."

"General Colt, we lost our sense of 'too late' when we became ghosts," replied Colonel Penhaligan. "Besides, I'll remind you that you are talking about your colleagues."

General Colt stared angrily at Penhaligan for a moment, then turned and stormed out. As he opened the door, he collided with Alice, who was crouching outside the door, listening at the keyhole.

32

A VISITOR

LAPSEWOOD AND THE MARQUIS STOOD BY THE DOOR
to the Vault, listening to the clinking sound of the keys sig-
nifying the approach of the guard.

"Remember the plan," said the Marquis. "We turn to
Ether Dust; then, as soon as you see a crack in the door, fly.
You head upward, and I shall go down. Whichever one of
us gets out will return to release the other. Good luck and
Godspeed. Let love of liberty lead us onward."

They could hear the cover in front of the keyhole being moved to one side and the key being quickly inserted.
Lapsewood watched the Marquis turn to Ether Dust and was
about to do the same when he heard his own name spoken.

"Visitor for Lapsewood," said Sergeant Brinks.

Lapsewood froze. He had a visitor? The key turned, unlocking the door. A crack of light appeared. The *thwack* of Brinks's Ether Beater bringing the Marquis down with a thud reminded Lapsewood, too late, about the plan.

The door swung open to reveal Sergeant Brinks standing over the beaten Marquis. Next to him, dwarfed by the Enforcer's size, stood Grunt.

"Grunt?" said Lapsewood.

"My old friend," he replied, offering his hand. Lapsewood took it, feeling so grateful to see him that he didn't even mind the dampness of his palm.

"You've got two minutes," said Brinks. "Inside, though." He pushed the Marquis and Grunt inside unceremoniously and slammed the door shut behind them.

"Some accomplice you turned out to be," grumbled the Marquis.

"I'm sorry, but you see, I know this man," said Lapsewood.

Grunt looked at the huge door that had closed behind him. "Sergeant Brinks?" he shouted.

"Don't worry, Mr. Grunt," replied the Enforcer, his voice muted by the thick door between them. "I'm not going anywhere."

"What are you doing here?" Lapsewood asked Grunt.

"Alice told me what happened."

"Alice knows I'm here?"

"Yes," replied Grunt. "I wanted to come because of all

the kindnesses you showed me when I started the job. It's quite a step up, but I'm working my way through the backlog now."

"Working your way through it?" said Lapsewood, dismayed that Grunt was succeeding where he had failed.

"Colonel Penhaligan says he's delighted with my work," said Grunt, grinning.

"'Delighted'?"

"That was the word he used. *Delighted.* Imagine that. I don't think anyone has ever used that particular word in reference to me before. I certainly never heard my wife use it, and she was a woman blessed with a rich and colorful use of the English language."

Grunt mopped away the gunk that had seeped over the top of his neck scarf.

While Lapsewood looked away in disgust, the Marquis seemed fascinated by the whole thing. "Hanged, eh?" he asked Grunt.

"Yes, sir," replied Grunt. "Newgate."

"They would have done the same to me, you know, if I hadn't picked up some rather interesting infections that saw me off first."

"One minute left!" shouted Brinks from the other side of the door.

"Grunt," said Lapsewood, grabbing him by the lapels and instantly regretting it, seeing the effect it had on the flow of gray goo from his neck. He released him. "You need to get me out of here. I need to get back to London.

I need to find whoever is exorcising spirits and stop them."

"Exorcising? I don't know anything about that, but I don't think you've much chance of visiting anywhere," said Grunt.

"No," said Lapsewood, thinking fast. "But you have."

"Me?"

"Yes, you. Take a leave for a day," said Lapsewood urgently.

"A leave for a day?"

Lapsewood spoke quickly. "Yes. Go to London. Go to St. Winifred's School in Whitechapel and get the other copy of the London Tenancy List off Doris McNally. Once you have that, you'll be able to use it to track down a Rogue ghost boy by the name of Tanner. He travels with a pack of spirit hounds."

"When I open that door again," warned Brinks, "don't even think about trying to escape, Marquis."

"Rogue ghosts? London? Spirit hounds?" said Grunt, sounding panicked. "No . . . I don't have the forms . . ." He frantically mopped away at the top of the scarf.

"This is more important than forms," said Lapsewood, grabbing him by the lapels and succeeding in increasing the flow of gunk. "You need to find Tanner and tell him that the Black Rot must be stopped. I have reason to believe that, left untended, it will draw something from the Void."

"The Void?" exclaimed Grunt.

"Oh, yes, that's exactly what happened in Paris," said the Marquis.

The door creaked open.

"Tell Tanner he needs to get ghosts into the infected houses by whatever means necessary," said Lapsewood. "That's the only way to stop it."

"Whatever means necessary," repeated Grunt.

"Yes, and, Grunt, say please."

Sergeant Brinks stepped inside, his Beater at the ready. "Time's up. Mr. Grunt, either follow me, or you've found yourself a new home."

"Good luck, Grunt," said Lapsewood.

Grunt looked at him uncertainly before following Sergeant Brinks out.

"Charming fellow," said the Marquis. "If you forgive the lack of personal hygiene, that is."

33

THE END OF NELL

Nell had spent her whole life pacing the streets of London. When she was a young girl, her feet had skipped along these cobbles as she sang prettily and sold flowers, only occasionally adding to her day's take with colorful hankies swiped from gentlemen's pockets. A few years on and Nell's steps were slower, and her attempts to look appealing were more studied and specifically aimed at the male population. By the time she was in her late thirties, with a string of financially rewarding, although ultimately doomed, relationships behind her, she had accrued much of what she desired and could afford to hire hansom cabs. Yet it was to the streets she always returned in the end.

Through poverty or wealth, joy or sorrow, friendship or loneliness, Nell had always wanted, above all, to be seen. She wanted the world to envy her, admire her, *notice* her.

Ghosts received no tip of a gentleman's hat, nor jealous glances from wives. Ghosts were invisible to the living. So Nell sought attention from other spirits. She had liked Mr. Lapsewood a great deal. He had been a proper gent, asking her to do up a button or two. She would seek him out and embarrass him again, prove that death might have robbed her of many things but that she still had the ability to ignite the spark in a man's heart, even if the heart in question had long since ceased to beat.

On the south side of Blackfriars Bridge she noticed an Enforcer heading her way, and she floated down to hide in the tunnel underneath. Her desire to be seen didn't extend to Enforcers. She was, after all, a Rogue ghost.

It was late. There wasn't a living soul around. Yet she sensed there was something in the shadows.

"Hello?" she called.

No echo for a ghost's voice.

"No need to be shy, love," she said. "If it's company you seek, come and see old Nell."

Nothing.

"Why are you hiding back there? There's nothing to be afraid of. You're newly ghost-born—is that it? Well, don't you worry. I'll show you the ropes. You can trust me."

Something moved in the shadows. Too dark to see. The bricks under the bridge were damp with moisture that dripped down to the pavement below. Black smoke edged forward. It was blacker than Ether Dust, but it began to take shape. A shadowy creature with a long snout moved on three legs.

"Oh," Nell sighed, disappointed. "You're a spirit hound." She had never seen such a black, black coat on a dog, alive or dead. Nor one of such size. It was almost the height of a human. It opened its great jaws and let out a soundless growl that Nell felt more than heard.

She stepped back, feeling a sensation she had not felt in many years. It took her a moment to realize it was fear.

"What are you?" she asked.

It was more than a dog. She couldn't peel her eyes away from the approaching blackness. She couldn't move. Something held her. The hound loomed over her, its great jaws above her. Deadly. Dark. Silent. She tried to turn to Ether Dust, but it wouldn't allow her, gripping her with its smoky black limbs. She screamed, but the beast opened its mouth and swallowed the sound.

Fear turned to pain.

Nell felt extreme agony as the hound devoured her, its teeth tearing into her body, wrenching her limbs from her torso, peeling her fleshless skin, unraveling her very soul.

In a matter of seconds, the ghost of Nell was no more.

34

MR. STERNWELL'S LAST WILL & TESTAMENT

IT WAS A BUSY WEEK AT CONSTABLE & TOOP. THE day after Mr. Gliddon's funeral, Sam was once again standing beside a grave in his role as mute. Today it was the funeral of Mrs. Eli, a cantankerous old woman whose relatives had struggled to supply the vicar with sufficiently fond memories for her eulogy. Sam was relieved that Mrs. Eli's ghost wasn't there to rant at her family's feigned sadness. While looking out for her, he noticed another spirit lingering nearby, trying to catch his eye. This one was a plain-looking, middle-aged gentleman with an honest sort of face and a belly that was obviously no stranger to a piled-high plate of food.

Sam took it as a good sign that the ghost did not try to speak to him during the funeral, instead waiting until the Eli family was safely inside the local tavern and Sam was taking a walk on Peckham Rye.

The ghost politely introduced himself as Mr. Sternwell of Borough, then explained, "I'm looking for some help with a small matter. I'm sorry to bother you about it." He had a soft, well-spoken voice that suited his benign appearance.

"What kind of help?" Sam responded.

"My will," he replied. "You see, I drew up a new one before I died, but my death was so sudden, I never had time to give it to my solicitor."

"If you tell me where to find it, I'll post it on," said Sam.

"Yes, well, unfortunately, it's taken me a while to track you down, and it's rather urgent now," admitted Mr. Sternwell.

"How urgent?"

"My solicitor is settling my accounts today," admitted Mr. Sternwell.

"What will happen if I don't help?"

"I'm afraid that would mean my fortune would go to my wife."

"Is that not the right person to inherit one's fortune?"

Mr. Sternwell shook his head. "Not in my case. We were estranged, you see. Not divorced, but we no longer lived together. I left my fortune to my dear Rosa, the only woman I truly loved." He smiled fondly.

"What will become of your wife with no inheritance?" asked Sam.

"Don't worry. The will leaves her enough—more than she deserves, in fact. Please, I'm begging you, help me out this once. I can't bear to see poor Rosa living the rest of her days in poverty. I swear I shall not bother you again nor speak of you to another soul."

Sam agreed to help him and returned to the tavern to ask Mr. Constable for the rest of the afternoon off. Sam never spoke to his father about the ghostly errands he ran, fearing that he would not approve, but Mr. Constable was always understanding. Mr. Constable did not ask for details, but, as usual, Sam was in no doubt that he knew what was going on.

"I won't go if I am needed in the shop," said Sam, giving him the opportunity to change his mind.

Mr. Constable smiled benevolently. "You are always needed in the shop, Sam, but I get the feeling you are need-ed elsewhere just now."

"My loyalty is to you, not Them," replied Sam.

"Helping out others is what makes us human," said Mr. Constable. "As my own father used to say, charity is the fuel of humanity."

With Mr. Constable's consent, Sam took his leave, then returned to meet Mr. Sternwell. They caught a train to London Bridge and walked to his house in Borough. It was an irritating journey, made worse by Mr. Sternwell's fretting about the time and constantly checking his pocket watch, which must surely have stopped ticking along with his heart. At the house, Mr. Sternwell struggled to remember where in the garden he had hidden the spare key and the floorboard under which the will was hidden. When Sam eventually pulled up the correct floorboard and retrieved the envelope, he received a splinter in his thumb for his troubles. The solicitor's office, Kessler & Abel, was several streets away, and Mr. Sternwell persuaded Sam he had to run if they were to make it on time, so Sam arrived out of breath and sweating profusely.

He was greeted by a junior clerk, who looked at him uncertainly.

"I'm here to see Mr. Kessler," said Sam, prompted by Mr. Sternwell.

"He's busy at the moment," replied the clerk.

Mr. Sternwell stuck his head through the door and peeked inside. "That's it. That's the settlement of my estate," he said. "That bloodsucking wife of mine is there, as is my beautiful Rosa. You must insist."

"I have a document that I believe to be of immediate relevance," said Sam to the clerk.

Reluctantly, the clerk agreed to check. He knocked on the door and, after a moment, returned to show Sam in. Inside the room, the bespectacled solicitor sat behind a large desk. Opposite him was a woman the same age as Mr. Sternwell, her white hair sharply contrasting with her black attire. Next to her was a much younger woman, wearing a red dress, with soft curls falling prettily around her heavily made-up face. They were sitting as far apart as was possible in the confines of the office.

"You have something of relevance to the matter of the settlement of the estate of Mr. Alfred Sternwell?" asked Mr. Kessler, the solicitor.

"Yes." Sam handed him the will.

Mr. Kessler examined it carefully, then spoke. "May I ask how you came by this?" He looked at Sam over the top of his glasses.

"My father works for the postal service," said Sam. "This was posted to you but mislaid. My father asked that I bring it to you."

"An inspired lie, indeed," said Mr. Sternwell.

"It seems genuine enough," said Mr. Kessler. "It is dated after the previous will in my possession, so legally we must go by this one."

"What does this mean? What does it say?" asked the older woman anxiously.

"You may well be worried, my dear," said the ghost of Mr. Sternwell.

"I'm afraid your husband left his entire fortune to Rosa," said Mr. Kessler.

Mr. Sternwell's wife burst into tears.

A smile spread slowly across the younger woman's face.

"But Mrs. Sternwell is looked after, too, is she not?" said Sam.

Both women and the lawyer turned to look at him.

"Did you open the envelope?" asked Mr. Kessler.

189

"No, but . . ." He looked at Mr. Sternwell.

"Nothing is more than she deserves," said Mr. Sternwell spitefully.

"I'm so sorry, Margaret," said Mr. Kessler.

"It's not your fault," said Mrs. Sternwell, still unable to stop the flow of tears. "It's her. She bewitched him. She took a silly old fat man and tricked him into leaving his fortune to her. Meanwhile, I, who stood by him all those years, I am left to rot without a penny to my name."

The younger woman stood, smoothed down her dress, and said, "All that money would have been wasted on you, you old bag. Anyway, so what? I made the old fool happy. Now he's made me happy."

Realizing what he had done, Sam turned to Mrs. Sternwell. He tried to apologize, but the words stuck in his throat. He turned and fled the building.

The ghost of Mr. Sternwell made no effort to follow. Sam had served his purpose. Sam felt sickened by the part he had played in ruining the widow's life. Failing to look where he was going, he collided with a hurrying businessman coming the other way and was knocked to the ground.

"Mind where you're going next time," snapped the man.

Sam felt disoriented. Confused. He had been in such a hurry getting to the solicitor's, he couldn't remember the way back. He needed to ask directions, but everyone was rushing, wrapped up in the importance of his or her own concerns. Not one person stopped to check Sam's well-being as he sat on the filthy pavement, instead swarming around him like a colony of ants. Busy, rude Londoners with no concern for their fellow men. Sam picked himself up and made his way along the street, desperate now to get home and escape the cesspool of a city that was London.

35
GRUNT IN LONDON

ARRIVING AMID THE SMOG OF THE CITY, GRUNT wondered why on earth he had agreed to help Lapsewood. The last time he had set foot in London, the ground had literally been pulled out from under his feet, and he had felt the sudden, violent tug of the rope around his neck as the baying crowds cheered. Among them Grunt had spotted the man who had killed his wife, except the fellow was so drunk, he failed to notice the moment when Grunt was hanged. Being such a private man, unaccustomed to showy public displays, this was the only time Grunt had ever stepped upon a stage, and yet this debut went unnoticed by the one man who really should have been paying attention.

It was a cruel world, and Grunt did not relish being back in it.

As he walked across London Bridge, he reflected that the old city seemed even busier, noisier, and fuller than it had when he had walked here as a living man.

Disoriented by the constant stream of people, horses, and vehicles passing through him, Grunt stepped off the bridge and hovered above the cold River Thames. The tide was in, and the murky waters of the river hurried on their way toward the estuary.

"Papers, please," said a voice from the bridge.

Grunt took a moment to realize that the request was directed at him. A thick-headed Enforcer with a low brow stood at the edge of the bridge, tapping his Ether Beater, more unthinkingly than threateningly. His name badge read ENFORCER DAWLISH.

"Yes, of course," said Grunt. He reached into his pocket and handed over his documentation.

The Enforcer studied it closely. "Says here you've got a desk job for the Dispatch Department," he said. "What brings you down here?"

"I . . . er . . . I'm on leave. You know, visiting family," lied Grunt.

"You got a Visitation Permit, then?" asked Dawlish.

"I . . . no . . . I thought since I won't be doing any actual haunting, I . . ."

"Still need a Visitation Permit, haunting or no haunting. Otherwise we'd have ghosts floating around all over

193

the place. Speaking of which, what you doing there hanging about in midair? You need a permit for that, too. That's how I knew you weren't no Rogue, you see. You don't find them drawing attention to themselves." He handed the papers back to Grunt. "Now, you can be on your way, but make sure you've got the right permits the next time you come down here."

"Yes, sir."

Grunt continued on to Whitechapel, traveling as Ether Dust to avoid any more encounters like that. Outside the school, Grunt met the ghost of a sailor who looked as if he had died from being eaten by a shark, judging by the teeth marks visible under his torn shirt. The sailor seemed friendly enough but warned him against going inside. "You mark my words, that place has fallen to the Black Rot, it has," he said. "One step inside and you'll be stuck there forever."

"But without the list, how will I find Tanner?"

"I'm afraid I don't know any Tanner," said the sailor.

"He's a Rogue ghost, a boy. He has spirit hounds traveling with him."

"Now, I did see a boy with a pack of hounds recently. He was heading down Bedlam way."

"Thank you," said Grunt.

Grunt turned to Ether Dust and flew south toward Kennington. Outside the lunatic asylum, he found the ghost of an old woman who had recently seen a boy matching Tanner's description. "He was checking that buildings still had their ghosts," she told him. "The 'ospital was on his list, but I told him there were so many spirits in there, it's a wonder there's any room for the livin'."

Grunt was halfway down Kennington Road when he finally found a pack of spirit hounds tied up to a streetlamp. He bent down to take a closer look at the revolting creatures.

"Oy, leave them alone."

Grunt turned around to find a young boy with another dog. "Master Tanner?" he said.

"Who's asking?" replied the boy.

"I'm not an Enforcer," said Grunt.

"I can see that."

Grunt gulped and felt a fresh globule of gray goo bubble up from his scarf. He quickly mopped it away.

"You know that's disgusting, don't you?" said Tanner.

"I have not come all this way to be insulted," replied Grunt.

"What brings you to these parts, then, if you're not in search of a good insult?" replied Tanner, grinning cheekily.

"I have a message from Mr. Lapsewood."

"Lapsewood? Where is he?"

"He's been detained."

"Detained? What, like locked up?"

"In a manner of speaking, yes."

"What manner of speaking?"

"Do you want to hear this message or not?"

"If he's been detained, what am I doing all this work for?" asked Tanner, holding up the London Tenancy List.

"He said you were to get ghosts into the infected houses. He said it was very important."

"Did he indeed?"

"Yes, and he said to say please."

Tanner smiled. "He's learning. But what? Get ghosts to step into prisons? That's no easy task."

Grunt explained as best he could about the Black Rot and how, left to its own devices, it would draw in something from the Void to satisfy its needs. "Lapsewood said to coax ghosts in by whatever means necessary," said Grunt.

"Coax Them?" exclaimed Tanner. "You can't coax ghosts, because ghosts don't want nothing."

"I don't know if that's true," said Grunt, thoughtfully. "I'd like to be able to give the man who killed my wife a piece of my mind."

"Of course." Tanner snapped his fingers. "That's it. How do you coax ghosts? You offer Them a service in return."

"What kind of service?" asked Grunt.

"The kind provided by a Talker," replied Tanner.

36
WHAT IF . . .

CLARA WAS STANDING OUTSIDE A PUB CALLED THE
Boar's Head. It was the address on her list that was nearest to Aysgarth House. In the second column was the name
Paddy O'Twain. If it really was a list of haunted buildings,
then Mr. O'Twain was the name of its resident ghost. Clara
had never been inside a pub and had to summon up the
courage to enter.

For some reason her thoughts drifted back to school,
when she used to play a game with the other girls called *What
If*, in which they would try to answer questions they had
dreamed up. Most of her friends came up with questions
like: *What if a prince wanted to marry you?* or *What if you could buy*

any dress in the world? But it was always Clara's questions that had them all in fits of giggles. *What if you were kidnapped by pirates? What if your parents were eaten by baboons? What if you could travel to the moon?* She thought about that game now as she wondered, *What if you found a list of haunted houses?*

The answer, she felt, was that you would go and investigate them.

Clara pushed open the heavy wooden door and stepped inside. The pub smelled of tobacco, beer, and sweat, but the atmosphere was convivial and not as intimidating as she had expected. Businessmen and tradesmen chatted and laughed among themselves. The large Irish landlady behind the bar with her red hair tied up atop her head asked, "What can I get you, lovey?" while pulling a pint with one hand and pouring a spirit with the other.

"I'm not here for a drink," replied Clara.

"You say you want a gin?" replied the lady, who was only half listening.

"No, I don't want a drink," repeated Clara.

The landlady handed a customer the pint, winked at him and said, more for his benefit than Clara's, "That's a shame, because it's only drinks we sell here."

The customers laughed.

"I'm looking for a Paddy O'Twain," said Clara.

"I'm afraid we're all out of those, too," replied the woman, earning another laugh.

"I think he used to work here," said Clara.

"Now, there's a debatable point if ever I heard one.

Paddy was my husband. I'm Mrs. O'Twain. And, well, let's just say that work was never a strong point of Paddy's." With all the customers served, the woman turned her full attention to Clara. "Now, why would a pretty young thing like you come here asking after my dead husband? You're no debt collector. So what is it? And please don't tell me you're a long-lost daughter come in search of her father, because I'd suspect you of reading too many novels. Besides, I'm afraid all you'd be set to inherit would be a houseful of drunkards and a bundle of debts."

"I'm not," said Clara. "May I ask how long ago he died?"

Mrs. O'Twain grabbed a cloth and wiped down the bar. "It's going on six years now, but debt collectors still come crawling out of the woodwork occasionally. I mean, I knew he was a useless old so-and-so, but it was only after he died that I discovered he owed money to half of London."

"I'm not here about his debts," said Clara. "I wonder whether you ever have a feeling that your husband is still with you." She had rehearsed the sentence beforehand.

"Thank the good Lord, no," replied Mrs. O'Twain.

"Not even his ghost?"

"Ghost?" she exclaimed with a sudden hoot of laughter. "The only spirits you'll find in this place are lined up against this wall."

A few of the customers at the bar were listening by now. They laughed heartily at this joke.

"Where did he die?" asked Clara, her confidence boosted by Mrs. O'Twain's levity.

"That very chair over by the window," said the landlady. "I was back in the old country visiting my poor ma, God rest her soul. Paddy was supposed to be minding the place but was instead doing his best to drink our profits. When I returned, I found him dead to the world, lying back, mouth open. But no snoring. That was strange. That's when I realized how dead to the world he really was. Poor old thing. Still, at least he went doing what he enjoyed. Sorry I can't be of more help."

Next on the list was an address in Eastcheap. Inquiries with the shopkeeper below revealed that the room above had indeed been leased to a man with the same name as that on Clara's list. The shopkeeper described him as a pale-skinned poet whose death from consumption had come as no surprise and seemed fitting for the type of man he was. However, he was not aware of any ghostly presence either.

Clara continued her ghoulish trail across London, finding none who would corroborate the existence of a ghost, until she reached the Drury Lane Theatre. She had, of course, heard stories of the Man in Gray before, but she had never heard anyone mention his name. According to the list, the resident ghost's name was Mr. David Kerby. If she could somehow connect the name with the theater's famous ghost, then she would be able to confirm that the list was genuinely a list of ghosts.

Arriving at the steps of the great theater, she told the doorman that she was seeking to discover the name of the Man in Gray.

"I never heard that he had a name," he replied. "I suppose *the Man in Gray* has a more dramatic sound to it, and since it's mostly the actors who see him, they prefer it."

"Have you ever seen him?"

"Never myself, but then, I'm always stuck out here."

"May I speak to someone who has?"

"I daresay you can," replied the doorman. "Let's ask this one. Eddie, ever seen the ghost?"

Walking up the steps was a young, good-looking man wearing a flamboyantly patterned coat. "Seen him? I think you'll find I'm playing him. Among a number of other roles, of course."

The doorman chuckled. "That's actors for you," he said, with a wink at Clara. "Always think you're talking about them. I'm talking about the Man in Gray."

"Oh, him," replied the actor. "Yes, the spirit who paces the theater. I have caught a glimpse of that specter a couple of times."

"What do you know about him?" asked Clara.

"Not much. I don't think he's an unpleasant sort of spirit. Some of the older actors say that he learns the lines of each play and that he will whisper them to you if you forget them. I've never forgotten my lines, so I wouldn't know about that."

"You don't get enough lines to warrant forgetting," said the doorman.

The actor smiled, taking the joke in good spirit. "It won't be long before I stride that stage not as the wailing ghost of Hamlet's father but as the great Dane himself."

"As a dog?" said the doorman with a loud guffaw.

The actor turned to Clara and said, "Some theaters save their clowns and jesters for the pantomimes. As you can see, at Drury Lane, we keep ours at the door."

BACK AT HOME, SITTING ON HER BED, CLARA THOUGHT about Lady Aysgarth. She wished she had tried to speak to her before that awful day. It was too late now. Her ghost had gone.

Staring at her curtains, Clara had a strange feeling, as though there was a presence in the house. It was almost as if something was watching her. If not Lady Aysgarth's ghost, then what? Something with a darker demeanor than Her Ladyship. There was a coldness to the house since her departure. Clara felt a shiver run down her back.

"Who's there?" she said. "Who's there?"

The door handle turned, and the door swung open.

"Clara? Are you all right?"

Her father stepped into the room. Clara ran to his arms and hugged him, breathing hard.

"I'm fine, Father," she said, gathering herself before pulling away.

37
STALEMATE

LAPSEWOOD WAS BEGINNING TO UNDERSTAND WHY so many prisoners of the Vault gave up their ghosts and turned to dust. He was feeling so thoroughly defeated and hopeless that he had finally agreed to a game of chess with the Marquis. It did nothing to improve his mood, instead adding to his prevailing sense of frustration and self-pity. Even the Marquis, who had certainly had long enough to come to grips with the eccentricities of his game, would get confused about which piece was which. Lapsewood suspected that he used this confusion to cheat, which he wouldn't have minded if it sped up the game and put them both out of their miseries.

"We're never getting out, are we?" said Lapsewood as he took a piece he believed to be the Marquis's queen using a piece of rubble he hoped was his knight.

"*Never* is not a word I favor," replied the Marquis. "A positive frame of mind—that's what you require, my boy."

"You've never even managed to get beyond the door," moaned Lapsewood despairingly.

"That I grant you, but how about if I were to tell you that every attempt at escape I have hitherto made was, in fact, all part of the most devilish plot, which I will now reveal to you if you care to listen, a plot that will surely secure both of us our freedom before the day is out? How would you feel about that?"

"Go on," said Lapsewood, deciding not to mention that the Marquis had just moved a rook diagonally across the board to put him in check. Lapsewood moved a pawn to block the impossible attack.

The Marquis lowered his voice. "As you know, it is impossible for us to pass through the walls and doors of the Bureau, and, as you also know, the Vault was built without holes or cracks."

Lapsewood agreed that he was aware of these facts.

"And yet there is one hole," the Marquis said. "A hole right in front of us. A hole in the door itself."

"Oh," said Lapsewood, one step behind him.

"The keyhole," explained the Marquis.

"Yes, but it has a cover," said Lapsewood.

"Indeed, it does, although I believe the correct word

is an *encrouchment*. Each time Brinks comes down here, he slides it to one side and then inserts the key, with which he opens the door."

"And then it swings shut when he removes the key," said Lapsewood.

"Yes, but what if it didn't? What if something was lodging it open? Then all we would need to do would be to dislodge that object and escape through the keyhole."

"What kind of object?"

The Marquis picked up a piece of rubble.

"Hey, that's my knight," protested Lapsewood.

"I'm so sorry. Where was it?"

"I think it was protecting the bishop."

"That's my bishop," replied the Marquis.

"Oh, perhaps it was threatened by it, then," admitted Lapsewood.

"Since it's my move, I'll take it and continue with my demonstration. The next time Sergeant Brinks comes down here, you will crouch behind the door with this knight and await the insertion of the key. I will attempt my usual escape so he doesn't suspect anything. Then, as he leaves, you will maintain the pressure on the knight. As he removes the key, the knight will take its place, lodging the cover open."

"What if he notices that it hasn't swung into place?"

"He will not suspect such a thing. He will have just thwarted my escape attempt, and I will tell him that you have retreated into the darkness with the rest of the hopeless souls."

"What if I push too hard, and the piece flies out the other side, or not hard enough, and it becomes lodged inside the keyhole instead?"

"No plan is without its pitfalls," admitted the Marquis. "But I believe we can do this. Once the piece is lodged, I will turn to Ether Dust and slip through. On the other side I will pull back the cover and aid your escape. It is brilliant, is it not?"

Brilliant was not the word that sprang to Lapsewood's mind, but a scarcity of options made it worth a go. However, he saved himself the pain of investing any genuine hope in the Marquis's scheme. If only the Vault had as many holes as the Marquis's plan; then escape would be easy.

38
JACK'S LAST BREAKFAST

FINALLY JACK'S LAST DAY AT CONSTABLE & TOOP had come. Jack had stuck to his part of the bargain, remaining out of sight and unheard. But still his presence had felt like an infection, slowly spreading its disease into Sam's life. He had stopped asking Sam to bring him alcohol but had continued to drop hints and insinuations about his father's childhood. Prior to Jack's arrival, Sam had heard nothing of his father's life in Whitechapel. Now that shady period of Mr. Toop's history occupied Sam's thoughts. His dreams were infiltrated by scenes of young Jack and Charlie Toop, running through the streets of London, pilfering, snatching, and laughing. Always laughing.

On Jack's final morning Sam cooked sausages and eggs.

"A hearty breakfast to see your old uncle on 'is way, eh?" Jack said.

Yes, thought Sam, *a hearty breakfast to give you the energy to run as far from here as possible.*

"I trust you have decided where you will go, Jack," said Mr. Toop.

"You don't want to worry yourself about my whereabouts," said Jack. "I wouldn't want you feeling you had to lie to any lawman who came looking for me."

"Harboring you here this past week has been enough of a lie," said Mr. Toop. "I asked whether you have decided your whereabouts, not where you'll be. You're well placed here to get down into Kent or travel to the coast."

"I went to the coast once," replied Jack. "I wanted to see all that water in one place. But it wasn't much to see, if you ask me. And the cold air that came off it interfered somethin' nasty with my chest. London air's good enough for me." He skewered a sausage with a fork and brought it to his mouth.

"You can't go back there now, Jack," said Mr. Toop. "You're a wanted man."

"Careful now, Charlie. You'll get me thinkin' you actually care."

"No matter what has happened between us, I'd not see you hang."

"Remember, according to your stipulation, we ain't brothers once I walk out that door. I'm just a man, and one who's murdered and all. You tellin' me you'd not see a murdering man swing by the neck?"

"You may have no regard for the sanctity of life, but I do," snapped Mr. Toop.

The kettle started to whistle.

"What about you, Sam?" asked Jack. "If they catch me, will you come watch your old uncle swing for 'is crimes?"

Sam stood up from the table to take the whistling kettle off the hob, leaving Jack's question unanswered.

"Wherever you're heading, I believe it's time you left," said Mr. Toop.

"You'd hurl me out in daylight?" exclaimed Jack.

"You have had your week," said Mr. Toop. "If you'd wanted to leave in the dark, you could have left last night."

"I'll leave at nightfall," asserted Jack.

"No. You'll leave now."

"Please, Charlie. Have mercy."

The two brothers glared at each other across the breakfast table. Jack's gaze was unrelenting, despite the desperation in his voice.

"Perhaps it would be better for Jack to leave this evening," said Sam. "In daylight there is too much danger that a neighbor might spot him. If he was caught, the question would come up of where he's been hiding this past week."

"Exactly," said Jack, smiling. "Listen to your boy, Charlie."

"At nightfall, then," conceded Mr. Toop. "But as soon as the sun goes, I want you gone, too, Jack."

39

DESTINY FOR THE DEAD

CROUCHING BY THE DOOR WITH THE PIECE OF RUB-
ble clutched between his thumb and forefinger, listening
to the jingle-jangle approach of the guard, Lapsewood
wondered what had happened to the dull, predictable, but
orderly existence he had led since he became a ghost. He
looked at the keyhole uncertainly. He knew that the chance
of success was lower than the Marquis had made out, but
the howling screams from the gloom reminded him that,
without hope, he might as well give up his ghost and join
the dissipated spirits now.

The Marquis tried to calm both their nerves with a
speech. "Destiny, some say, is the pre-written story of our

lives," he announced. "But there is no such destiny for the dead. We, my friend, shall be the authors of our own destiny, so let us write this chapter together and make it end on a happy note."

Lapsewood was only half listening. The footsteps stopped outside the door. He could hear the guard pulling his keys from his belt. Lapsewood raised the piece of rubble to the keyhole.

The Marquis saluted grandly, then turned to Ether Dust. Lapsewood saw a flash of light through the keyhole as the cover was moved to the side and the key inserted. He watched the tip of the key turn. He moved back to allow for the swing of the door, but it moved quicker than he anticipated. He jumped back to avoid being hit and lost his grip on the piece of rubble.

He groped in the dark, trying to find it. He heard the familiar sound of the Marquis being whacked by the guard's Ether Beater and collapsing to the ground.

"Morning, Marquis," said Sergeant Brinks.

"One day, Sergeant Brinks?"

"Not on my watch, Marquis," replied the guard.

A third voice spoke. "Why are these old Europeans always so damned fancy? I swear, they put more effort into their makeup than the girls back home do."

Lapsewood recognized the voice immediately as the southern American drawl of General Colt.

"The Marquis likes to provide me with regular exercise with his escape attempts," said Sergeant Brinks.

"Escape from the Vault? That's madness," said General Colt.

"Oh, this one had lost his mind long before he came down here," said Sergeant Brinks. "You married a pig in life, didn't you, Marquis?"

"How dare you talk about my wife like that!" replied the Marquis. "Snuffles was a good woman."

Sergeant Brinks and General Colt laughed. The Marquis was trying to give Lapsewood enough time to complete his job, but he still couldn't find the piece of rubble.

"I'm here to talk to Slapwood," said General Colt.

"Ah, now, I'm afraid that poor Lapsewood has joined the dissipated souls," said the Marquis.

"I told you that would be the case," said Sergeant Brinks. "Most of them go that way."

"Really?" said General Colt. "Then why's he hiding behind this door?"

Lapsewood looked up to see that the general had stepped inside the cell and was now standing over him.

"Hello, sir," he said.

"Get up." General Colt turned to Sergeant Brinks. "I'd like a minute to talk to this prisoner."

"I've never known such a popular one for visits as this one," replied Sergeant Brinks. "You can have two minutes, while the Marquis gets better acquainted with my Beater as punishment for lying about Lapsewood."

He closed the door, leaving General Colt inside with Lapsewood.

"Now, listen up, Slackwood," said General Colt. "I don't have much time."

"Are you here to release me, sir?" asked Lapsewood hopefully.

"Have you any idea how much paperwork that would incur? Don't answer that. No, there's no time to release people."

"So why are you here?"

"The thing is, I realize now I may have been a little hasty in suspecting you of being some kind of duplicitous agent working to undermine my department."

"Thank you, sir," said Lapsewood uncertainly.

"What have you to thank me for?" barked General Colt. "After all, I was the one who had you thrown in here in the first place, and as I've explained, there'll be no getting you out. I wouldn't go thanking me."

"No, sir."

"Damn it, you've made me lose my train of thought."

"Sorry, sir."

"Stop apologizing, and stop interrupting. I'm trying to explain something. We haven't much time. The fact is, I've looked into your findings, and I believe this Black Rot poses a very serious threat if left undealt with."

"You do?"

"Yes. But if we go through correct procedure, it'll be weeks—months, even—before something is done. That's the problem with this country. It can't move for the red tape that binds it up. If I'd died in my own country, I daresay I'd see how efficiently an organization like this could be run. But there you have it. I was killed in an illegal duel on your miserable gray island. You follow me?"

"Not really, sir."

"Of course you do. You and me, Blackwood, we're going to shake up this stuffy old place."

"We are, sir?"

"We are, sir," replied General Colt.

"But I'm stuck in here."

"That's right. But if you weren't, you could get back to London, find your little Rogue friend, and sort out this problem, couldn't you? Although we could not be seen together."

"But—"

"Time's up!" shouted Sergeant Brinks, opening the door.

"Good," said General Colt. "We'd just finished."

"Had we?" asked Lapsewood.

The Marquis staggered back in, looking dazed from his encounter with Sergeant Brinks's Ether Beater.

"Yes, all done," said General Colt. "Except for me to wish you good luck." He grabbed Lapsewood's right hand and squeezed it. Lapsewood felt something cold pushed into his palm.

"Yeah, good luck," added Sergeant Brinks, clearly amused by the idea.

The door slammed shut.

"Ah, well," sighed the Marquis. "Another plan thwarted.

But I do feel we learned some valuable lessons here. The next attempt will surely work."

Lapsewood opened his palm. "I think you're right," he said.

"You do?" said the Marquis, genuinely surprised.

Lapsewood held out the content of his hand for the Marquis to see.

"What is that?" he asked.

"It's a key," replied Lapsewood.

40

THE LAST WORDS OF ENFORCER DAWLISH

ENFORCER DAWLISH PROWLED THROUGH ST. JAMES'S Park, his Ether Beater drawn. He was closing in on his target. It was no Rogue ghost he was hunting tonight. The problem with Rogues, as Enforcer Dawlish saw it, was that they could see him coming a mile off. As soon as they did, they turned to Ether Dust and were gone before he even got a chance to draw his weapon. As a policeman, back when he still had air in his lungs, his favorite aspect of the job was clouting criminals with his truncheon. The problem with Enforcer work was that it lacked that solid satisfaction of a job well done.

This was where spirit hounds came in handy. They were

much more susceptible to Enforcer Dawlish's clumsy approach, and so they made ideal targets. Also, since they were not officially recognized by the Bureau, there was no rule preventing him from beating them as hard as he could manage before they scampered off, their rancid tails between their rotten legs.

He didn't feel any guilt about his nightly dog hunts; the dogs themselves felt no pain, and it gave him an extraordinary amount of pleasure when he felt the end of his baton connect with the head of a mangy mutt.

Embankment, Soho, and Piccadilly had provided slim pickings this evening, so he had ventured into St. James's Park, where packs of spirit hounds often gathered. He heard a noise on the other side of the lake. A growl. Dawlish smiled. The hunt was on. He moved stealthily across the lake. Mostly the dead dogs were stupid enough to walk straight up to him in hope of getting some affection, but the creature lurking in the darkness tonight was obviously more timid.

"Nice doggy," he said. He drew his Ether Beater and raised it in preparation.

He saw a wisp of black smoke disappear into a bush. He drew nearer. The animal was jet black and a good size. It would make for a satisfying beating. Enforcer Dawlish gripped the handle of his Ether Beater tightly.

"Come on, fella," he said. "Don't be shy."

Still no movement.

A challenge, thought Dawlish. *This makes for a change.*

He moved in and took a swing, but his Ether Beater went straight through the beast's head. Dawlish was confused. This was no living dog, and yet he couldn't hit it. The dog opened its great jaws. Enforcer Dawlish tried to move away but found his movements constricted. The dog was holding him in place.

"Good doggy?"

Those were the last words of Enforcer Dawlish. His final dog hunt ended with his body being torn apart and devoured by the creature that lurked in the shadows.

41
ONE TREE HILL

AFTER BREAKFAST, SAM LEFT HIS UNCLE UPSTAIRS and went down into the shop to get on with his chores, which today involved polishing the paraphernalia that filled the glass-fronted cabinet. As Mr. Constable always said, the display items needed to look their best if they were to reflect the care and attention that the customers of Constable & Toop could expect. Sam had removed the selection of lid ornaments, inscription plates, and coffin handles and placed them on a red cloth on the desk when he sensed a presence behind him.

"Sam Toop," said a boy's voice. "Now, if you ain't a tricky one to track down."

"I won't help you, so you might as well leave," said Sam, keeping his back to him.

"That ain't very nice after we got on so well at the church and all."

Sam turned to find the ghost of the boy he had met in Shadwell. "Oh, it's you."

"The name's Tanner."

"What do you want?" asked Sam irritably.

"I searched all over for this place, you know, asking everywhere I went. Most ghosts tend to know at least one undertaker. You never forget the man who profited from your death. But it took a lot of asking and a lot of ghosts before I hit upon a fella who'd been put into the ground in one of those lovely death boats your old man is making back there." Tanner pointed to the workshop door, behind which Mr. Toop could be heard sawing a piece of wood.

"Why did you want to find me? I thought you had no need of a Talker."

"Things have changed."

"So have I. I don't help ghosts anymore."

"Don't be like that." The floorboards above them creaked. Jack was on the move. Sam lowered his voice. "So you can find another Talker," he said. "I'm not helping you. I've had it with helping ghosts."

"This ain't your normal sort of help."

"None of Them are normal," snapped Sam. "They all think they're different. But they're all the same. Mothers, fathers, wives, husbands. 'Tell them I love them, tell them where the money is hidden, tell them not to pawn that old trinket.' I've had enough of it."

Tanner slipped behind the desk and expertly picked up a pen between his forefinger and thumb.

"Stop that," said Sam.

Tanner dipped it into the inkwell. "I was only going to write you a note asking for your help." A drop of ink splashed onto the desk.

"You can't make me help you that way," said Sam. "You're like the rest of Them, trying to spook me into doing what you want. I won't."

"All I ask is that you hear me out," said Tanner. "This isn't one of your selfish ghost problems. This is important. Now, you going to help me or what?"

"Put the pen down," said Sam. "All right. I'll hear you out. Only not here."

"Where, then?"

"The top of One Tree Hill in an hour."

The boy smiled. "See you there, Sam Toop."

One Tree Hill was a place Sam went when he wanted to get away from everyone. When he was younger, he would go there after being teased by his classmates. He went there now when the ghosts got too much for him or when he needed to escape the shop and the morbid profession into which he had been born. Mr. Constable always said that theirs was a noble trade, helping to mark the passing of unique and precious lives, but Sam sometimes wondered if they were not more like vultures, preying on grief and extracting money from the vulnerable. Sam had heard enough ghosts grumbling about their own funerals to know that the dead were never satisfied. Plus, they cost money that could be better spent on food, schooling, and medicine. Bodies could be thrown into a hole with no ceremony or burned in a crematorium for half the expense, and who would be the worse for it?

Grieving relatives tried to find comfort in the idea of an afterlife, but Sam, who had witnessed it for himself, saw no comfort in what he had seen. Every day he saw the restless spirits pacing the same streets they had walked in life, leaving no footprints, making no sound. The dead he saw had found no enlightenment. No nirvana. No joy.

At the top of the hill Sam could see London's hazy skyline, the great dome of St. Paul's, the countless rooftops of the city's cramped population, and the factories of Borough churning out the black smoke of industry.

"Lovely view from up here," said Tanner, materializing next to him.

"Just tell me what you want," said Sam.

"You remember that church where we met?"

"Of course." How could Sam forget the strange black substance that had rendered him unconscious?

"You were in there before I entered, which means you were there when Li'l Mags went in."

"Your dog?" said Sam.

"Yeah, my dog. You saw what the church was like."

"I don't know what I saw that night."

"It's called the Black Rot. We have to stop it from spreading. Houses are losing their Residents. That's when it sets in. I need someone who can persuade ghosts to replace them."

"I've had it with all of you," snapped Sam, unable to hide his anger. Jack was right: ghosts were selfish. Mr. Sternwell's deception over his will had been the last straw, but Sam could think of countless examples of similar behavior. "I'm through helping ghosts."

"I'm not talking about helping ghosts. I'm talking about saving London."

"I don't care about London either," replied Sam. "It can all go to hell."

"The way things are going, it's more likely to be the other way around," said Tanner wryly.

"That's not my problem."

Tanner stared angrily at Sam. "The dead ain't no one's problem," he said. "Just like the poor. Let them ruin themselves with drink. Let their children die like rats. The whole lot of them may as well rot away in their own filth."

"I'm talking about the dead, not the poor."

"The poor sit in the dead's waiting room," stated Tanner.

"I can't help you," said Sam. "No one can help you." He turned and walked down the hill.

TANNER SHOUTED AFTER HIM, BUT SAM TOOP DIDN'T turn around. Tanner felt furious. He was frustrated that he had wasted all that time searching for a Talker who refused to help. He channeled his emotions into the tips of his fingers and picked up a pebble. For a moment he considered throwing it at Sam, but instead he turned and lobbed it into the trees.

"I couldn't help but overhear," said a gravelly voice.

Tanner turned. A man with bloodshot eyes and leathery skin stood behind him. He was a living man, and yet he was looking directly at him.

"My nephew wouldn't 'elp you, would 'e?" he said.

"Your nephew?"

"I'm Jack Toop. Pleased to meet you." The man leaned forward, bringing his face close to Tanner's. "I couldn't help but overhear your request. Shame 'e wouldn't 'elp you out."

Tanner had met Jack Toop's type before. The way he rubbed his hands together, the way he hunched his shoulders as though in constant readiness to duck out of sight. Men like him could be thieves or killers, and they were never good news. Never. In life, Tanner had feared them. In death, however, they posed no threat to him.

"I've got a proposal for you, boy," said the man. "A proposal to 'elp you out of your little predicament."

"You mean you'll help me get ghosts into the houses?"

"Oh, yeah, I'll get ghosts into 'ouses. Nothing could be easier. But you got to 'elp me out in return. Do you think you can do that?"

"Help you out with what?"

"I need some spyin' done. It'll take hardly any time. How

about we make a deal: for every ghost I get inside one of your 'ouses, you do me a little bit of spyin'. How about that?"

"You really think you can convince them to go in?" asked Tanner.

Jack laughed. "Don't worry about that. I'll drag 'em in kickin' and screamin' if necessary."

"All right," said Tanner. "We've got a deal."

Jack grinned. "I'd shake your 'and if I could. Now, give us an 'ouse, and, as an act of goodwill, I'll do the first one for free."

Tanner picked an address from the list at random and read it out loud. "Aysgarth House, Three Kings Court, Fleet Street."

"No problem. I'll get you a ghost inside before mornin'," said Jack.

42
BREAKING OUT

LAPSEWOOD TURNED THE KEY GENERAL COLT HAD given him and heard the satisfying click of the Vault door unlocking. Then he felt the Marquis's hand on his shoulder.

"May I?" the Marquis asked.

"Of course."

The Marquis pushed the great door open, and they both stepped out.

"Breathe it in," said the Marquis. "That, my friend, is the sweet aroma of liberty."

Lapsewood nodded. Ghosts could not smell, but this was no time to quibble. He pushed the keyhole cover to one side and locked the door. "We don't want Brinks getting suspicious," he said. "He needs to think we simply gave up the ghost and dissipated."

"Agreed," said the Marquis.

"Right, let's go," said Lapsewood.

"Perhaps we should say a few words to mark the occasion," said the Marquis. "What a fickle mistress freedom has been to me over the years, and yet how smitten I have always been with her. In spite of her inconstance—"

"Maybe we should save the speeches for later," suggested Lapsewood, fearful about spending any more time outside the prison than was necessary in case Sergeant Brinks should make an appearance.

"You are right. There is a time and a place for oration, and this is neither the time nor that place," replied the Marquis, still speaking louder than Lapsewood would have liked. "Where to now?"

The two men began to walk up the stairs.

"There's an entrance to the Paternoster Pipe two floors up," said Lapsewood. "From there you can get to the physical world and go where you choose."

"No, I will stick with you." The Marquis gripped Lapsewood's elbow.

"That's good of you, but there's no need."

"I will hear no argument. Where are we going?"

"I need to find a way into the Central Records Library."

The Marquis gasped. "The CRL?" He spoke in hushed awe. "Why would you risk rearrest by venturing in there?"

"In order to solve this problem, I must find my friend Tanner. He will be working his way through the London Tenancy List, so I need a copy of it to find him. Assuming Grunt was successful in obtaining Doris McNally's copy, the only version that remains is the safety copy, which is filed in the CRL."

"This scheme is bold, daring, and utterly insane. I like it. It reminds me of a time while traveling through Arabia when I decided to steal a sultan's camel."

"Why?"

"I forget the reason, but rest assured that when it comes to adventure and escapades, you have seen but a few colors of those in my palette. Lead on, sir. You are my Moses. I am your Israelites."

The Marquis was undoubtedly the most insane person Lapsewood had ever encountered. He had no idea whether his presence would prove beneficial or a hindrance, but equally he could see that he was saddled with him now. Besides, perhaps insanity was a useful quality when it came to breaking into the Central Records Library.

43

THE GIRL IN THE KITCHEN

AN EAR-PIERCING SCREAM FILLED AYSGARTH HOUSE. Clara sat bolt upright. In her sleepy state she vaguely wondered whether Mrs. Preston, the cook, had seen a mouse again. But the scream grew in volume and intensity and turned into hysterical babbling. Clara quickly dressed and went out onto the landing. Looking down into the hall, she saw Mrs. Preston being comforted by her mother. Her father was standing at the kitchen door with Hopkins close behind him.

"Who is she?" Mrs. Preston was managing to say between her sobs. "Who is she?"

"She's . . . no one," replied Mrs. Tiltman. "She's no one."

Clara stepped onto the stairs. "What's happened?" she asked.

"Clara, go back to your bedroom at once," barked her father. He spun around and closed the door, but not quickly enough to prevent Clara from seeing that the kitchen floor was stained with a dark red liquid. "Clara, do as I say this minute," ordered Mr. Tiltman.

Clara was not used to hearing her father speak in such a way. He looked at her as though daring her to contradict him. She turned and went back to her room but, once she was out of sight, slammed the door shut from the outside and sat down on the landing so she could still hear.

"Hopkins, go to the police station and fetch an officer," said her father.

"Should I not remove the body first, sir?" he replied.

"The police will take care of that," said Mr. Tiltman.

"But what about your breakfast, sir?" said Hopkins.

"Good God, man, that hardly matters at this point," stated Mr. Tiltman.

"But who is she?" asked Mrs. Preston, who, in her hysterical state, appeared unable to say anything else.

"Please take Mrs. Preston into the drawing room," said Mr. Tiltman to his wife. "Hopkins will find a street vendor to buy tea on his way back."

"But I don't understand who she could be," said Mrs. Preston.

"The police will deal with these questions," said Mr. Tiltman.

"That's right, Mrs. Preston," said his wife. "You've had a terrible shock."

"But the door was locked last night," continued the cook. "How can she have found her way in?"

Mrs. Tiltman made no attempt to field those questions as she led the overwrought cook into the drawing room.

"Now, Hopkins, please make haste," said Mr. Tiltman. "The sooner the police get here, the sooner everything will be well. I am sure this is just a terrible accident."

Clara lingered outside her door for a moment. The temptation to go downstairs and see for herself the horror that she was now imagining was overwhelming, but her father was still down there, and she did not want to reignite the fury she had seen, so she opened her bedroom door quietly and slipped inside. She pressed her back against the door and closed her eyes.

A body. A dead body found in her kitchen. Clara knew she should have felt sickened and scared by the idea, but she did not. She felt excited. Reporters would come to the house. She had read accounts of such stories. They would name it something like "The Gruesome Murder at Aysgarth House."

Clara wondered if there was something wrong with her that she could feel so excited. But it wasn't just that; something else was different about the house today. The sense of dread had gone. That indefinable, invisible presence that had borne down on her so heavily over the last few days had lifted. The warmth had returned.

There was a dead body in the kitchen, and yet, for the first time since Reverend Fallowfield's exorcism of Lady Aysgarth, Clara felt safe in her house.

44
EMILY'S NEW HOME

THE ONLY TIME EMILY WILKINS HAD SET FOOT inside a place as grand as Aysgarth House was when her mother had held the position of maid to a family in Islington. So, even now, standing in the kitchen as a ghost, looking down on her own bloodied body, she didn't feel it would be right to venture beyond those rooms assigned to the servants. She found the sight of her dead self upsetting and was relieved when, at last, Hopkins, the butler, returned with two police officers to remove the body.

Upon seeing the corpse, the younger of the two policemen put his hand to his mouth and retched.

"Just a street urchin by the look of things," said the elder, who had white wispy whiskers sprouting untidily from his chin and neck. "Probably got into an argument with her boyfriend."

"Bit young for that kind of thing, isn't she, sir?" said the younger man, forcing himself to look.

"You'd be surprised. I seen 'em younger than this walking the streets. Prettier, too."

"Funny she should find her way into this house."

"Must have found the door open and stumbled in." The older man walked to the back door and eased it open with the side of his boot. "Yep, look. Blood on the handle."

"The cook swears she locked it at night," replied his colleague.

"That hysterical old bird?" snorted the other. "She's worried about losing her position."

"But what if it's the truth?"

"Listen to me, Sidmouth. How long have you been on the beat now?"

"It's coming up to three months now, sir."

"Three months? Twelve years is my tally. And when you've been patrolling these streets as long as I have, you get a nose for these kinds of things. You have to ask yourself what is more likely: a dappy old cook forgetting to lock a door, or a street urchin with her throat cut picking a lock and breaking into a kitchen?"

"Perhaps it was some kind of burglary gone awry, sir."

The older man sighed and stepped onto the porch. "You see how the blood leads to the house? You mark my words:

this little one gets into some kind of dispute with her fella, has her throat cut, then stagger, stagger, stagger, plop, she drops dead on the kitchen floor. Come on now, wrap up the body, and let's get it out of here."

The younger man knelt down next to the dead body.

Emily floated down to his side with the strangest feeling, as if she was paying her last respects to herself. The policeman closed her eyelids and set about wrapping up the body for removal. "So young," he muttered under his breath.

"So young," repeated Emily.

She felt sorry for the distress she had caused Mrs. Preston, and for the upset her appearance had caused in the house. She wished she could leave, but the outside wall remained as solid as if she were still alive, so she remained in the kitchen.

After a few hours, her curiosity grew. Since she could not be seen, what harm was there in exploring the rest of the house? Without thinking, Emily stepped through the wall into the hallway, feeling the freedom of the realization that the rules of the living no longer applied. She drifted up the stairs. The lightness of her new body was disconcerting. It felt as though the merest breeze could blow her away.

The dining room, with its matching green curtains and patterned wallpaper, was beautiful. She poked her head into the cabinets to admire the gleaming silver cutlery and white porcelain plates. She wondered if such objects actually made the food taste better. In the drawing room she wished she was able to enjoy the softness of the cushions. But her favorite room was the daughter's bedroom. In spite of her short hair and plain dress, Clara Tiltman was the handsomest girl Emily had ever laid eyes on. Emily investigated her wardrobe and found some far prettier dresses. She wondered why Clara had chosen the dowdier one to wear. And why did she sit writing at her desk instead of playing with the toys she had hidden away at the back of the cupboard or with the splendid miniature theater by the window?

Emily was sitting by the theater, admiring its every detail, wishing she could move the pieces, when Clara's gaze drifted up from her desk and looked straight through her. Emily felt so unnerved by this that she turned to Ether Dust and drifted up to the attic window. She spent the rest of the day looking out on the Strand, thinking how all her life she had endured such squalor, with no possessions, no permanent home, no toys or pretty dresses. Only now, in death, could she observe what it would have been like to have been born into wealth.

45
THE RESPECTABLE MR. REEVE

WHEN HE LOOKED UP AT THE GHOST OF THE GIRL AT the attic window, Tanner could see that Jack Toop had fulfilled his side of the bargain. The girl was young. Perhaps that had made her easier to coax into the house, but Tanner didn't want to ask how Jack had done it. She was there, and that was all that mattered. The Black Rot had subsided from Aysgarth House. The house had its new ghost. Tanner drew a line through the letter *i* on the list.

"Satisfied?" muttered Jack from behind the collar of his black frock coat.

Tanner nodded.

"Then it's your turn. Follow me."

Jack walked swiftly through the Aldwych, around Covent Garden, always taking the busiest streets, crossing the road to avoid the police but also steering clear of the beggars and crooks who frequented the quieter, shadier alleyways.

On one of the roads off the Seven Dials Jack slipped into an alley between a pawnbroker's and a secondhand-clothes shop. There they remained, watching the passersby, until he pointed out a man wearing a pale blue coat and carrying a silver-tipped walking stick.

"That's 'im," said Jack.

"Who is he?" asked Tanner.

"'Is name is Reeve."

"He looks respectable enough to me," said Tanner.

"'E's the biggest ne'er-do-well in the whole of this stinkin' city."

"What do you want me to do? I already told you, I won't go haunting. Tricks is one thing, but scaring attracts the wrong kind of attention."

"I told you, I just want you to spy on 'im for the day," said Jack.

As the man named Reeve passed tradesmen and shop-keepers on the street, they tipped their hats to him. In response he nodded back so benignly that Tanner wondered if Jack wasn't mistaken in his assessment of the man. Reeve tossed a coin into a beggar's hat, then stepped through a door into a pub called The Crown.

"'Is office is at the back of that pub. I'm interested in anythin' 'e says that relates to me."

"What connection do you have with this man?"

"For many years I worked for 'im."

"So what prevents you from approaching him now?" asked Tanner.

"You ask too many questions. You know what you need to do."

"I just find it hard to believe that you could have any connection to him at all," said Tanner, "let alone enough of one that he would waste time talking about you."

"I ain't asking you to believe anything, just to watch 'im." Jack chuckled darkly. "Besides, Mr. Reeve would 'ave the world think that 'e's a respectable businessman. But you mark my words, lad, Mr. Reeve is as sinful as the devil 'imself."

"If I'm to spend my time doing this, then you must continue with your work," said Tanner.

"Of course. Give me an address, and I'll find you a ghost by nightfall."

"Two," said Tanner. "If I am to follow your Mr. Reeve all day, you can fill two houses."

"Two it is, then."

Tanner read out two addresses from the list, then drifted across the road to spy on Mr. Reeve.

46
LAST CALL

THE LANDLADY OF THE BOAR'S HEAD, MRS. O'TWAIN, hadn't noticed anything odd about the man with the three-pointed birthmark who entered the pub as she was ringing the bell for last call. The Boar's Head was home to as many different kinds of customer as there were kinds of folk in the world. Often it was filled with journalists drinking and gossiping in the name of work. Businessmen came to escape their offices by day and their families by night. The rich, the poor, the reputable, and the disreputable—every walk of life came through its doors. As her husband used to say, liquor was the great equalizer, and you couldn't tell a lord from a chimney sweep when they were under a table.

Mrs. O'Twain had served a number of religious men, too. Anglicans and Catholics might argue about what happened to the wine they took at Holy Communion once it entered the body, but both agreed on the importance of it going in to begin with.

"What will it be, padre?" she asked. "You're just in time."

"You have a spirit here," he replied.

"We have a wall full of them. Which can I interest you in?" she said, taking his strange manner as indication he had visited a number of public houses prior to arriving at this one.

"A spirit of a different kind concerns me. My name is Reverend Fallowfield."

"You want something you can't see?" she asked, confused.

"None can see the spirits of which I speak," he said. "Those spirits who walk among us. Unhappy souls."

Mrs. O'Twain rolled her eyes. "Oh, you're like that girl, are you?"

"What girl?" demanded Reverend Fallowfield.

"A well-to-do young lass, she was. Little more than fifteen, but polite enough. She came here asking after my dead husband. I thought she was a . . . well, I don't know what I thought she was, but as it turns out, she never knew my Paddy in life. She was hoping to meet his ghost." She chuckled.

"Her name, this girl?"

"I never thought to ask. What's all this sudden interest in my husband's ghost, then?"

The priest seemed temporarily lost in thought. By now, a couple of the regulars were listening in.

"This chap bothering you?" asked one of them.

"He says he's interested in my Paddy," she replied.

"Debt collector?" asked another.

"Ghosts are the debts we collect in life," said Reverend Fallowfield. "I pay them off. I banish them to the other side, where they belong."

"My Paddy never hung around here enough in life, always roaming around looking for more trouble to land himself in. I see no reason he'd linger here in death."

"Unless the dead like a drink, too," said one of the regulars, laughing.

"In which case I'd notice the depletion in my stocks," replied Mrs. O'Twain.

The joke got more laughter than it deserved, but then, they all did this far into the evening.

"I was not asking a question," said the priest angrily. "Your husband's spirit stays here because he cannot leave."

Mrs. O'Twain felt a pang of annoyance now, and her resolve to speak her mind was strengthened by the inclusion of others in the conversation. "If he is here, then he is no burden. Which is more than could be said of him in life."

"Spiritual decay," pronounced the priest. "They exist among us without our permission. They pollute us."

"Oh, and now you'll be telling me that for a small donation you'll rid me of this unseen tenant who's bothering no one, will you?"

"I will not charge you for the exorcism," said the priest. "It is your decision if you wish to make a donation after you have seen this public house cleansed."

"I tell you, I've heard some scams in my day," said Mrs. O'Twain, "so I'll give you credit for at least coming up with a new one. But it is a scam, and in the end you're no better than the counterfeiters I chased out last Wednesday."

The priest slammed down his fist in anger, but as he did so, his elbow collided with a man behind him, sending the remainder of the customer's drink splashing to the floor. The two regulars instantly stood up, and the priest backed away.

"I'll ask you not to come in here causing trouble again," said Mrs. O'Twain. "Now, I suggest you buy this man a beer to replace the one you just spilled."

The priest scowled. He thrust a hand into one pocket and pulled out a coin, which he tossed across the bar.

"It'd better be real," said Mrs. O'Twain.

"You dare question my authenticity?" barked the priest. "I who will rid this city of every stinking devil that lurks in its shadows? You mark my words, I shall do it."

With that, the priest turned and left the pub to cheers and laughter from the other customers.

47
MR. REEVE'S PLACE OF BUSINESS

TANNER STOOD IN A CORNER OF THE WINDOWLESS room. With its elegantly carved desk, neatly arranged ornaments, and grand oil paintings hanging from the wood-paneled walls, Mr. Reeve's office looked like that of a flourishing business. Its tranquility seemed out of keeping with its location at the top of a staircase at the back of a public house. Tanner moved through the wall into the pub, where a burly-looking brute called Mr. Bazeley acted as Mr. Reeve's secretary, although he had a broken nose and rolled-up sleeves revealing a pair of strong arms more fit for fighting than note-taking. Mr. Bazeley sat at the bar, taking the names of visitors, then announcing each one before they entered Mr. Reeve's office. Some of them he assisted in leaving. His build alone should have been enough to make those who were unwelcome go, but occasionally he had to resort to more physical methods of persuasion.

In his office, Mr. Reeve was protected from having to witness this brutality and was able to conduct his affairs in a serene, businesslike manner. The majority of his time seemed to be taken up with money-lending, involving large sums being lent with high interest rates and harsh punishments threatened on failure to repay. Tanner wondered what any of this had to do with Jack Toop. Did Jack owe him money? Or, more likely, was he one of the men employed to carry out the threatened violence on Mr. Reeve's behalf?

Late in the morning, just before lunch, a man entered wearing dark, ragged clothing, his collar turned up and a hat pulled down over his face to cover his shifting eyes.

"Please, take a seat, Bill," said Mr. Reeve.

"You gotta help me, Mr. Reeve, sir," he said. "The coppers caught my partner, and he'll give 'em my name if it's the difference between prison and hangin'. I know he will."

"Now, Bill," replied Mr. Reeve, "you know me well enough to realize that making demands is no way to ask for help. If it's help you want, you need to ask. You need to outline exactly what I can do for you and what you will do for me in return. You know this, Bill."

"I need protection. I need you to keep the law off my back. After all, I done this job for you, didn't I?"

With his money-lending clients, Tanner noticed, Mr.

Reeve had adopted an air of professionalism, like that of a well-to-do businessman. Talking to this man, however, brought out a different side of him. His voice lowered in tone. It sounded gruffer. Edgier. Harder. "I never told you to break into that house."

"I done good work for you," protested the man named Bill.

Mr. Reeve sat back in his leather chair and steepled his fingers. "You think someone like me needs to send someone like you onto the private property of a law-abiding citizen? No, Bill, you do that by your own choice. Yes, I may help relieve you of the burden of your acquisitions, finding a buyer and getting you the best price, taking the most modest of percentages for my endeavors, but that is all."

"You've made enough money out of me. You owe me some help now."

"I'm trying to explain that I already help you. I turn your silver candlesticks, snuffboxes, and jewelry into coin, Bill. If there's any owing, it's the other way around."

"What do I owe you?" yelled Bill, slamming his fist down on the desk.

Mr. Reeve calmly looked at Bill's fist until Bill removed it. Then he replied in a cold, measured voice. "Respect," he said. "And it ain't very respectful, you coming in here with your demands."

"I'm sorry, Mr. Reeve, sir," whined Bill. "I don't mean no disrespect. I'm just saying, one word from you, and I'm off the hook."

"It seems to me that it's your partner who will be saying or not saying the word. My advice to you would be to take a little holiday, get out of town for a bit."

"Leave London? Where would I go? How would I live?"

"There are plenty of people who live in places other than London," said Mr. Reeve, with a smile. "Why, Bill, the world is full of them."

"I've got no money on me. If I go back to my dwellings to get my stash, they'll surely nab me," said Bill. "You need to lend me something. You've skimmed enough off what I've stolen over the years."

"You aren't listening, Bill. You were free to sell your items wherever you chose. You chose to sell to me. You never grumbled about my prices before. But now you have this spot of bother, and you act like I'm the thief."

"You are a thief," said Bill, spitting out the words. "Your hands are as dirty as mine. Dirtier, even. For all your fancy clothes and office, you've got every burglar in London coming to you."

"I don't know what you expect from me," said Mr. Reeve. "The police have your partner, and you clearly don't trust him not to give you away. What can I do to prevent them from coming after you?"

Bill stood up. "I know you got people you could ask, people in the police."

Mr. Reeve rose slowly to his feet as well. "Sit down, Bill," he said.

Bill sat back down on the hard wooden chair. Mr. Reeve

remained standing, leaning over him. "Why would I waste my time trying to get you off when I've got men just like you lined up and willing to do your work? The police, though, they don't see it that way. Their job is to catch people like you. You ask me, that's a bit like trying to rid the world of cockroaches or flies. No matter how many of you they catch, more will always crawl out and take your place."

"Then I'll give 'em your name," said Bill desperately. "I'll take you down, too."

Mr. Reeve sat back down and let out a low, throaty laugh. "I think you missed my point about the flies," he said. "A fly flies into a window, and the window is fine. The fly, though . . ." He slammed his palm down on the desk. "You mention my name, and nothing will come of it, but the consequences for you—well, Bill, you'll get swatted."

Bill stood up. "I see how it works now. This is what you did to Jack, was it? You cut him adrift, too."

"Jack Toop was a better thief than you'll ever be," said Mr. Reeve. "Never once got caught, did Jack. You can't be wanted if no one knows you exist. But then he went and did something foolish, didn't he? He killed one of their own. The police don't like it when you do that. Then they got wind of his name. Now they all want him: Jack Toop, the copper killer. If he's as smart as I think he is, he's done what I'm suggesting you do and left town."

There was a knock at the door.

"Enter," said Mr. Reeve.

Mr. Bazeley stepped inside.

"Ah, Bazeley. Bill was just leaving. Escort him out, will you?"

Tanner followed the two men down the stairs, listening to Bill's protests as the bigger man strong-armed him out through the pub and into the street.

That evening, back in the shady alley, Tanner relayed the conversation to Jack.

Jack smiled. "Good work, lad."

"He said you killed a copper?" said Tanner.

"That's none of your business," replied Jack. "I want you to go back tomorrow."

"What of your work?" asked Tanner. "Did you find Residents for the houses?"

"Oh, yes. Both vacancies are now filled," said Jack.

48

THOSE WHO MOURN

Two days after Jack's departure, Sam was at another funeral, silently watching a tiny coffin being lowered into the ground. Today the piece of silk draped over his funeral baton was white. Children's burials were always the worst. The funeral cortege of a man who had reached a respectable age would usually find its way to the tavern next to the cemetery, where liquor and games of skittles would shift the mood from misery to fond remembrances or funny stories about the deceased. But there was nothing funny to be said about an infant who had barely reached his second month, and there wasn't enough alcohol in the world to numb the pain of a couple who were burying their third child. As Mr. Constable had said, *"Ours is not a profession that values regular customers such as these."*

The mother shook with each violent, pained sob. On occasions such as this, Sam was grateful that his role as mute prevented him from speaking. What could anyone say to this poor woman who had gone through labor three times but had no children to show for it? With each one's death, another slice of hope was cut from her heart. Her husband kept his own feelings tucked behind his gray eyes, standing as still as a statue.

Several years ago, when the role of mute was new to Sam, he had been moved to tears seeing the look on a young widow's face. After the funeral, Mr. Constable had taken him to one side to have a word.

"We are undertakers," he had said. "Some of our profession—most, perhaps—become immune to the sadness and personal tragedy that is our daily business, but that is not our way. My father used to tell me that we should never cease to feel for our clients. To do so would be to divorce ourselves from that which makes us human. And yet, this is a job. We have a responsibility to our customers. It is up to them how they demonstrate their grief. Some cry; some do not. Some conduct themselves with reserved dignity in public; then, once behind closed doors, the floodgates will open. Some beat their chests and wail. Others eulogize or drink to the memories of their loved ones. It is our business to respect each decision. A grieving widow unable to shed a tear for her departed husband may be embarrassed by a stranger who weeps openly. We each are prisoners of our emotions. Our role is to allow the grieving the opportunity to grieve. It is not for us to dictate how, nor to grieve for them."

Sam had never cried at a funeral again.

The husband at this service finally found the strength to place an arm around his wife's shoulders and lead her away from the grave, unknowingly taking her right past the ghosts in the cemetery who sat mourning their own lives. Sam knew all the regulars. Most came to cry over the gravestones that bore their names. In some cases these lumps of stone were all the evidence that remained of their existence in the first place. Others angrily awaited visits from their relatives, bemoaning loudly the poor maintenance of gravestones and the lack of flowers. Only one of them came hoping to comfort his family when they visited. His name was Mr. Ravenstock, and Sam had known him in life and death. Seeing Sam, he waved. Ghosts like him were few and far between. Most cared for no one but themselves.

Sam thought about Tanner. Sam had still been angry when he had met the boy on the hill because of Mr. Sternwell and the will. He had calmed down now. With the clarity of hindsight he could see that Tanner had not been asking for a favor for himself. He was trying to prevent that strange black substance from spreading, and yet Sam had turned him away. Sam had always seen his ability as a burden to be borne, but what if it was also a gift to be used? What if he could make a difference, not just to the dead but to the living, too? Mr. Sternwell had betrayed Sam's trust, but Sam could not allow one betrayal to destroy his trust in others.

He looked down the hill toward the distant skyline of London and resolved to speak to Mr. Constable about taking the rest of the afternoon off. He had to find the boy Tanner.

49

BREAKING IN

The Central Records Library was situated behind a brown door on the twenty-second floor of the Bureau. Lapsewood had held a post as librarian's assistant there when he first began work at the Bureau, so he knew that, providing he acted quickly and confidently, it was possible to get out with the list without arousing suspicion.

The problem was getting in.

By the door stood an Enforcer with half his head missing, revealing a brain that had not been very large even when it was complete. Lapsewood and the Marquis peered around the corner at him. Hoofmarks on what remained of his face indicated that he had been trampled to death.

"We can't get past him without permission papers," said Lapsewood.

"I will distract him," said the Marquis. "As soon as you see his back turned, turn to Ether Dust and slip through the door."

"What are you going to do?" Lapsewood asked, nervously wondering whether the Marquis was any more adept at getting into places than he was at breaking out of them.

The Marquis smiled and winked. "I have a few tricks up my sleeve."

"But if he discovers that you're a Rogue ghost, you'll be taken straight back to the Vault."

"True. Valor requires jeopardy, my boy. For when the jaws of danger snap—"

"Again, shall we save the speeches?" Lapsewood interrupted.

"Yes," said the Marquis. "Perhaps you're right."

The Marquis pushed back his shoulders, puffed out his chest, and marched around the corner. "Stand at attention when your superior approaches," he barked.

"Yes, sir," said the Enforcer, saluting.

"That's better. Now, I have some rather good news for you, Enforcer . . . er . . ."

"Bloom, sir. Enforcer Bloom."

"That's right," said the Marquis. "We in upper management are on a recruitment mission. We're looking for fresh talent to move up the ranks. And you, Bloom, have come to our attention."

"Have I, sir?"

"Oh, yes. How long have you been guarding this door now?"

"I'm not sure, sir."

"During your tenure you've shown aptitude, initiative, intuitive instincts, and exceptional cognitive reasoning."

"Really?" asked the Enforcer, scratching an exposed part of his brain.

"You have. How do you feel about a nice, comfortable desk job?"

"I like this job, sir."

"Standing in front of a door? That's no role for a man of your abilities."

"Isn't it?"

"No. Besides, this is an order from on high." The Marquis spoke sternly. "If you have a problem with the decision, you can take it up with Admiral Hardknuckle. Now, run along. I'll stand guard at the door until your replacement turns up."

"But—"

"Come on, man, get a move on before I have you court-martialed for disobeying an order."

"Yes, sir." Enforcer Bloom did as he was told. He marched around the corner and walked straight into Lapsewood. "Sorry," he said. "I wasn't looking where I was going."

"No, no, it was my fault," replied Lapsewood.

Enforcer Bloom hurried down the corridor, and Lapsewood joined the Marquis. "That was excellently done," he said.

"When it comes to deception, one must pander to the target's vanities. Give them no opportunity to question the assertions you make. For it only takes—"

"Marquis," interrupted Lapsewood. "It won't take him long to discover there's no desk job waiting for him."

"Very true. I'll remain here while you go in."

The Marquis opened the door, and, with a short nod of gratitude, Lapsewood stepped inside the Central Records Library.

50

SAM AND TANNER

Sam had made the decision to go in search of Tanner, but how was he to find him? Luckily, Sam had spent enough time among the ghosts of London to know who to ask. Still dressed in black from the funeral, he took the bus to the city, where he found the three victims of the Great Fire of London sitting at the base of Christopher Wren's monument. The most horrifically burned was a man called Pertwee, who, in spite of his appearance, was an extremely charming, friendly fellow.

Sam had once helped Mr. Pertwee by passing on a message to his descendants regarding a mistake in the secret family recipe for balm cakes. Mr. Pertwee was on good terms with a good many ghosts due to having died with a deck of cards in his hand, meaning he had plenty of visits from those in search of a good game of whist. Sam supposed that if he had the rest of eternity with nothing to do, he might want a diversion such as a game of cards.

The ghosts all talked while they played, making Mr. Pertwee a useful source of information. Taking him aside, Sam described Tanner to him. Mr. Pertwee told him that the boy had been seen in the past couple of days up Seven Dials way.

The sky was darkening by the time Sam reached the Seven Dials. Large drops of rain were landing in the road when Sam spotted Tanner step out of a pub.

"Tanner," he said.

The boy turned and looked at him. "Why, if it ain't the Talker who don't like to talk."

"Can we speak somewhere privately?" asked Sam. He said it quietly but was heard by a passing woman who threw him a dirty look and hurried on her way.

"I suppose," said Tanner.

Tanner led him to an alleyway. It stank so badly, Sam almost gagged.

"You'll have to be quick," said Tanner. "I'm expecting someone."

"I wanted to apologize," said Sam. "I've come to offer my help."

"What's brought this on?"

"What you said. About the Black Rot. I felt it that night. It got inside me. Rector Bray wouldn't even enter that church.

259

You were right. It affects us all. It has to be stopped."

"All this happened before I came to see you. Why the change?"

"I think I'm supposed to help you," Sam said slowly.

"'Supposed to'?"

"Yes, I think perhaps that's my purpose."

"You're losing me now, sunshine." Tanner grinned. "You had a vision or something? God appear on the back of a white goat telling you to fulfill your destiny?"

"No, it's not like that. It's just—"

Tanner interrupted. "Because you're not the only Talker in the world, you know."

"I know, but it's not that common, is it? When we first met, you said my being the son of an undertaker explained why I could see you. There are plenty of undertakers with plenty of sons and daughters who aren't Talkers. Why me?"

"I suppose you're just lucky, ain't you?"

"Lucky!" exclaimed Sam. "All my life I've lived with the knowledge that I'm different from everyone else. I'll never be normal. That's not 'lucky.'"

"Listen, we've all got our problems." Tanner looked around nervously.

"I'm trying to tell you that I want to help," stated Sam.

"Yeah, well, you're too late. I've got someone else helping me. And he didn't have to wrestle with his conscience before saying yes. He's helping me, and I'm helping him."

"Who?"

"Your uncle."

"Jack?" said Sam, aghast.

"Yeah, Jack."

"He's a murderer."

"It may have escaped your notice, but I'm already dead."

Sam tried to take it all in. "Jack's getting ghosts into houses for you?"

"Yeah. He's doing that for me while I spy on some old fella in this pub for him."

"You shouldn't be mixing with people like Jack."

Tanner laughed. "I mixed with people like that my whole life. It's what you have to do when you're born with nothing. Only now they can't hurt me no more, and I'm using him rather than the other way around."

"Jack will only bring you trouble," said Sam.

"Listen here, your uncle's doing good work for me. If you don't believe me, go to Aysgarth House off Fleet Street. That was an infected house before Jack persuaded a ghost to enter it. Now it's all right. I ain't under any delusions about Jack's character, but I told you, he's working for me as much as I'm working for him."

"How's he getting the ghosts in?"

"Who cares?" Tanner shrugged. "Probably with tricks and deceit, like what you would have done. He's going to be here any second, so unless you're after a family reunion, I suggest you scat."

Sam had no desire for an encounter with Uncle Jack in this stinking dark alley, so without another word he turned and fled.

51
THE KITCHEN KILLER

Inspector Savage beckoned the young police constable to enter his office. "What is it, Sidmouth?"

"There've been two more, sir," replied the constable.

"I'm not a mind reader, Sidmouth. Two more what?"

"Two more murders like the one in the house off Fleet Street. That's five in total."

"You mean, five street urchins killed?"

"No, sir. Three children, a lady of ill repute, and an elderly drunk."

"So in what way were they similar?"

"All the bodies were dragged into residential buildings after they were killed."

Constable Sidmouth had Inspector Savage's full attention now.

"Anything taken?" asked Inspector Savage.

"No, sir."

"What was the method of death?"

"The same. Throat slit by a sharp blade."

"That's how Heale was killed," said Inspector Savage.

"Heale wasn't dragged anywhere, though, was he?"

"No," he admitted. "But it makes you wonder if Jack Toop isn't behind all this. Not content with killing one of our own, he's now gone on a killing spree. He's mocking us with these murders. He's challenging us." Inspector Savage banged his fist down on the desk.

"That name, sir—Jack Toop," said Sidmouth.

"What about it?" snapped Inspector Savage.

"I don't understand where it came from. We've no records of a man by that name ever being arrested. There are no notes about him as far I can tell. How can you be so sure that's the name of the man we're looking for?"

"I have a reliable source," said Inspector Savage irritably. "You're a young man, Sidmouth. Don't go thinking you know everything yet, because you don't."

"Some of the lads are calling him the Kitchen Killer," said Sidmouth.

"I'm sure the newspapers will appreciate their help, but it isn't our job to name these people. It's our job to catch them. It is up to us to find Jack Toop and put a stop to this trail of murder."

"You think he'll strike again, sir?"

"I have no doubt, Sidmouth. If Jack Toop has declared war on us, it's time for us to retaliate."

"But we don't even know what he looks like."

"There'll be plenty out there who do. I'll see Jack Toop swing for this if it's the last thing I do."

"If he is the Kitchen Killer, sir."

"Stop using that name, Sidmouth. We start giving these animals titles, and they'll start believing they're important."

"Yes, sir. Sorry, sir."

52

FRESH BLOOD

IN A SMALL, QUIET COURTYARD OFF FLEET STREET
Sam found the house Tanner had mentioned. A plaque
next to the door read AYSGARTH HOUSE. He wanted to un-
derstand how Jack was fulfilling his half of his bargain with
Tanner. To do that, he had to speak to the ghost inside that
house. He climbed the stairs and knocked on the door.
The rain had grown steadily heavier since Seven Dials, and
Sam's black funeral attire was soaked through.

An elderly butler answered. "Yes?"

"I'm here about the chimneys," said Sam.

The butler looked him up and down. "You don't look
like a chimney sweep," he said. "Besides, we have a contract

with Mr. Compton to clean our chimneys."

"Yes, that's who I work for. He said to meet him here."

"The chimneys aren't due for cleaning this week," said the butler.

"This is Aysgarth House, isn't it?"

"It is."

Behind him a man's voice said, "Who is it, Hopkins?" A smartly dressed gentleman appeared, clearly superior in status to the butler, judging from the confidence in his voice and the way the butler stepped out of his way.

"He says he's come to meet Mr. Compton, the chimney sweep here, Mr. Tiltman, but Mr. Compton is not due today," replied Hopkins.

"He definitely said to meet him at Aysgarth House," said Sam. "But if he's not inside, I'll wait outside for him. Sorry to bother you." He turned around.

"Don't be silly," said Mr. Tiltman. "It's pouring rain. You can come and wait in the drawing room. I'm sure Mr. Compton has just gotten mixed up and will be here presently."

"But, sir . . ." said the butler.

"What?" asked Mr. Tiltman.

"You know how Mrs. Preston and your wife feel about visitors since . . . the incident."

"Oh, nonsense. They wouldn't have me turn away this polite, if rather soggy, young man to catch his death while waiting in the rain." He turned to Sam. "What's your name, lad?"

"Sam Toop, sir."

"You're not planning to gain entry to rob or murder us, are you?"

"Not at all, sir."

Mr. Tiltman laughed. "I didn't think so. Hopkins, the day we lose our humanity because of actions by those who have lost theirs is the day that we may as well give up. Come on in, Sam Toop."

Hopkins opened the door wide, and Sam followed Mr. Tiltman through the hall into the drawing room.

"So you're learning the trade from Mr. Compton, are you?" asked Mr. Tiltman, who had a disarmingly friendly nature and raised eyebrows that implied the world was endlessly amusing.

"Yes," replied Sam.

"This may be the last time he cleans these chimneys."

"You have a new contract?"

"No, we are to move."

"Why would you move from this house?" asked Sam, looking around admiringly.

"I would not, but my wife would," replied Mr. Tiltman. "Which, if you know anything about marriages, means I would also. She wants to move us to the outskirts of London and condemn me to a life of train journeys to and from my work in the city. I've no idea where yet, but I imagine my estate agent will find somewhere suitably ghastly."

"Honor Oak is pleasant enough and well positioned for such a journey."

"Is that true? I shall mention the name to my man. Anyway, at the risk of appearing rude, I have some work I must attend to. Do you mind if I leave you dripping here until your master arrives?"

"That's fine. Thank you for letting me in. I'm sure he won't be long."

"Very well. Nice to make your acquaintance, Sam Toop."

Mr. Tiltman closed the door behind him, leaving Sam alone in the room. Sam wondered that a man with such a house could be so trusting and not assume that Sam might steal some ornament, then make his escape. He walked to the door and listened for footsteps. He didn't want to betray Mr. Tiltman's trust, but he needed to find the house's ghost.

"You'd better not be planning on stealing nothing from this house. This family has been through enough as it is," said a voice from behind him.

He turned to see the ghost of a ragged little girl standing there.

"I'm not going to steal anything," said Sam.

In different circumstances Sam might have laughed at how the girl jumped as she realized that he had heard what she said.

"You can see me?" she said, astonished.

"My name is Sam. I'm a Talker."

"I'm Emily. What's a Talker?"

"It's a living person who can see and hear the dead. How did he get you in here?"

"Who?"

"The man who got you into this house. How did Jack Toop persuade you to enter?"

"You know his name? You know that man's name?"

"Yes. He's my uncle. How did he convince you?"

"He didn't convince nor persuade me," said Emily. "He slashed my throat and dragged me in."

Sam's eyes were drawn to the slit in Emily's throat. He had to steady himself as Emily's words sank in. He remembered Jack showing him his knife, with its sharp blade and stained handle. He remembered Inspector Savage talking of a previous victim having his throat cut.

It was suddenly extremely clear what was happening. Jack was using Tanner for something, and in return Jack was filling infected houses with ghosts for Tanner. But Jack wasn't negotiating with the ghosts. He hated talking to ghosts. Jack was taking innocent people off the street and murdering them. He was killing them for their ghosts.

Emily was talking. She wanted to know why she had died, but Sam didn't know what to say. He couldn't bring himself to utter anything other than, "I'm so sorry . . ."

"Father?" The voice came from the hallway. The door opened, and another girl stepped in, this one very much alive. The girl's hair was as short as a boy's. She had large hazel eyes and was undoubtedly the most beautiful thing Sam had ever set eyes on.

"Who are you?" she asked.

"I'm Sam," he replied idiotically. "I'm waiting for . . ."

But he couldn't remember the name of the chimney sweep, and his voice trailed away.

"Who were you talking to just now?" she asked.

"No one," said Sam. "That is to say, I was speaking to no one but myself."

"You haven't told me who 'yourself' is," said the girl.

Mr. Tiltman entered the room behind her, and Sam was struck by the family resemblance. "Clara," he said. "I see you've met Master Toop. He's waiting for Mr. Compton."

Sam felt confused. Emily was still talking to him, demanding an explanation about why she had been killed. He glanced at her and saw Clara following his gaze.

"He's very clean for a chimney sweep," said Clara.

"I'm learning the trade," replied Sam.

"Yes, I suppose it must take some training to get so dirty," said Mr. Tiltman, making Clara laugh.

"I have to go," said Sam.

"But Mr. Compton hasn't arrived yet."

"I don't think he's coming," replied Sam.

"Very well, then." Mr. Tiltman moved out of his way.

Sam saw him exchange a glance with his daughter, both of them clearly amused by his behavior, but Sam couldn't concentrate enough to even attempt to act normally. He had to escape this house. He felt terrified by what he had just learned and paralyzed by the girl's beauty. Emily was crying.

"I'm sorry," said Sam, making for the door.

The Tiltmans looked confused at the apology, not realizing it had not been meant for them.

53

THE CENTRAL RECORDS LIBRARY

Lapsewood stepped into the Central Records Library, trying to look as if he was supposed to be there, but it had been a while since he had been inside and he couldn't help looking up to take in its splendor. It was without a doubt the most spectacular room in the Bureau. Its walls rose up higher than the highest cathedral, and every one was filled with books and files detailing all aspects of post-life business since record-keeping began. Also adorning the walls were great ladders on runners that librarians used to reach required records. The use of ladders was another example of how the Bureau attempted to normalize the business of being dead. Occasionally one of the more doddering librarians would topple and be forced to turn to Ether Dust while the ladder clattered to the floor, but it was strictly forbidden to float up to a shelf.

Correct procedure required Lapsewood to take a request docket to the inquiries desk for validation, then take the validated docket to the record request desk, wait for an available assistant, and hand over the docket, which would have to be verified with the same officer who had validated it before it was put into the queue of requests to be dealt with. All this could take weeks.

Instead, Lapsewood found a directory that would tell him the section of the library he was looking for. While he was flipping through it, a librarian arrived, also wanting to use the directory, but didn't think to question Lapsewood's authority. The idea of someone doing anything unprocedural was virtually unthinkable, so no one thought it. By the time Lapsewood had found what he was looking for, there was a line of librarians waiting behind him.

When he located the section he needed, he found ten blank-faced librarians waiting patiently for the ladder. Turning to Ether Dust would attract too much unwanted attention, so Lapsewood looked for a way to cut in line. No easy task, when there were so many signs on the walls warning of the dire consequences that awaited line cutters without the correct documentation.

Lapsewood watched the elderly librarian slowly make his way down. He tapped the shoulder of the man at the back of the line. His name tag read MR. BRYSON.

"Mr. Bryson?" he said quietly.

"Yes?" said the librarian.

"I've a message from Mr. Doddrington. You're to go to the front of the line."

The man looked at Lapsewood as if he had just suggested something utterly unspeakable. "Me? Why?"

"Your priority rating has been upped. You should go now before the next librarian goes up."

"Do you have fast-track documentation for me?" asked the librarian, twitching nervously.

"It's being generated as we speak."

"Should I not check it with Mr. Doddrington?" said Mr. Bryson.

"No time," said Lapsewood. "Come on, now."

Without further argument Mr. Bryson walked to the front of the line just as the previous librarian stepped off the ladder. "I'm sorry," he said to the next in line. "I have been given permission to cut in line."

As Lapsewood had hoped, the other librarian demanded to see his paperwork. Lapsewood moved out of sight to avoid being dragged into the dispute. It wasn't long before voices were raised, accusations were being flung, and threats were being made. More of the librarians in line got involved. Choosing his moment carefully, Lapsewood slipped past the throng and quickly climbed the ladder, unnoticed by the bickering librarians.

He found the correct shelf and looked for the London Tenancy List. It wasn't there. He checked again. Perhaps it had been put back in the wrong place. But there was no list. He quickly climbed down the ladder, where the argument was still in full swing, and made his way over to the inquiries desk, in search of the signing-out ledger.

The old female clerk behind the desk was looking anxiously over at the corner of the room where there was an unacceptable amount of noise.

"What's going on over there?" she asked.

"There's some kind of ladder dispute," replied Lapsewood. "Perhaps you should remind them of the rules regarding noise."

"Yes, I will," she said. "Will you mind the desk?"

"Certainly."

As soon as she stepped out from behind the desk, Lapsewood found the huge ledger and turned to the page where the list had been signed out. There, under the name of the signing-out clerk, was the name *Alice Biggins*. Lapsewood stared at it for a moment but was brought to his senses when he realized that Mr. Bryson had spotted him and was pointing him out to the desk clerk. It was time to go.

54
A NEW GHOST

CLARA NO LONGER KNEW WHAT SHE WAS WRITING. She only knew she couldn't stop. It was certainly not the well-argued unpicking of Reverend Fallowfield's trickery her father had requested. There was no doubt in Clara's mind that the exorcisms she had witnessed in her home and St. Winifred's School were as genuine as they were cruel and brutal. She wrote page after page, putting down her thoughts, trying to order them, to give them structure, to make sense of them. She wrote about her brief encounter with Lady Aysgarth's ghost. She wrote about the ghost in the school and the list of haunted buildings that had ended up in her hands. She wrote of her frustration at having such a list when she was unable to communicate with their ghostly inhabitants.

Reverend Fallowfield was never far from her thoughts, but she had not referred to him in front of her parents since the visit to the school. Aunt Hetty had been the last person to bring up his name, during a recent visit when she announced that, although he was undoubtedly gifted, he really only ever did the same thing. Hetty had hoped he might extend his act to include, say, the summoning of the ghosts of famous historical figures, but he had dismissed that idea out of hand, and Hetty had found alternative entertainment in a Spaniard who claimed to be able to eat absolutely anything. Mr. Tiltman seemed reluctant to have this new person over for a dinner party, fearing that he would have to buy yet more replacement cutlery.

Clara allowed her parents to believe that she, too, had lost interest in Reverend Fallowfield, just as they hoped she would one day drop the notion of becoming a journalist. The newspapermen who had visited after the discovery of the dead girl in the kitchen had certainly not made the profession seem any more glamorous to her. Intrusive, rude, sniveling men who smelled of tobacco and augmented every quote with a string of sensationalist adjectives, they were more interested in the bloody details than in the reason behind the girl's death. Still, Clara read every word of their overblown reports, while her mother went to great lengths to avoid them. Since the incident, Mrs. Tiltman habitually checked that the doors were locked and spoke incessantly about moving away from the city, causing a number of heated rows with her husband.

Clara knew that eventually her father would give in. Her days in London were numbered. Her mother would get her own way, and they would move to a boring town on the outskirts. Clara didn't want to leave the city. Nor did she want to abandon Aysgarth House. Since the discovery of the murdered girl in the kitchen, the place felt different. It felt the way it used to when Lady Aysgarth's ghost had still been there.

It is as if the ghost of the murdered girl has replaced that of Lady Aysgarth, Clara wrote.

She stopped and reread the sentence. Yes, that was exactly what it felt like. She looked at the toy theater. Perhaps it was her imagination, but she could have sworn she saw something move. She took a couple of steps toward it. She glanced at the window. There was no breeze outside, and the window was shut tightly, anyway, preventing any draft. Yet one of the paper actors had moved. She was sure of it.

"Hello?" she said.

Nothing.

"Hello?" she repeated.

There was no movement.

When a bell rang, Clara nearly jumped out of her skin, but it was only Hopkins announcing dinner. She glanced at the miniature theater one more time before leaving the room.

55

AN APPRENTICESHIP OF THIEVERY

SAM PLACED THE PLATE OF EGGS ON THE TABLE AND sat down to breakfast with his father.

"Thank you, Sam." Mr. Toop carefully folded his newspaper and picked up a knife and fork.

Sam had not spoken to him of his discovery about Uncle Jack. His father had protected Jack from the police once already. Would he do it again if he knew what was happening? Since Jack's disappearance, Mr. Toop had taken to buying a newspaper every day. Sam didn't need to ask why. He understood that his father was looking for news of his brother's arrest. Whether he was hoping they would capture Jack or that he would get away, Sam was unsure. All he knew was that his father had once been close to his brother. As close as brothers. As thick as thieves.

"Anything in the paper?" asked Sam.

"The usual assortment of death and theft," Mr. Toop replied wryly.

"Theft is a subject you know something about," said Sam quietly.

Mr. Toop folded the paper. "So, Jack told you of our past. You're upset," he said.

"Not upset," replied Sam. "I know that for those who have nothing, stealing can seem like the only option. You have always taught me that."

Mr. Toop picked up his empty mug. "Is there more tea in the pot?"

Sam stood up to pour his father another cup.

"I taught you it because I believe it to be true," said Mr. Toop. "Not as an excuse for what I did. Nor does it alleviate my guilt. I am ashamed of what I did then."

"So you choose to forget," said Sam.

"Memory does not allow such simple, selective decisions. In my experience, fond memories are too easily lost. It is the terrible ones that lodge themselves firmly in one's mind."

"So why put Jack in my room with me? You must have known he would tell me."

"Perhaps I wanted him to," confessed Mr. Toop. "I never chose to hide anything from you, Sam. It is just that some things are difficult to say. After all this time . . ." He trailed off.

"Jack said you only got your apprenticeship because you stole from the carpenter and that you abandoned him after that."

"We were a pair of thieving children. There is much about pickpocketing that appeals to a child. Running, sneaking, shouting, adventuring . . . the thrill of a chase. But it is not a game. Or if it is, it is an extremely dangerous one. In stealing from Old Man Chester, I saw an opportunity to escape. I allowed myself to get caught so I could throw myself on his mercy. It was a most cynically rehearsed performance. But heartfelt all the same. Whether he saw it for what it was, I do not know, but he took me under his wing all the same."

"So you left your brother?"

"Jack had already found his own apprenticeship," replied Mr. Toop.

"Jack did an apprenticeship, as well?"

"Of sorts, yes. His was an apprenticeship of thievery. His mentor was a man named Reeve. An attic burglar at the time, but a smart one. In every sense. He dressed well, even when he didn't have two coppers to rub together. All the pickpockets looked up to him, but Jack idolized him. He wanted to *be* him. He made his choice and I mine."

"How old were you?"

"Eleven and twelve. Young to make such life choices, I suppose."

"What happened to Mr. Reeve?"

"I have no idea. Caught? Dead? Still thieving? There

are few options for such men, none of which is desirable."

Sam picked up his father's empty plate. "I have one more question," he said.

"Yes."

"Jack mentioned my mother, so you must have seen him at least once more when you were grown up."

Mr. Toop looked away, avoiding Sam's gaze. "Jack and trouble are like smoke and fire. You find one, the other won't be far away. Whenever he has come back into my life, I have regretted letting him back in. Now, Sam, I must get to work."

Mr. Toop left the room, clearly flustered. Sam picked up the newspaper and noticed the headline. *The Terrible Murders of the Kitchen Killer.* The story told of a monster roaming the streets of London slitting the throats of the impoverished, then dragging them into strangers' homes to die. As he read the gruesome details of the murders, his hands began to shake until he was unable to read a single word.

"Jack," he muttered. "Jack. What have you done?"

281

56

THE RESPONSIBILITY OF MURDER

IN THE DARK ALLEY OF THE SEVEN DIALS, TANNER
had furnished Jack with another two addresses from the list.
Tanner then crossed the road and went into the pub, slipping through the wall of Mr. Reeve's office for his third day
spying. The previous day had provided no further revelations, and today, once again, much of the day's business
involved money-lending and was conducted in a professional manner with an underlying threat of violence. Dubious behavior, no doubt, but nothing out of the ordinary
and nothing about Jack.

Along with the usual debtors, Mr. Reeve met and made
deals with thieves, beggars, brothel-owners, swindlers,

embezzlers, and pickpockets. There appeared to be no criminal occupation so low or depraved that he didn't have some involvement in it. At midday there was a line of people waiting in the bar to see him, but when a man with a pockmarked face entered, Mr. Bazeley allowed him to walk straight in. A rake-thin young woman with mournful blue eyes who had been begging Mr. Reeve for a loan went pale with fear when the man entered the room, and Mr. Reeve quickly announced their business done with.

"Detective Inspector Savage," said Mr. Reeve. "To what do I owe the pleasure?"

"There's no pleasure in this visit," replied Inspector Savage.

"I'm sorry to hear that. What's troubling you?" asked Mr. Reeve. "You do seem troubled."

"Murder, Mr. Reeve. Bloody murder."

"The worst of all crimes, Savage."

Inspector Savage tossed a newspaper onto Mr. Reeve's desk.

He picked it up, read the headline, and snorted. "The Kitchen Killer?" he said, raising an eyebrow.

"Read it," said Inspector Savage.

"I don't appreciate being told what to do in my own place of work—you know that. Nor do I get my information from such unreliable sources as this."

Inspector Savage scowled and offered no apology. "This man kills his victims by cutting their throats," he said.

"I'd swear these newspapermen have a greater thirst for

blood than the most scurrilous criminals," said Mr. Reeve.

"Heale was killed in the same way."

"Yes." Mr. Reeve met Inspector Savage's gaze defiantly.

"Heale's murder was the work of this man, Jack Toop. Or so you told me."

Tanner's ears pricked up at the mention of Jack's name.

"That was what I heard," said Mr. Reeve. "You've not found him, then? What more than a man's name and address do you need to bring him to justice? Would you have me round him up and deliver him to the hangman for you?" He spoke angrily.

"I chased Jack Toop from that address myself. We lost him down Peckham Rye."

"Jack was always a good runner." Mr. Reeve smiled fondly.

"In Honor Oak I came across a shop with his name. An undertaker's."

Mr. Reeve laughed. "Appropriate enough. Jack's certainly buried a few people in his time."

"The proprietor was also a Toop, but he claimed to have no knowledge of Jack."

"What was this man's Christian name?"

Inspector Savage pulled out a notebook and flicked it open. "Charles Toop," he read aloud.

"Charlie Toop," said Mr. Reeve. "Now, there's a name I haven't heard in some time."

"You know him?"

"Yes, I know him. That's Jack's brother."

"So he was lying."

"Yes. You searched the premises, I take it?"

"You don't need to tell me how to conduct my business," snarled Inspector Savage.

"I thought that was exactly what I had to do," replied Mr. Reeve.

"Now, listen here. I only have your word that this Jack Toop even exists," Savage complained.

"Oh, Toop exists all right. And Charlie is his brother. It's not me who's lying to you."

Inspector Savage leaned close and spoke quietly. "You'd better not be, Reeve."

Reeve did not back down. "I'm not one of the common crooks you spend your days chasing," he said. "I'm paying you good money, Savage. More than the pittance you earn from the law. But that money can stop at any time. As Heale's death showed, no man is safe in this city. Now, I have given you Jack's name. I suggest you find him, arrest him, lock him up, then hang him. Maybe he is your Kitchen Killer. Maybe not. My guess is not. Jack may be a killer, but he isn't a mindless killer. As a gesture of goodwill I'll put some feelers out for you, but if you're serious about catching Jack, you need to go back to Charlie's shop and make him talk."

"You're certain he knows something?"

"I can tell you how to find out for sure . . ."

Tanner had stopped listening. He was hovering over Mr. Reeve's desk, reading the newspaper article. It listed the addresses where the bodies had been found. He didn't need to check his list to know that they were the ones he had given to Jack. This was Jack's solution—not persuading ghosts, but creating them. Sam had been right. Tanner had thrown his lot in with a very bad man, and now terrible things were happening. People were being killed, and it was Tanner's fault. Tanner turned to Ether Dust and flew through the wall into the pub. So intense was his anger and guilt that he knocked a freshly poured pint of ale clean off the bar as he whooshed past, sending it smashing onto the wooden floor.

57
POOR MRS. PRESTON

Since the appearance of the dead girl in the kitchen, Aysgarth House had been a very different place to live. Gone was any air of levity. In its place, an unpleasant tension lingered. Obsessed with moving out of London, Mrs. Tiltman had grown increasingly frustrated with her husband's attempts to pretend that everything was fine.

"What ever happened to that article you were writing about that man Fallowfield, Clara?" asked Mr. Tiltman from behind his newspaper.

"I'm still working on it," replied Clara.

"Well, you'd better get a move on. It looks as if the old fraud's about to go public."

"What do you mean?" asked Mrs. Tiltman coldly.

"This advertisement says there's to be a public exorcism at the Drury Lane Theatre. It mentions Fallowfield's name," he said. "It says the place has been haunted for years."

"The Man in Gray," said Clara, remembering what the doorman had said.

"I'm impressed," said her father. "You have been researching the subject."

"So he's putting on a show?" asked Clara.

"Fallowfield is inviting skeptics to debunk his show. The gall of the man. He's throwing down the gauntlet. You know how much I like a good gauntlet-throwing. Let's go." Mr. Tiltman's eyes sparkled with childlike excitement.

"No. I forbid it," said Mrs. Tiltman.

"'Forbid'?" replied Mr. Tiltman, catching Clara's eye.

"You think the two of you can go down and poke fun at the whole thing, but, no, I won't allow you to take Clara, not at night. No," stated Mrs. Tiltman, folding her arms defiantly.

"She'll be with me," said her husband. "London is no less safe than it ever was."

"'No less safe'?" exclaimed Mrs. Tiltman. "How can you say that with this killer roaming the streets?"

"Darling, please keep your voice down." Mr. Tiltman spoke sternly. "Mrs. Preston will hear."

"Mrs. Preston?" pronounced Mrs. Tiltman. "What about me? I can barely stand to leave the house these days. I can't sleep. I'm scared to step outside. I'm scared to stay

288

in. I will not have you taking Clara out at night while this monster is at large."

Mr. Tiltman sighed. "It was an unfortunate incident, and that is all."

"A burst pipe or the stubbing of a toe is an 'unfortunate incident,'" countered Mrs. Tiltman. "This was something else. How long must you keep us here, living in abject fear?"

"If you are worried, take a holiday. Take Clara to visit your aunt. The country air will do you good."

"No, we need to move, George. All of us. We need to get out of the city."

"I don't want to go," said Clara.

"The decision is not yours," snapped her mother.

"Father doesn't want to leave either," replied Clara.

"You will not speak to me that way," said Mrs. Tiltman.

"I don't think we should be hasty in reacting to this. It was a terrible shock for us all," said Mr. Tiltman.

"Yes, it was," shrieked Mrs. Tiltman. "Finding that poor, murdered girl in a pool of blood in our kitchen. It was certainly a shock."

With her back to the kitchen door, Mrs. Tiltman couldn't see Hopkins standing in the doorway, holding a tray. Behind him in the kitchen, Mrs. Preston burst into tears.

"Are you happy now?" asked Mr. Tiltman.

"'Happy'?" replied Mrs. Tiltman, who was also crying. "No, I'm very far from happy."

"That poor woman has been through enough," said Mr. Tiltman.

"Can't you see? It's not just about her. The body was found in our house. Ours. We have been invaded by this horror. Can't you see that? Our house is stained with that girl's blood." Mrs. Tiltman stood up, knocking over her chair, and fled the room.

"Darling," pleaded her husband, following her out.

Hopkins said, "I had better see to Mrs. Preston, miss."

"Yes," replied Clara.

Eventually everyone calmed down, and dinner was brought and consumed in a frosty, reserved atmosphere.

Afterward, Clara went to her room. "It's you, isn't it?" she said, unsure where to look. "It's your ghost. You're the girl who was dragged in here, aren't you? You made my theater actor move. Do it again—show me you're here."

Nothing happened.

"Please. I want to help."

Still nothing.

Clara couldn't have known that Emily's ghost was downstairs in the kitchen, standing next to Hopkins, trying her best to comfort Mrs. Preston.

58
THE RETURN OF INSPECTOR SAVAGE

SAM WAS HELPING HIS FATHER WHEN THERE WAS A knock on the workshop door. Mr. Toop looked up from the piece of wood he was planing. "Yes?" he called.

The door opened, and Mr. Constable appeared. "Sorry to interrupt, Mr. Toop," he said. "This gentleman would like a word."

Behind him stood the man with the pockmarked face.

"Inspector Savage," said Mr. Toop.

Sam could tell that his father was spooked by the policeman's return.

"Charlie Toop," said Inspector Savage.

"I prefer Charles."

"I prefer Charlie. As in Charlie and Jack Toop."

"I'm afraid I don't know what you're talking about." Sam's father sounded flustered.

"I think you do," said Inspector Savage.

"If you have something to say, I'd appreciate your coming out and saying it." Mr. Toop spoke angrily. "As you can see, I have no corpses for you to flavor today, Inspector."

"I'd be careful with your jokes, Mr. Toop. I'm here to discuss your brother. We have reason to believe he's back in London and up to his old tricks. I'd like to know everything you know."

"I already told you—"

"That you have no brother? Yes, you did imply that, and I do not appreciate being lied to." Inspector Savage's manner was calm but assertive. "You are Charlie Toop. You grew up in the district of Whitechapel with your brother, Jack. Your brother is guilty of murder, and if you are found to be protecting him, the law will see you swing for your part in this unsavory business."

"Father—" began Sam.

"Sam, please leave this to me," snapped Mr. Toop. He turned to Inspector Savage. "We parted ways many years ago. We chose different paths, Jack and I, so when I said I didn't have a brother, I meant I didn't have a brother anymore."

"No," said Inspector Savage. "You lied to me, Mr. Toop, but that's going to stop now."

Mr. Toop said nothing.

"I can make life very difficult for you if I want," said

Inspector Savage. "I can start asking questions that haven't been asked for some time, investigating things that haven't been investigated, if you get my drift. Or you can cooperate and let me know everything you know."

Mr. Toop looked at his son, then back at Inspector Savage. "Not here," he said. "We'll speak upstairs."

Inspector Savage nodded.

"Sam, finish off this coffin," said Mr. Toop. "I won't be long." He led Savage up the staircase.

Sam turned to Mr. Constable, but Mr. Constable turned away and muttered, "Best do as your father says," and he allowed the door to swing shut behind him.

59

A FRENCH INTRUSION

TANNER LINGERED IN THE AIR AS ETHER DUST, mixing with the smog and the fog and the stinking tobacco smoke that polluted London's air. Jack stood in the shadowy alleyway. Tanner swirled around his body, seeing now the unmistakable stains on Jack's grubby black frock coat. The blood of his victims. Jack rubbed his hands together to warm them. His fingerless gloves revealed stubby fingers with blackened filth around the edges of the nails. In its leather sheath was the blade he had used to cut his victims' throats. In his pockets were the few coins they had been carrying, taken as souvenirs of their murders.

What kind of man chose murder when there were other

options available? Tanner thought about that poor girl in the attic window. Now he understood the look in her eyes. Not the sadness of a ghost imprisoned, but the bewilderment of a girl whose life had been taken for reasons far beyond her own understanding.

"Come on out," snarled Jack. "I know you're 'ere. I can smell you lot out. Death has its own stench, don't it?"

Tanner materialized in front of him, his fists clenched, his eyes burning with dark anger.

"What's the matter with you?" asked Jack.

"I know what you're doing," replied Tanner.

"What? Talking to you?"

"You're killing people."

Jack shrugged. "What d'you care? I'm getting you ghosts, ain't I?"

"I never asked for murder."

"You asked for help, and that's what you're gettin'."

"Help as a Talker."

"Talk? Who wants to talk to a whining ghost? You expect me to persuade and negotiate when there's shortcuts available?" Jack pulled his knife out and jabbed it through Tanner's chest.

In spite of himself, Tanner flinched.

"Anyway, I'm only killin' them with no lives," said Jack. "Drunks, urchins, whores. They should 'ang a medal on my chest. I'm cleanin' up London."

"They've been calling you the Kitchen Killer," replied Tanner.

Jack smirked. "Jack Toop, the Kitchen Killer," he said with a wistful smile. "Yes, that'll do."

"They're closing in on you, Jack. The police have your name. Reeve told them you killed that copper."

"Did he?" breathed Jack. "He'll live to regret giving me up, 'e will. Then he'll die to regret it, too. Give me another of your addresses, and I'll drag 'is body inside. That way I can go visit 'is ghost, and 'e can watch as I take over 'is empire."

"I will not be a part of this," said Tanner.

"Suit yourself. You've served your purpose now. I had my suspicions that it was Reeve, but I had to know for sure. Reeve's goin' to get what's coming to 'im. I want 'im to look into my eyes while the blood drains from 'is body."

"I hope they catch you."

"Don't be like that," said Jack mockingly. "You should be proud of yourself. You're the first ghost that ever proved useful."

Jack stepped into the street and swiftly disappeared among the crowd. Tanner thought about the five lives ended because of him. The dead liked to speak of being ghost-born to make it sound more pleasant, but Tanner knew that nothing could sweeten the violence of death. He remembered his own. He didn't know the name of the sickness that had killed him, but the pain of dying lingered on in his memory. Nothing that could happen in life hurt like the feeling of having it torn away. Refusing the Unseen Door and remaining a ghost was to retain the memory of that pain forever. That was why the pull of the door was so hard to resist; it promised to wipe away that pain.

Tanner turned. Something had caught his eye.

"Who's there?" he called.

A ghost materialized. He was a well-dressed man with a thin mustache and greasy, slicked-back hair. He smiled.

"What do you want?" asked Tanner.

"*Bonjour*," said the man.

"Eh?"

"Typical ignorant English ghost," said the ghost.

Tanner didn't like the way the man looked at him. He began to turn to Ether Dust but felt two cold, metallic hands suddenly clamp around his wrists, preventing him from escaping. "What are you playing at?" he demanded.

"I am not here to play, Monsieur Tanner," replied the man. "I am here to work."

60
ALWAYS ALICE

THE PAST FEW WEEKS HAD CHANGED LAPSEWOOD. After a lifetime and, subsequently, a deathtime of treading the careful path of conformity, he had finally been set free. He had walked among the living as a ghost, acted upon his own initiative, been thrown into, then broken out of, prison. He had even found his way into the Central Records Library without being caught. If ghosts had reflections, his would have looked very different now as he walked purposefully along the corridor with the Marquis by his side. Moving around the Bureau as an escaped convict was surprisingly easy. With the exception of personnel guarding restricted areas, no one asked for their papers. Of course, it did help that no one knew they were missing.

They stopped in front of an entrance to the Paternoster Pipe Network.

"Thank you," said Lapsewood, grasping the Marquis's hand. "You have been a great help."

"Spoken with such finality," replied the Marquis.

"The danger in which I must now put myself is for me alone, and there will be no need for distractions. You can take the Pipe to the exit and find exile in the physical world."

"A very good speech, and I will reluctantly agree to this parting," replied the Marquis. "But I will save my final oration for the moment we are reunited."

Lapsewood smiled. "I must go speak with Alice Biggins. It's likely I'll be rearrested."

"Then don't do it," urged the Marquis. "Find another way."

"No, this is the only way," said Lapsewood. "If I'm the only one investigating the Black Rot, why did Alice get that list out of the CRL? No, something is going on."

"I can see you are determined to walk this path alone," said the Marquis. "So, with a heavy heart, I wish you good luck and good-bye."

The two men shook hands, then turned to Ether Dust slowly, so that, for a moment, all that remained were two hands clasped together. Then they flew into the Paternoster Pipe and parted ways. The distaste Lapsewood had always felt for the Paternoster Pipe Network did not seem relevant anymore. He no longer felt the need to pretend he was still alive. Walking the streets of London unseen by the crowds of living people had made him realize he shouldn't be ashamed about being dead. The dead had as much of a role to play as the living. They had as much right to their existence. The physical world may have been home to the living, but it was also the legacy of the dead.

Lapsewood materialized on the twenty-fifth floor and once more laid eyes on the unmatched beauty of Alice Biggins. She was sitting behind her desk, looking as beautiful as ever. She stared at him. He stared back. For a moment, neither spoke.

Then she uttered, "How can you be—"

He raised a finger to his lips, cutting her off mid-flow.

"Is he in there?" he asked, pointing to Penhaligan's office door.

"Yes," she replied.

He had forgotten how that voice made him feel, as though all his energy had been sucked out and replaced with a soft, sweet, contented mush.

"I saw that you were arrested. Have you been released?" she asked.

"Sort of," replied Lapsewood.

"I didn't like the idea of you being stuck down there," said Alice. "Is it as awful as they say?"

"I'm here about the list," he replied.

"The list?"

"The London Tenancy List."

"Oh, that. Why do you care about that?"

"Where is it now?"

"He wanted it." She pointed to Colonel Penhaligan's door.

"How did you get ahold of it so quickly?"

"Quickly?" exclaimed Alice. "It took me weeks to get that."

"Weeks? When did you take it out?"

"I don't know. A month ago?" she replied. "I think he gave it to Monsieur Vidocq."

"Vidocq?"

"That's right. The Prowler. French, nice mustache."

"Yes," replied Lapsewood irritably. "I remember him. Why would Penhaligan give the list to him?"

"Don't ask me. He doesn't tell me anything. Oh, Lapsewood, it is nice to see you."

"You've . . . you've missed me?" Lapsewood felt wrong-footed.

"Oh, yes. The way Mr. Grunt dabbed his neck all the time made me feel awfully queasy. But he's gone now, too, hasn't he?"

"Has he?"

"Yes, the last time I saw him, I told him about you being in the Vault. I haven't seen him since."

"And what about Vidocq? Where is he now?"

"Out in the physical world, I suppose. No idea where, though. You know what it's like with Prowlers. Everything's all so secretive, isn't it?"

"I'm going in to see him." Lapsewood looked at Penhaligan's door. That door had filled him with so much dread before. Now it was just one more obstacle.

"You haven't got an appointment. You know what he's like about unscheduled interruptions."

"The time for appointments is over," said Lapsewood.

61

EMILY'S PLAY

IT WAS WHEN EMILY THOUGHT ABOUT HER MOTHER
that she first animated Clara's toy theater. As the pain of
losing her mum filled Emily's body, she saw a puppet actor
twitch. After a few more experiments she realized she could
manipulate it whenever she felt strong emotions. The trick
was to feel the emotion without getting dragged down by
spiraling, self-destructive thoughts.

Her motivation did not come from a desire to make an
impact upon the physical world. Emily simply wanted to
play with the most magnificent toy she had ever laid eyes
on. Only when Clara began to watch the theater intently
did Emily consider that she could use the paper actors to

communicate with her. Clara sat patiently for hours, waiting for Emily to perfect her performance. Emily came to worry that she was taking too long and that Clara would lose interest, but eventually she got it right.

Her play opened when she led out onto the stage a little girl dressed in rags. Emily didn't know she had picked Cinderella to play the part of herself.

"This is you?" said Clara, instantly understanding.

Ever so delicately, Emily reached her other hand into the theater and tapped the back of the character's head, making Cinderella nod in answer to the question.

"You're the poor girl from the kitchen."

Another nod.

"Do you know who did it?"

Emily shook the character's head to indicate *No*.

"What happened?" asked Clara.

Emily had never laid eyes on her murderer, but she'd found the figure she felt best suited his rasping voice. The character she had chosen to play Jack was King Rat, the villain from *Dick Whittington*. Even the tail curling from his backside didn't seem out of place with how she imagined the man who had dragged her, bleeding, through the streets of London. Slowly she pushed him across the stage, behind Cinderella's back. He pounced, and Cinderella fell.

Clara watched, fascinated, as King Rat dragged Cinderella off the side of the stage. She gasped when Emily plucked a red petal from a bowl of dried flowers on the windowsill and let it flutter down onto the spot where Cinderella lay.

"He killed you and dragged you inside. Why?" whispered Clara.

Nothing moved; Emily could not respond to such open questions.

"Are you able to leave the house?" asked Clara.

Emily dragged Cinderella to the back of the stage, demonstrating that the outside walls were as impassable for her as they were for Clara.

"You're stuck here, all by yourself," said Clara.

Emily brought another character onto the stage. It was Cinderella again, only now her tattered rags had been transformed into a beautiful gown. Emily knew that Clara understood what she meant when she saw a tear form in Clara's eye. The transformed Cinderella represented Clara. Emily was showing her that she did not feel alone, because she had Clara for company.

"If my mother has her way, we will have to move," said Clara sadly. "The fear is affecting her health. She gets worse every day. Father is worried about her. I am worried about her. I do not want to leave London, but neither do I want to see my mother suffer so much. Living south of the river, one may as well be dead . . ." She stopped. "Sorry, that was thoughtless. It's just, I cannot bear to be torn from this place. Tomorrow we catch the train to see a house my father has found. Somewhere south. I don't want to leave you, but I don't think I can stop it now."

Emily wished she could cry, too, but no tears would come, and her dead eyes remained dry and clear. She let

305

Cinderella flutter to the ground and found the mechanism that operated the theater curtain. She lowered the red curtain in front of the stage to indicate that the play was over. If Clara left, Emily would be utterly alone in this house.

Alone forever.

62
THE BALLAD OF PADDY O'TWAIN

NONE OF THE REVELERS IN THE BOAR'S HEAD no-ticed Reverend Fallowfield return to the pub as he slipped inside, a hood pulled over his bald head. Neither the living customers enjoying the warmth on that cold winter's night, nor the ghost of Paddy O'Twain saw him enter and find a seat in a corner. Had Mrs. O'Twain not been so occupied with customers, she would have spied him and reminded him that the seats were for paying customers only. But Mrs. O'Twain was distracted by a gang of spirited young Irishmen leading the entire pub in a rousing sing-along. Paddy's was an unheard voice as he joined in with ballads he hadn't heard in years, while his wife was busy batting off one of the more amorous members of the gang. Paddy didn't mind that. He had never been a jealous man in life and was not going to start being one now. He was having the time of his death.

Even when Reverend Fallowfield began to mutter to himself in the corner, no one paid him any heed. The Boar's Head had seen its fair share of mutterers over the years.

The first Paddy knew of the priest's presence was a sudden, violent tug in his chest. He wondered whether it was a side effect of his latest batch of spirit ale, but a second tug soon convinced him otherwise. Before he knew what was happening, he had been dragged across the bar onto the table in the corner and was spinning around like a puppet with tangled strings.

Reverend Fallowfield threw off his hood to reveal the three-pointed birthmark on his head. His burning eyes focused on Paddy.

"Devil spirit," said Reverend Fallowfield. "Now we see your terrible form."

The raucous rendition of "The Irish Washerwoman" petered out as, one by one, each singer noticed the strange occurrence in the corner of the pub. Mrs. O'Twain pushed her way through, demanding to see what the trouble was. When she saw her dead husband suspended above a table, spinning around, she gasped. "Paddy?"

Paddy O'Twain felt very much the way he used to feel when his wife would discover him downstairs late at night working his way through a bottle of whiskey.

"Ah, well, hello there, dear," he said.

"'Ah, well, hello there, dear'?" she squawked. "You return from the grave, and that's all you can bring yourself to say? Those are the words with which you choose to haunt me?"

"'Haunt'?" said Paddy. "Now, that's a strong word."

"Silence!" cried Reverend Fallowfield, his clawlike fingers tightening their grip, making Paddy wince in discomfort.

"Oh, it's you again, is it?" said Mrs. O'Twain, turning to confront the Reverend. "I thought I made it clear what would happen if you returned."

"You doubted my assertion," hissed Reverend Fallowfield. "Now see for yourself the demon that lies within your place of sin."

"That's no demon, Father. That's my husband."

"No longer!" exclaimed Reverend Fallowfield. "Before you, you see a shape of your husband, but this thing, this apparition, this aberration is no longer human. God had no part in making it. 'Twas a redder hand that formed this creature."

"Steady on, now," said Paddy.

"He still sounds like my husband," said Mrs. O'Twain, causing laughter from the drunken crowd.

"I am here to release this spirit from its imprisonment," said Reverend Fallowfield.

"Release," said Paddy. "Yes, that would be good. You're making me dizzy with all this spinning, you are."

Reverend Fallowfield muttered something under his breath. He raised his hands, and the muttering grew louder. "Damnable spirit, uninvited wretch, unrequested, unwanted . . . unliving. The other side awaits you. You must begone from this place. You must begone."

Mrs. O'Twain, who could see plainly enough the discomfort these words caused her husband, shouted, "Leave him alone! I told you I didn't want this."

"It is not for you to decide," replied Reverend Fallowfield. "This trespasser shall be chased out, eradicated, exterminated. Begone, foul spirit. Begone."

Paddy's discomfort turned to pain. He could feel himself being pulled in all directions, as though wild horses were tied to every part of his body. Dark cracks appeared all around him. He could no longer focus on his wife's face.

"I'm sorry, dear," he managed to utter before pain was all that he knew, and Paddy O'Twain was torn apart into nothingness.

63

THE HELLHOUND

THE NIGHT SKY OVER LONDON WAS DARK, BUT ITS
streets were aglow with yellow lamplight and teeming with
life. In among all that life, two of its dead made their way
through the streets, houses, and yards, heedless of the physical obstructions that hindered the living souls.

Monsieur Vidocq dragged Tanner bodily behind him,
clutching the chain between the two metallic hands clasped
tightly around Tanner's wrists. Tanner struggled to get to
his feet, but each time he did, Monsieur Vidocq picked up
his pace. From the alley in Seven Dials, he took him down
Shaftesbury Avenue, then along Piccadilly.

"What do you want with me?" screamed Tanner.

"A Rogue ghost consorting with a Talker is one thing," said Monsieur Vidocq. "Having him commit murder is quite another."

"If you were listening to all that, then you'll have heard that I didn't know what he was doing. I never told him to kill no one."

"Then what exactly *were* you doing?"

"I was trying to get ghosts into the infected houses."

"And why would a Rogue ghost want to do that?"

"The Black Rot," said Tanner. "We've got to stop the Black Rot."

"*La Pourriture Noire*," said Monsieur Vidocq. "What concern is that to you?"

"We were investigating it," replied Tanner.

"'We'?"

"Lapsewood and me."

"Ah." Monsieur Vidocq stopped, giving Tanner enough time to stand. "Lapsewood."

"Yeah, he's one of your Bureau lot, ain't he? He'll tell you. I was helping him."

"And he told you to enlist the help of this Talker, did he? Most interesting."

"Yes, well, no. Not exactly, but—"

"So you are both implicated in this scandal?"

"I already told you, I didn't know—"

Vidocq interrupted him. "—that he was killing people. Yes, you said. Unfortunately for you, ignorance is no excuse."

"So what are you going to do?" asked Tanner defiantly. They were standing by the park. During the day it would have been as busy as any part of London, but at night without streetlights it was a dead space in the city. The only living souls to venture in at night were those who desired the seclusion its darkness offered. Monsieur Vidocq yanked on the chain, pulling Tanner off his feet and dragging him across the grass.

"You planning on locking me up or what?" said Tanner.

"An arrest requires a great deal of administration. I myself find the whole thing very frustrating. Especially when there are more appropriate methods of dealing with your indiscretions."

"What *are* you going on about?" asked Tanner.

"You have no idea what you are involved in. You cannot comprehend what you have done. And yet, for someone so ignorant, you have been the cause of much trouble."

"Listen, I didn't know that Jack Toop was killing people," protested Tanner.

"This is not about the Talker," said Monsieur Vidocq.

"What, then?"

"The anomalies."

"The what?"

"*Les chiens*, the hounds. You fed them to the houses."

"I was using them to test if it was safe."

"'Safe'?" Monsieur Vidocq laughed. "Not a word I would use. The church in Shadwell had been infected so long, it had drawn something terrible from the Void, a formless

313

thing of unimaginable horror, a different kind of darkness . . . what some might call a demon."

Deeper into the darkness Monsieur Vidocq dragged him.

"A demon?" said Tanner.

"*Oui*, a demon. This thing was trapped within the confines of the church. With no body, it wore the building as its clothes. Even the living could sense its presence, and yet, imprisoned as it was, it could do no harm. Not until you found a solution for it, how to release it."

"A solution?"

"It was a formless demon in search of a body. And you provided it with one. You gave it the body of a hound."

"Li'l Mags ran in," protested Tanner. "I tried to stop her."

"Ah, you English do so love your animals." Monsieur Vidocq had slowed down as they approached a large bush. The sounds of the city were distant and dreamlike. If not for the shimmer of the streetlamps, Tanner could have believed they were standing in the middle of the countryside. He spotted something shift in the darkness, ghost-silent and blacker than night.

"This demon took the hound's form and escaped the church," said Monsieur Vidocq. "The damage you have done is . . . what's the word? Oh, yes, *formidable*."

"What does it want?" asked Tanner, struggling to free himself from the cuffs, fearful of the approaching creature.

"It wants your soul," said Vidocq. "This thing you created feeds on the souls of ghosts. With each one it devours, it grows larger."

"I didn't mean for any of this to happen. We were trying to help. We were just using the hounds to check that the houses were safe. We're on the same side. We have to stop it."

"Stop it? *Non*." Vidocq shook his head. "Feed it, Monsieur Tanner. We must feed it. And the same side? I don't think so. You see, your fate is to be devoured by the creature you created. It is neat, is it not?"

Vidocq swung the chain and hurled Tanner into the darkness. He stumbled and tripped and felt something land on top of him. It held him down.

"*Au revoir*," said Monsieur Vidocq.

The creature loomed over Tanner. Its cavernous mouth drooled. He could see its black teeth and eyes like shadows in the darkness. It lowered its huge head and moved in for the kill.

Pinned to the ground, Tanner stared into the jaws of despair. Regret flooded his mind. He wished he had never turned his back on the Unseen Door. There was no chance of tranquility now. This creature would tear him apart and feed on his soul.

A cold breeze blew through the park, but neither ghost nor hound felt its chill.

"Go on, then!" shouted Tanner. "You might as well get it over and done with."

The hound did not move. Its warm breath stank of devoured souls. Its black eyes were alive with death.

"I said, you might as well be done with me," said Tanner.

The hound growled. Tanner shut his eyes and waited. And waited.

When he opened them again, the beast had moved. It edged back, releasing him from its grip. Tanner scrambled to his feet. His instinct was to turn to Ether Dust and go, but the handcuffs prevented him. The hound stared at him. He stared back and realized he knew those eyes.

"Li'l Mags?" he whispered. "Is that you?"

The hound lowered its huge head and stepped forward. Tanner reached up and, ever so cautiously, tickled it under its chin. It pushed its chin into his hand.

"Li'l Mags," Tanner exclaimed. "It is you."

He reached up to stroke her again, but the hound snarled. He raised his hands to protect himself, and it snapped its jaws shut on the chain between the handcuffs, breaking straight through, releasing Tanner. The handcuffs and chain fell to the ground.

"Good girl, Li'l Mags," said Tanner.

The hound threw its head back and howled, then turned and ran, its black shape moving toward the shimmering lights of Piccadilly. Understanding what he had to do, Tanner gave chase.

64

A WIDOW'S GRIEF

SAM WAS RELIEVED INSPECTOR SAVAGE HAD NOT thought to interrogate him as well as his father. The inspector clearly knew that Jack Toop was back to killing, and, unfortunately, Sam knew why he was. He had no desire to protect his uncle, but neither could he reveal the truth. To make himself an informer would be to invite too many questions, the answers to which would then become a matter of official record. Sam had no desire to go public with his supernatural abilities. He did not know what had been said during Inspector Savage's interrogation, and Mr. Toop did not bring up the subject until the following morning over breakfast.

"I never should have let Jack stay," he said. "I should have sent him away that night or else turned him over to Savage when he lay in that coffin."

"Why didn't you?" asked Sam.

Mr. Toop forked a mushroom into his mouth and considered his answer. "For years we were all each other had. Jack and I. He was my little brother. I suppose I felt protective, though Jack never really needed my protection."

"What about the other time he came back, before I was born?" Sam was still thinking about Jack's mention of his mother. "What happened then?"

Mr. Toop carefully cut the rind off the bacon. "If I tell you, you won't be able to unknow it."

"I need to know," said Sam.

Mr. Toop put down his cutlery and pushed his plate away. "I suppose you do," he said. He fell silent again for a moment. "I've never told you the truth about how your mother and I met."

"You told me you met when she came here to bury her father."

Mr. Toop pushed the tips of his fingers together until they turned pink with the pressure. "We met when she came to bury her husband."

"Her husband?"

"There was nothing untoward in what we did," said Mr. Toop quickly. "Your mother was a widow when we met. She wore black for the year that followed his death, and we were discreet with our affections. Friendship came first. We never once acted upon our feelings, but when you fall in love, you are as helpless as a leaf on a breeze."

"Why have you never told me this before?"

Mr. Toop walked to the window, keeping his back to Sam.

"Her father disapproved. He wanted her to continue wearing black long after a year of mourning. I think he would have had her remain in her widow's weeds for the rest of her life, but we had fallen in love. Only one thing stood in the way of our marriage. Him."

"Couldn't you have married without his consent?"

"Your mother would not. So we did the only thing we could do. We waited for the old man to die."

"I don't see what this has to do with Jack," said Sam.

"That's when he came to visit. It had been a long time since I'd seen him. We went for a drink, and I confessed my troubles. I told him that I wished the old man would get on with it and die, so your mother and I could begin our lives. The next day, your mother came to the shop. I knew at once something was wrong. She told me how a burglar had broken into the house that night and killed the old man as he lay sleeping in his bed. He was smothered by his own pillow."

"Jack did it," whispered Sam.

"I had no idea what he had become," said Mr. Toop.

"Did you ask him to do it?"

"No," said Mr. Toop. "No . . . No . . ."

Each time he spoke the word, it sounded more like he was trying to convince himself.

"Were you pleased he had done it?" asked Sam.

"Your mother and I were married a month later. She fell pregnant with you soon after that. It was what we both wanted."

"Were you pleased he did it?" repeated Sam.

"It was a terrible, unforgivable thing to do. I know that. Had I been there, I would have stopped it. But was I grateful for the result? Yes, Sam, I was. The result was you."

Sam could feel his world collapsing in on him. He felt nauseated. Dizzy. He tried to make sense of what his father had told him, but there was too much to take in. Mr. Toop said no more, but the ringing in Sam's head was deafening. He had to get out. He stood up.

"Sam, please," said his father, but he left the room and ran downstairs.

He went through the shop and into the street. It was a cold day, and Sam was not wearing his coat, but he liked how the wind numbed his exposed skin, making him feel on the outside how he felt on the inside.

He walked past the grocer's. Richard Gliddon was inside stacking shelves. Seeing Sam, he raised his hand in greeting, but Sam didn't stop. He walked onto the railway bridge. A train was pulling in. Steam billowed up from the funnel. Sam hitched himself up onto the wall to look down at the platform and saw three figures step off the train.

The steam dispersed, and Sam saw Mr. Tiltman. By his side was a woman Sam took to be his wife, but it was the third figure who drew Sam's gaze. Walking behind her parents, dragging her feet and rolling her beautiful eyes, was Clara.

As they emerged from the station, Mr. Tiltman spotted him and waved.

"Master Toop," he said. "What a small world it is."

Mr. Tiltman's words reminded Sam of the lie he had told during their last encounter and how strange he must have seemed, running out like that.

"I took your advice about this area. We are here to see a house," said Mr. Tiltman, speaking with as much ease and charm as before. "What brings you out here?"

"I'm visiting family," replied Sam.

"No chimneys to sweep today?" said Clara.

Sam stared back at her, uncertain what to say.

Mrs. Tiltman coughed pointedly.

"I'm sorry, my dear," said Mr. Tiltman. "This is my wife. Young Sam here sheltered with us from the rain while waiting for his master, Mr. Compton."

"Pleased to meet you," said Mrs. Tiltman. She turned back to her husband. "So, where is your estate agent?"

"It would appear that he's late," replied Mr. Tiltman.

"Perhaps I can point you in the right direction," said Sam. "I know the area quite well."

"How kind," said Mr. Tiltman. "We're looking for a house called The Elms."

"I know that house," said Sam. "I can take you there."

"We wouldn't want to put you out," said Mrs. Tiltman.

Sam was finding it difficult not to stare at Clara. "It's no trouble," he said. "It's just the other side of the hill."

"Is there no taxicab we can take?" asked Mrs. Tiltman.

"There is a carriage service not far from here," said Sam. "I could run and see about hiring one."

"What a helpful young fellow you are," said Mr. Tiltman. "But no, we are happy to walk, so if we're not putting you out, then please lead on."

Sam led them up the hill. Due to the impracticalities of Mrs. Tiltman's city footwear and the roughness of the road, she and her husband fell behind, while Clara and Sam walked ahead. He kept his eyes firmly on the road ahead of him.

"Do you really work for Mr. Compton?" asked Clara.

"I . . ." Sam didn't want to lie. "Not exactly, no."

"And you really were talking to someone in our drawing room before I came in, weren't you?"

"I told you, I was talking to myself."

"You're quite peculiar, you know. Coming to our house in the pouring rain, talking to yourself, then appearing here in the middle of nowhere with no coat on the coldest day of the year."

A moment of uncomfortable silence fell between the two of them. Sam was unsure how to respond, so he asked, "Why is your family moving out of Aysgarth House?"

"It is not my choice," replied Clara. "It's a silly thing that brings us here."

"How silly?"

"A girl was found in our kitchen."

"A girl?"

"A dead girl. It was reported in the papers."

"You consider the discovery of a murdered girl in your kitchen a silly thing?" replied Sam.

"How do you know she was murdered? I said nothing of it."

Sam was thrown by this. "I . . . I suppose I must have read about Emily in the paper," he said.

Clara stopped walking and grabbed Sam's arm. He glanced at her hand, and she quickly removed it. "There was no name in the paper," she said. "The girl's identity is unknown."

"Really?" In spite of the biting wind, Sam felt a bead of sweat form on his forehead.

Clara's face was animated now and her eyes so wide, Sam wondered that they had not swallowed him up. "You spoke to her, didn't you?"

Seeing Mr. and Mrs. Tiltman getting closer, Sam started walking again.

"Were you speaking to my ghost?" said Clara, racing to keep up with him.

"Yes," said Sam, realizing he had nothing to lose. "I spoke to Emily."

"How wonderful!" exclaimed Clara. "You could help me. You see, I've been writing about ghosts."

"A ghost story?"

"No. I'm writing about real ghosts."

Sam usually hated talking about his supernatural ability,

but he liked the way Clara had started looking at him since he came clean. He wondered if this was the feeling his father had spoken of, the feeling of being like a leaf on the breeze.

"What can I do to help you?" he asked.

"We could interview the ghosts of London."

"Why?"

"Because it's interesting."

They had reached the gate to the house. Mr. and Mrs. Tiltman were catching up with them. Sam knew he was running out of his time alone with Clara. He had no interest in talking to ghosts, but if it meant he got to see Clara again, he would interview every spirit in the world.

"Come to my house tomorrow," said Clara.

"I have a funeral tomorrow."

"Oh, I'm sorry."

"No, I mean, I have work."

"Sweeping chimneys *and* funerals? What an interesting business you're in."

Sam smiled.

"Then come the following day," said Clara.

Pure joy bubbled up from Sam's toes and warmed his shivering body. Finally, something good had come from his terrible curse.

"What are you two talking so intently about?" asked Mr. Tiltman.

"Ghosts," replied Clara.

"Why can't you at least try to act like a normal human being for once in your life?" asked Mrs. Tiltman.

"I blame parental influences," said Clara.

"Thank you for showing us the way, Master Toop," said Mr. Tiltman, offering Sam his hand.

Sam shook it. "It was on my way," he said, inwardly swearing it would be his last lie to this family.

"Also, you appear to have cheered up my daughter," said Mr. Tiltman. "So thank you for that, too. Now, let's take a look around this house. I believe the housekeeper next door has a key. Although it will need to be nothing short of spectacular to justify that walk. I swear, a hill like that would either keep a man in good health or else kill him stone dead. And I fear with me, it would be the latter."

65
COLONEL PENHALIGAN'S AGENDA

LAPSEWOOD ENTERED COLONEL PENHALIGAN'S office and locked eyes with the man he had spent the last ten years fearing.

"Alice," bellowed Colonel Penhaligan. "I don't recall scheduling a meeting with an escaped convict."

"No, sir," said Alice, appearing behind Lapsewood. "I'm afraid he wouldn't take no for an answer, sir."

Colonel Penhaligan turned back to Lapsewood. "Insisted, eh? That doesn't sound like the donkey I remember."

"I'm not a donkey," replied Lapsewood.

"So I'm told. Or perhaps you're simply a donkey with delusions of grandeur," said the colonel. He dismissed Alice with a wave. She glanced at Lapsewood and closed the door behind her. "What do you want, Lapsewood?" he asked once they were alone.

"The truth," Lapsewood stated.

"You'll have to be more specific."

"You knew about the Black Rot when you transferred me."

"What's led you to that conclusion?"

"Why else would you have obtained the safety copy of the London Tenancy List?"

"Perhaps you should tell me."

"You gave it to Monsieur Vidocq."

"Why would I do that?" he asked, reaching for a cigar.

Lapsewood took a deep breath. "I think you wanted to find a solution to the problem yourself so you could prove General Colt's incompetence and dismiss him. You told me yourself that you wanted to get rid of him."

Colonel Penhaligan clipped off the end of the cigar. "If that were the case, why would I send you to help him?"

"He wanted a Prowler. You sent him someone unqualified for the job, someone who hadn't set foot in the physical world since becoming a ghost, someone who . . ." Lapsewood faltered. "A clerk who had fallen behind with his paperwork."

"So you're saying I sent him useless deadweight," said Colonel Penhaligan, smirking.

"Yes, sir," said Lapsewood. "But you underestimated me."

"Finally, something we agree on. I did underestimate you," said Colonel Penhaligan. "But I am sorry to tell you that, apart from that, everything else you have said is a matter of purest fancy. The fact that General Colt is a lazy, American oaf is precisely why I recommended him for the role in Housing in the first place."

"You recommended him?" said Lapsewood.

"Oh, yes." Colonel Penhaligan smiled and lit the cigar. "A competent man would have spotted the problem much earlier on. I needed someone who was too busy practicing his golf swing to bother with the business of actually running a department."

Lapsewood felt thrown by this confession. "But . . . what about the Black Rot?"

"As I said before, I've been a ghost a long time. When I saw what happened in Paris, I saw the potential. But in Paris there was no plan. I saw that if I could provide an efficient exorcist with a list, he would be able to act much more efficiently in ridding the city of its Residents."

"You put the list into the hands of a living person?" Lapsewood couldn't believe it. Not only had Colonel Penhaligan done something far worse than any of *his* transgressions, but he was openly confessing to it. What was more, he appeared to be enjoying Lapsewood's horrified reaction.

"Lapsewood, you are the most entertaining donkey I've ever encountered. I certainly underestimated you. You have proved to be utterly invaluable."

"Invaluable?"

"Utterly so." The colonel blew a mouthful of smoke into his face. "I presume you've learned by now what happens when an infected building is left untended for long enough?"

"The chateau in Paris drew something from the Void," said Lapsewood, remembering what the Marquis had told him.

"Exactly. Formless spirits feeding off the souls of ghosts. The one in Paris devoured every ghost that entered. Even the living could sense there was something wrong with the place. But it was unable to get out, you see. It was trapped in that chateau, devouring all who entered. In the end it took fifteen French Enforcers to force it back through to the other side. The whole thing was a downright mess. But you and your Rogue friend, Tanner, found a way to unleash the one we cultivated in Shadwell. You got the demon out. Cigar, Lapsewood?"

"No, thank you. I don't understand, sir."

Colonel Penhaligan snapped shut the lid of the cigar box. "The anomalies. Brilliant. Without souls, the hounds make perfect vessels for the demon to travel inside. You created a hellhound, Lapsewood." Colonel Penhaligan grinned. "That's not an official name, of course. We're some way off from properly classifying it."

"We did what?" said Lapsewood, aghast.

"Don't look so worried. It's a good thing."

"With respect, how can it be a good thing to create a hellhound, sir?"

"What you're failing to see is that the Black Rot isn't a disease. It's a cure." Colonel Penhaligan tapped the cigar into an ashtray. "In time, all of your dogs will go the same way. As we speak, the Shadwell hound is roaming the streets, devouring Rogues. Soon London will be overrun with the canine creatures, wiping out every wretched Rogue ghost in this overpopulated city. I'll succeed where Admiral Hard-knuckle's Enforcers have failed."

"We can't let that happen," exclaimed Lapsewood, so angry that he felt he could have knocked a door off its hinges. "You're mad, sir."

"Ee-ore," brayed Colonel Penhaligan, with a low chuckle.

"Then I'll do something."

"What will you do?"

"I'll go over your head."

"Over the head of the Head of Dispatches?" barked the colonel. "You, an escaped convict? You don't understand, do you? I am on the verge of solving London's Rogue ghost problem. I'm the hero in this story."

"But—"

"Would you like to hear another interesting thing?" Penhaligan interrupted. "Since this is the last time we're likely to see each other? Do you know why you fell behind on your paperwork?"

"No," admitted Lapsewood.

"I tripled your workload," proclaimed Colonel Penhaligan. "I needed an excuse to send General Colt the worst possible person for the job. That was you. So I redirected more work into your office than you could handle to make it look as if you were falling behind. Now, if you'll excuse me, I've a letter to dictate. Alice!"

"Yes, sir?" said Alice, appearing at the door.

"I need to send Admiral Hardknuckle an urgent memo about an escaped convict by the name of Lapsewood."

"Yes, sir," she replied, glancing at Lapsewood with sorrowful eyes.

"This isn't the end," said Lapsewood.

"It is for you," countered Colonel Penhaligan.

But Lapsewood had not been speaking to him. He had been looking at Alice.

"Go," she mouthed.

Lapsewood nodded, then turned to Ether Dust and escaped into the Paternoster Pipe Network.

66
THE WORK OF THE DEVIL

REVEREND FALLOWFIELD SAT IN THE COFFEE SHOP with an open newspaper in front of him. He had picked up a taste for good coffee in Paris but had struggled to find anywhere in London that served anything remotely drinkable. As if that wasn't bad enough, there was the matter of the overfriendly waitress who hovered over him holding the coffeepot, unable to see that he wanted to be left alone.

"Terrible business, them murders," she said, holding the pot threateningly near his cup without actually pouring.

"Yes," replied Reverend Fallowfield curtly.

"What sort of man could do such a thing, Father? Surely that would be the devil's work."

"The devil does his own work," replied Reverend Fallowfield. "This is the work of man."

"What kind of man, though? That's what I can't understand," continued the waitress, undeterred by his blatant hostility.

When finally she poured the coffee and found another customer in need of attention, Reverend Fallowfield pulled out a piece of paper tucked into his tunic. He ran a crooked finger down the list and found an address. He looked back at the newspaper. The same address was listed. He checked the others. Each one cited in the article was on his list. Each one had been ticked off his list. What did it mean? Were these killings meant as a threat? A warning? It would not be the first; Reverend Fallowfield had made a great many enemies over the years. There were many in the church who objected to the clerical collar he wore in spite of his never having been ordained. They failed to understand that he answered to a higher authority than the corrupt institutions of churches.

"Sorry," said the waitress, returning. "Did you want my attention?"

"No," he snapped.

"Only, you were talking. I thought maybe you wanted something else. A refill, perhaps?" She looked at his untouched cup.

"I was talking to myself," he replied, irritably.

"Oh." She let out a burst of intolerably loud laughter. "Not to worry. I do that myself sometimes. They say it's the first sign of madness, but I've got plenty more of those. I think we're all a bit mad, don't you?"

"I was saying that perhaps you were right," he said. "Perhaps this killer is doing the devil's work."

"Well, let's hope they catch up with him. Hanging's too good for such people."

"Yes," said Reverend Fallowfield, picking up his cup of coffee to drink. "Yes, it is."

67

AN ENTERTAINING
EXORCISM

MR. TILTMAN STEPPED OUT OF THE TAXICAB BY THE
entrance to the Drury Lane Theatre. A sign outside read:

FOR ONE NIGHT ONLY:
AN EVENING OF EXTRAORDINARY ENTERTAINMENT
LIVE EXORCISM
REVEREND FALLOWFIELD VOYAGES INTO THE OCCULT
AND UNVEILS THE TRUE STAR OF DRURY LANE:
THE GHOST OF THE MAN IN GRAY

Mr. Tiltman helped his daughter onto the pavement,
too.

"The London nightlife," he said, taking a deep breath. "There's nothing quite like it."

Mr. Tiltman's words were tinged with the sadness of one who was appreciating that which he would soon be denied. The offer he had put in on the house in Honor Oak had been accepted. The Tiltmans were moving to The Elms.

Mr. Tiltman paid the taxi driver and led Clara to the theater, where he purchased two tickets for the circle.

"So, how shall we expose this fraud?" he asked, as they made their way through the lobby and up the great staircase.

"I told you. I do not believe Reverend Fallowfield to be a fraud," replied Clara.

"Oh, Clara," said Mr. Tiltman. "The world is full of men like him, preying on the gullible for his own financial benefit. They dwell in politics and in finance. Religion has its fair share. But this Fallowfield is more akin to the tricksters who stand on street corners with three cups and an unfindable penny."

"I disagree. The man with the three cups knows he is tricking his victims. Reverend Fallowfield believes in his own powers, and, I'm afraid, so do I."

"So you think we will see a real ghost tonight?"

"I have no doubt of it, and I believe I can prove it," said Clara.

Mr. Tiltman clapped his hands together in delight. "I feel a wager coming on. Name your terms."

"If I am right, we stay at Aysgarth House," said Clara.

Mr. Tiltman smiled and shook his head. "Out of the

question. The decision has been made. More reasonable terms, please."

Clara had known this to be a long shot. "Ten shillings, then," she said.

"I will give you three shillings, the price of the ticket, if you can prove it."

They shook on it, and Clara felt a tingle of excitement at being out with her father, being treated like a grown-up, even if it was only for one night.

"How do you propose to prove this claim, then?" asked her father.

"I'll show you."

Clara had already noticed that the man checking tickets at the door to the house was the actor she had met on her previous visit to the theater.

"Tickets, please," he said.

"Excuse me," said Clara. "I have a question."

"If it's why this great theater is interrupting an excellent performance of *Doctor Faustus* for a novelty act, putting trained actors such as myself, Mr. Edward Gliddon, on the door, then I can't help you."

"It's about the ghost," said Clara. "The Man in Gray."

"Oh, him," said the actor, not recognizing her from their previous encounter.

Her father looked on, amused but saying nothing, allowing his daughter to take the lead.

"As someone who has seen the ghost and heard much about him, can you tell me his name?" asked Clara.

"I've never heard any mention of it. I don't believe it's known."

"You're sure? No one knows his real name?"

"That's correct, as far as I know."

"Thank you." She turned back to her father. "Let's go in."

Mr. Tiltman handed the tickets to the disgruntled actor, and they made their way to their seats. "What does that prove?" he asked.

"No living person knows the name of this ghost," she said. "But I do. If Reverend Fallowfield reveals his name as David Kerby, then I'm right, and you owe me three shillings."

"This is your proof?"

"The only way for me to cheat would be if I were in league with Fallowfield, and you have my word that I would not speak to the man again, let alone work with him."

Mr. Tiltman inwardly congratulated himself on his part in helping to produce such a clever and funny girl. He shook her hand again. "I agree to your terms," he said. "Although I have no idea how you might be sure of such a thing, if no one knows it."

"Maybe I have researched the theater and found the name."

"Have you?" inquired Mr. Tiltman.

"Or maybe I have a list of ghost names," continued Clara.

"It is times like this when I wonder whether I was wrong

to bring you up in such a progressive way. Dr. Wyatt's two daughters would never dare act so mysteriously with their father."

"Nor so interestingly," countered Clara.

"True," admitted Mr. Tiltman.

The theater was far from full, but it was a sizable crowd that had turned up to see this spectacle. A hush fell as the lights were dimmed and the curtain was raised. No fanfare or puffs of smoke introduced Reverend Fallowfield as he stepped onto the stage. In fact, he looked a little like a man who had taken a wrong turn to find himself there.

"Good evening," he mumbled.

"Speak up," yelled a voice from the stalls, causing the whole theater to collapse into laughter.

Reverend Fallowfield scowled back at the heckler, then said, "I am here to reveal to you the devils who walk among us, the half lives of the undead, the aberrations who stand in contempt of God's almighty decree that the earth shall be for the living while the dead will be confined to hell or rewarded with heaven." As he spoke, his voice grew louder and louder. "I am here to rid this house of one such unpaying tenant. I am here to reveal to you, then vanquish from this place, the ghoul known as the Man in Gray."

"Where is he, then?" yelled a voice.

"Did he have to pay three shillings a ticket, too?" added another.

"He is among us. I can sense the putrid stench of his ghostly presence," said Reverend Fallowfield.

"I think that's the drains," cried someone, causing more raucous mirth.

"You will not be laughing soon."

"I thought this was a comedy show," shouted another heckler.

"This is no 'show' at all," responded Reverend Fallowfield angrily. "No guile or trickery will be used. What you see here tonight is real. That is my guarantee to you."

"I want my money back," yelled another.

"You can have your money back if you are not, at the end of the night, convinced that you have witnessed a genuine exorcism this evening. Now, let us commence."

Reverend Fallowfield slowly raised his arms and muttered incantations. The hecklers shouted out, jeered, or threw peanuts, but in his trancelike state he paid little heed.

"Spirit, show yourself," cried Reverend Fallowfield.

A couple of drunken men in the front row repeated his words mockingly. But the laughter stopped when a woman seated in a box let out a piercing scream.

Clara nudged her father and pointed out the cloud of dust drifting down through the theater, its particles catching in the dimmed gaslight. The dust gathered in front of Reverend Fallowfield on the stage.

"Spirit, reveal your form," he commanded, holding his arms up dramatically.

The smoke took the form of a human body. A pair of shoes and yellow stockings appeared. Then a gray coat took shape. Finally there emerged the face of an extremely surprised-looking gentleman wearing a large tri-cornered hat. The audience gasped. Even the hecklers were silenced.

"Tell us, cursed demon, are you the spirit known as the Man in Gray?" asked Reverend Fallowfield.

"'Cursed demon'?" said the ghost. "How rude. But, yes, that's the name I'm known by, although, as you can see, it's an entirely inaccurate epithet. These yellow stockings were not cheap. Although I can say this of dying in them—I certainly got my money's worth."

"Silence." Reverend Fallowfield held up an open palm, then turned to the audience. "Does anyone here have a question for this spirit?" he asked.

"What's his name?" bellowed Mr. Tiltman.

"What is your name?" repeated Reverend Fallowfield.

"I can hear, you know," said the ghost. "My name, sir, is Mr. David Kerby."

Mr. Tiltman looked at his daughter with wide-eyed admiration. She smiled back. "Now I have two magic tricks to unravel," he whispered.

"Who else has a question?" asked Reverend Fallowfield.

More questions were asked and answered. The ghost told the audience of his life and of the circumstances surrounding his death. He told them of all the great plays and actors he had seen over the years. He confirmed that, yes, he had been on occasion guilty of whispering lines to forgetful actors. Once he had gotten over the initial shock of being visible, the Man in Gray began to enjoy his moment in the limelight.

Soon the audience grew doubtful that this was anything other than a visually spectacular trick. One vocal dissenter suggested that the appearance of transparency was achieved with the clever application of paint, lighting techniques, and carefully arranged mirrors. In response Reverend Fallowfield invited two volunteers up onto the stage, including the man from the door, Edward Gliddon. Reverend Fallowfield held the Man in Gray in place, then instructed Mr. Gliddon to walk through the ghost. As he did so, the audience gasped and watched with unblinking fascination. The second volunteer was an especially vocal heckler. Having watched Mr. Gliddon walk straight through, he decided to stop in the middle of the ghost. Mr. Kerby objected strongly, but it got a great laugh from the crowd. When the man still refused to move, Mr. Kerby announced that, looking inside his head, the gap between his ears was so cavernous, it was a wonder he was able to put one foot in front of the other at all. This got the biggest laugh of the evening, and finally the man moved.

Reverend Fallowfield asked the volunteers to remain on stage for the finale to ensure that no trickery took place. He also asked for the lights to come up and suggested that everyone in the auditorium make sure they had a good view of the stage. "I will only be able to expel this spirit from the theater once," he announced.

"I'd really rather you didn't," said the Man in Gray.

"You have dwelled here too long," responded Reverend Fallowfield. "You will be exorcised."

"No!" screamed Clara, suddenly on her feet.

"Sit down," said a woman behind her.

"He has done nothing wrong," said Clara.

"He *is* something wrong," replied Reverend Fallowfield. "If you have not the stomach to watch this, little girl, then I suggest you leave."

"No." This time it was Mr. Tiltman on his feet. "This so-called man of God came to my own home with his begging exorcism. My daughter is right. You should leave this ghost be. He has done no harm."

Reverend Fallowfield peered up at them. "I will rid this city of every damnable spirit, every demon, every devil that infects it," he said.

"You're a bully," said Clara. "These ghosts deserve our sympathy, our pity, our charity. They did not choose to be as they are. Look at Mr. Kerby in his silly yellow stockings. Imagine being stuck in those stockings for the rest of eternity."

The audience tittered, and many of them turned to get a better view of this new heckler.

"You came here for an exorcism, and that is what you'll get," yelled Reverend Fallowfield.

"That's true," said a voice from the stalls.

"Yeah, let him get on with it," said another.

"No, this girl is right," said Edward Gliddon. "This ghost has been a part of this theater for many years. Who are we to destroy it? And for what? The sake of one night's entertainment?"

"I paid good money for this," said the other man on stage.

"Perhaps you should have saved your money for some real art," replied Mr. Gliddon. "You ignoramus."

"Right, that's it."

The heckler landed a punch in the side of the actor's face, sending him staggering back into Reverend Fallowfield. Knocked off his feet, Reverend Fallowfield was unable to retain his hold on the ghost. The Man in Gray vanished. The audience was, in equal measures, angered and amused by this new development, and it wasn't long before the fight on the stage had spread into the auditorium itself, the ripples of violence working their way through the stalls as more and more joined in the brawl. The last Clara saw of Reverend Fallowfield, before her father suggested they get out, was as he crawled toward the wings on all fours.

68

THE ELEVENTH HOLE

THE BUREAU WAS A REMARKABLE FEAT OF PHANTAS-
magorical engineering, one of the best examples of which
was the eighteen-hole golf course on the sixty-third floor.
General Colt had never played the game in life, considering
it to be a colossal waste of time. In death, however, he had
found himself with an endless supply of time, and so he had
taken up the hobby with gusto. To his surprise, he took to it
at once and, these days, played as often as he could.

He was in the middle of a game with Mr. Wandle of Li-
censing and had just missed the eleventh hole after slicing
his ball into the rough. General Colt was searching for it
when he heard a voice whisper, "General . . . General."

"Who's that?" he demanded.

A cloud of Ether Dust settled into the shape of a ghost, and Lapsewood materialized in front of him.

"My God, Clapwood, what are you doing here? I told you we can't be seen together."

"Lapsewood, sir. We need to talk."

"Penhaligan has rushed through an emergency warrant for your arrest. You were supposed to go unnoticed."

"I had no choice. My investigation led me to him."

"To Penhaligan?" barked General Colt.

"It's probably best to keep your voice down," whispered Lapsewood.

"I already spoke to Penhaligan," continued General Colt. "He's making a motion or some such bureaucratic claptrap that's going to take years to get anywhere. That's why I came to you in the first place. I put a lot at stake, slipping you that key."

"I understand that, sir. What I'm saying is that Penhaligan doesn't want to stop it. He's responsible for the Black Rot. He created the problem."

"Created it?"

"Yes, he's trying to get rid of Rogue ghosts."

General Colt looked disbelievingly at Lapsewood. "Have you been at the spirit ale?"

"No, sir. I swear it's true. He gave a copy of the London Tenancy List to an exorcist by the name of Fallowfield. He means for him to exorcise every last Resident in London."

"Those lists are written using spirit materials. How

could he have given it to anyone in the physical world?"

"According to Opacity guidelines, it is possible for ghostly items to be transferred to the living if a ghost is at seventy percent or above on the Opacity scale."

"I can't see how that would get rid of Rogue ghosts."

"It wouldn't. Not in itself, but there's something else. It's a demon from the Void in the body of a spirit hound. It is prowling the streets as we speak, devouring any soul that comes into its path."

Through the trees, General Colt could see Mr. Wandle waiting patiently on the green. He ducked down and grabbed Lapsewood by the lapels, dragging him down with him.

"Listen, Lambswool, this is serious."

"That's what I've been saying, sir. What should we do?"

"It's a tricky one, I'll give you that. Are you sure about all this?"

"Penhaligan confessed the whole thing to me."

"And yet if it came to trial, it would be the word of a respected member of upper management against that of an escaped convict with a history of consorting with Rogue elements."

"You could testify on my behalf," suggested Lapsewood.

"Damn it, Larchwood, it's not that easy," replied General Colt. "If I put my own neck on the line and we ended up both going down, then there would be no one left to do the right thing."

"I suppose," admitted Lapsewood doubtfully. "But I was

only a convict because you sent me to the Vault."

"Yes, I guess that was a little rash of me in hindsight, but right now we have to deal with the current situation."

"What are you saying, sir?"

"You have to do this on your own."

"On my own?" said Lapsewood. "Back at the Vault you said we'd shake up this stuffy old place."

"And so we will. I'm going to be there right behind you when you come back with proof of Penhaligan's involvement."

"What kind of proof?"

"Something that will stick. Then we can take that conceited colonel down a notch or two. They'd probably give me a promotion for something like this."

"You, sir?"

"I mean we. Get me proof, then we'll show them all. You and me, Lapsewood. You and me."

It was the first time General Colt had gotten his name right.

"But, sir," said Lapsewood, "surely the most important thing is to stop the exorcist and prevent the hellhound from swallowing any more souls?"

"Of course. Do that, too. Hey, look, my ball." General Colt picked up a golf ball from the undergrowth.

"But can't you help?" asked Lapsewood.

General Colt pulled off his large hat and scratched the bullet wound in the center of his temple. "There are some things a man must do on his own. This is one of them.

348

Now, you'd better be off before Mr. Wandle spots you. I'd better get back to my game. I really think I can claw it back and beat the old goat this time."

"But, sir—" protested Lapsewood.

"Good luck, Laxwood. Let me know how you get on." General Colt turned and walked away, tossing and catching his golf ball, whistling to himself.

69
A FATHER'S GUILT

WHEN SAM REQUESTED THE MORNING OFF TO GO visit Clara, Mr. Constable suggested they take the train up together, as he had no appointments and had been meaning to visit a supplier of coffin handles in Bloomsbury. Sam didn't mind traveling with his father's partner, but he was relieved that he didn't ask him the reason for his trip. He wasn't ready to tell anyone about Clara. Not even Mr. Constable.

Mr. Constable and Sam found a train carriage to themselves. Sam had barely spoken to his father since their revelatory conversation about his mother, so he was expecting one of Mr. Constable's well-intentioned conversations about the importance of family. Sure enough, as the train pulled away, Mr. Constable said, "You've learned a lot about your family these past few weeks. More, perhaps, than in all the years that preceded them."

"I've learned that my father stole as a child and, as an adult, was responsible for the murder of an innocent man," replied Sam.

"Difficult things to learn at any age," said Mr. Constable. "Your father has had to overcome a great many obstacles in his life, but he remains the most loyal, good-hearted man I have ever had the pleasure to meet."

"You have always taught me it is our actions that define us," said Sam.

"When you reach our age and look back on your life, I guarantee you will feel ashamed of a great many things: transgressions you have made, people you have hurt, cruelties you have spoken. Even in my dull life, there are things I would rather not dwell on."

"But murder . . ." said Sam.

The word hung between them as the train rattled onward.

"Have you always known about this business with my mother's father?" asked Sam.

"Yes," said Mr. Constable, maintaining eye contact. "I suppose that makes me a liar, too."

"It was for my father to tell me. I imagine he asked you to keep it from me."

"He didn't have to," replied Mr. Constable. "He wanted to protect you."

"From the truth?"

"From the pain."

Sam had never experienced a conversation with Mr. Constable that was so stilted. When the train pulled in at the next station, a smartly attired gentleman looked at the carriage but, thankfully, thought better of it and chose another one.

Mr. Constable sighed. "Your mother took her father's death hard. That his death unlocked the door to her own happiness was no consolation. Your father had to live with that guilt."

"So you agree that he was guilty?"

"No," stated Mr. Constable. "It was worse than that. He felt guilty when he was not. At the time he confided in Jack, he had no idea what his brother had become. They argued shortly afterward, and Jack left. He would not return until the day you saw him. But he left in his wake the consequences of his actions, and your father took on his guilt, with a conscience that Jack never possessed. Guilt is a terrible thing. It corrodes from within. It is something your father always wanted to protect you from."

"What have I to feel guilty about?"

Mr. Constable fell silent.

"I don't want any more secrets," said Sam.

"Even those that protect you?"

"Even those."

"Your mother didn't die of a fever. She died giving birth to you, Sam," said Mr. Constable. "Your father kept this from you for fear that you would blame yourself for her death."

Sam tried to let the words sink in, but they merely splashed around the edges of his mind, like water on stone. His mother had died bringing him into the world. How many more lies had his father told him?

Sam's voice quavered as he asked, "Did he blame me?"

"Never," said Mr. Constable, without a moment's hesitation.

The train trundled past a raised hedgerow. Dappled sunlight shone through, flickering on Sam's face. He shut his eyes until a factory wall blocked it out.

"That's why I can see Them," he said. "That's why I can see ghosts. Death must touch you. Jack got it from murdering, I from my mother's death."

There passed another moment of uncomfortable silence except for the rattling of the carriage.

"What was she like?" asked Sam.

"A fine woman," said Mr. Constable. "There was never a more troubled beginning to a love affair, but your parents loved each other more fervently than any couple I've ever known. The gossips talked, as gossips will. First the courting of a widow, then the timely death of her dissenting father. Your parents were unable to trumpet their love to the world. Their wedding was an understated affair. Your mother was a troubled woman, but she eventually found happiness. The month before she died, she told me she was the happiest she had ever been. Do you know why?"

Sam shook his head.

"You, Sam. She was pregnant with you. She was so looking forward to meeting you and to spending every hour with you. You made her happy, Sam."

The train made another stop, where a woman climbed aboard with her two young children in tow. To the mother's embarrassment, the children were so excited about the train journey that they barely stopped chattering. Mr. Constable, however, was his usual charming self and engaged the younger boy in an amusing conversation regarding the workings of a steam train, a subject about which the boy turned out to be a great authority. Sam, for his part, was grateful for the distraction.

He knew now that he could see death because of his birth. Every dead soul he saw with his right eye was a reminder of the woman who had died so that he could live.

70

GRUNT'S DECLINE

Lapsewood felt like a new ghost. Arriving in London, he didn't materialize in a dark back alley this time. Instead, he chose the middle of the busy thoroughfare of the Strand. Even the tram that trundled straight through him, giving him a distasteful view of the contents of its passengers' shoes, didn't put him off. It would take more than a faceful of bunions to upset this new Lapsewood. All his life, and his subsequent death, he had watched the world from the sidelines, too fearful to do anything other than what was expected of him. Now he was dealing with things himself. He had been devastated when Colonel Penhaligan had taken away his job, but he could no longer imagine returning to his desk job with its endless paperwork. General Colt had asked Lapsewood to complete this enormous task alone because he was too cowardly to endanger his own position, but that didn't matter to Lapsewood. For once in his life he was going to do the right thing rather than the easy one. He would find Tanner, stop the exorcist, and vanquish the hellhound back to the Void. The only problem was that he had absolutely no idea where to start.

On the pavement outside Charing Cross Station where the taxicabs gathered, a man waved the latest edition of the *Evening Standard* in the air.

"Standardstandardstandard," he shouted, "the Kitchen Killer kills again."

Lapsewood glanced at the headline. If the living really knew what death was like, would they be more careful with their lives? he wondered.

"Five murdered," cried the newspaper seller. "Confused coppers can't cope."

A uniformed policeman with his hands behind his back stopped beside the man and coughed. "Ahem."

The newspaper seller tipped his cap to the officer and shouted, "The city's finest constabulary is close to cracking the case. Standardstandardstandard."

The policeman nodded approvingly and moved on.

Lapsewood turned to Ether Dust and left in search of Nell. She would be able to help him track down Tanner. However, after several hours, there was still no sign of her. In fact, there were far fewer ghosts on the streets than the last time he had visited. Several hours of fruitless searching later, he eventually found a spirit lying in a doorway. He was hitched up on one elbow, with a half-drunk bottle of spirit ale in one hand, mumbling quietly to himself.

"Grunt?" said Lapsewood. "What are you doing here?"

"Lying down," replied Grunt, sounding worse for wear. "And drinking. You want some?" He offered up the bottle.

"No, thank you," replied Lapsewood. "What happened to you?"

"You were right. Getting out of that place did me a world of good. I'm much happier now." To prove it, Grunt let out a loud sob and took another swig of ale.

"You're drunk."

"Yep," agreed Grunt. "It's not the same, you know, getting drunk with spirit ale. Do you remember what it was like getting drunk when you were alive?"

"I was never a drinker," said Lapsewood.

"When you're alive, it numbs the pain. After I found my wife dead, the first thing I did was find myself a bottle. Our pain, though, it's different, isn't it? Memory, Lapsewood. That's our pain. It takes something stronger than spirit ale to take that away."

"Yes." Lapsewood noticed how the ale had turned the gray goo that leaked out of Grunt's neck an alarming shade of purple.

"I think people should be ghosts first," said Grunt. "If we were dead before we were alive, we'd appreciate it more, wouldn't we?"

"Perhaps we are," said Lapsewood. "Maybe a new life lies on the other side of the Unseen Door."

Grunt emitted a snort of unamused laughter at the notion.

"Did you find Tanner?" asked Lapsewood. "Did you give him the message?"

More laughter. "I gave him the message, all right. Haven't you heard?"

"Heard what?"

"Your boy Tanner has got someone murdering people."

"Murdering?" said Lapsewood, thinking he must have misheard him.

"Yep. For their ghosts," slurred Grunt. "They call him the Kitchen Killer."

"I . . . I . . ." Lapsewood was at a loss for words.

"What with Tanner's killer terrorizing the living and this black demon hound that roams the city feeding on the souls of ghosts, there's very little hope left in London. Haven't you noticed how few Rogues there are around? Us ghosts are a dying breed." He laughed so much that the fluid bubbled up through the gap in his neck.

"I have to speak to Tanner," said Lapsewood. "I'm sure he can't have meant to . . . I mean, I never said . . ."

"'Whatever means necessary.' Those were your exact words."

"I have to put this right," said Lapsewood determinedly.

"That's what I tried to do. I tried to put things right."

"What do you mean?"

"I haunted him, Lapsewood."

"Who? Tanner?" said Lapsewood, confused by how one could haunt a ghost.

"No." Grunt spat. "That villain who killed my wife. I haunted him good and proper. I didn't have a license to, and I don't care. They can throw me into the Vault if they want. It can't be any worse than this."

"What did you do?"

Grunt took a big swig from the bottle, and Lapsewood watched as half of it oozed back through the neck scarf.

"I threw a cup at him," he said.

"A cup?"

Grunt nodded. "A tin cup."

"The man who killed your wife, whose crime you were hanged for? You threw a tin cup at him?"

"The strange thing is that it didn't make me feel any better."

"No," replied Lapsewood flatly.

"He was terrified, scared out of his wits, and yet even then I wished I could swap places with him. I'd rather feel fear than nothing. But the next day, there he was, in the pub, telling it like it was a funny story. That's when I realized there's nothing we can do, us ghosts. Nothing. Working at the Bureau makes us feel like we're making a difference, but we're not. With all our licenses, forms, and permissions, what difference does it make? None that I can see. That's when I found this bottle. Are you sure you won't have a drink?"

"Thank you, but no," said Lapsewood. "I *can* do something. I can put right what I've made wrong."

"I'll drink to that," said Grunt. "Good luck, Lapsewood."

"Good luck, Grunt."

71
AN UNEXPECTED VISITOR

CLARA HAD SPENT ALL MORNING WAITING FOR THE knock on the door. Today she would finally communicate with a ghost. Not just any ghost either. Her ghost. She was excited to see Sam again, too. With his mournful eyes and quiet disposition, he was easily the most interesting person she had ever met.

But when the knock finally came, just after eleven, Clara was alone in the house and felt unsure what to do. Her father was at work, her mother was visiting a shop to discuss furnishings for the new house, and Hopkins had asked permission to accompany Mrs. Preston to the shop, seeing as she was so nervous about leaving the house these days.

Even Clara understood it would not be right for her and Sam to be alone in the house. She resolved to ask him to wait outside until Hopkins and Mrs. Preston returned.

However, when she opened the door, it wasn't Sam who stood on the doorstep.

"Hello, my dear," said Reverend Fallowfield.

"What do you want?" she asked, as rudely as possible.

"You ruined my show," he replied.

"You said it wasn't a show."

"I was there to *show* people what I do."

"Go away. There's no one else here," she replied.

"Oh, yes, there is." Reverend Fallowfield pushed past her and stepped inside. He sniffed the air like a bloodhound picking up the scent of its prey. "You have a new one. A fresh demon."

"Get out," she exclaimed.

"He's working against me, this Kitchen Killer, filling the holes I make. But I will rid this house of its new tenant as easily as I rid it of the previous one."

"No!" shouted Clara.

"You would defy me?" he pronounced. "I am on a mission from God."

"You're mad."

"I have been touched by the Almighty, not madness. Those hypocrites in the church call me a heretic. It's a word used by those who do not understand the true gift I have."

"Get out of my house." Clara felt panicked.

Reverend Fallowfield pushed her away. "I must clean this

lair of Satan. I must cleanse the world of those who dare defy God's natural order. Earth is for the living. The dead must go to almighty heaven or damnable hell." He raised his hands. "Spirit, show yourself."

"No!" screamed Clara. "No!"

Fallowfield grabbed one of Clara's wrists and squeezed hard, twisting her arm behind her back, causing her to bend over in pain. He strong-armed her into the drawing room, slammed the door shut, and turned the key, locking her on the other side.

"Let me out! Get out of my house!" Clara screamed at the top of her voice. On the other side of the door she could hear Reverend Fallowfield muttering incantations, but there was nothing she could do to stop him. "Please," she sobbed. "Leave her alone."

72
JACK'S FINAL VICTIM

MR. REEVE HAD ALWAYS VALUED JACK TOOP ABOVE the other thieves who worked for him. Jack was the closest thing he had to family, but when Jack got ideas above his station, Mr. Reeve had curtailed Jack's ability to operate in the city. He had chased him out, so he was surprised when Jack Toop stepped into his office. While Mr. Reeve's face gave away nothing, his right hand, unseen by Jack, reached into a drawer in the desk and extracted a knife, which he kept hidden from sight.

"Jack," he said. "Close the door behind you."

"Expectin' someone else, were you?" replied Jack.

"Bazeley announces my visitors. You know that, Jack."

"Bazeley won't be announcin' no one no more."

Mr. Reeve shook his head as though dealing with a badly behaved child. "You've been doing a lot of killing recently. Careless, Jack, very careless."

"I was never that," said Jack. "All these years and they never caught me once. They didn't even 'ave my name until you gave it to them." Jack leaned over the desk, but Mr. Reeve showed no sign of being intimidated.

"I want to help you, but I can't do that with you in London where you're a wanted man. You get yourself up to Liverpool, I know a man who will take good care of you."

"I'm sure you do." It was the first time Jack had smiled since entering the office.

"Don't be like that, Jack. Sit down, won't you?"

"I'll stay standin', if you don't mind." Jack stepped away from the desk and paced the room, all the time keeping his eyes on Reeve. "When would you say it all started going wrong for me?"

"Around about when you got caught up to your elbows in some copper's blood," replied Mr. Reeve. "And that was no one's fault but your own. As I said, you got careless, Jack."

"I killed Heale because you asked me to. You said he started askin' for too much."

"I didn't tell you to get caught."

"I didn't," growled Jack. "You put Savage on to me."

"Savage?"

"Yeah. I know now that he's on your books, too. I know now you gave him my name and told him where I was."

Under the table, Mr. Reeve's knuckles went white as he tightened his grip on the knife. "And you tell me, Jack. Why would I want to lose you? You were always a good thief. The best, Jack. Why would I want to lose such a good thief?"

Jack drew his knife. Its handle was stained with dried blood, but its blade was clean. "No," he said. "You tell me."

"Ambition is a dangerous thing," said Mr. Reeve. "For years we worked well together, you and me, but then you started sniffing around my business, trying to turn my own people against me, trying to steal from me, Jack." Mr. Reeve's voice grew louder and louder.

"I helped build this empire of yours," replied Jack. "I been helpin' you out all my life, and yet there I was, still riskin' my neck breakin' into 'ouses, while you sat pretty in this office, playin' at being respectable."

Mr. Reeve nodded. "You wanted me out of the way, Heale wanted more money, and Savage needed reminding of who was the boss. Him catching you killing Heale was the perfect solution."

"Except I got away."

"Ah, well, yes, but here's the thing, Jack. You've gone and turned yourself into a celebrated murderer now. Anonymous Jack is now the Kitchen Killer." He laughed. "You're famous, Jack. Notorious. You're the most famous man in London, and when Savage brings you in, they'll make him commissioner, and he'll owe it all to me. You see, even when you think you're winning, you'll still never beat me. I'm better at this than you, Jack. That's why you're a thief. That's why that's all you'll ever be."

Jack lunged forward, aiming his knife at Reeve's throat. Mr. Reeve blocked him, stopping the knife with the flesh of his forearm. He then rammed his own knife into Jack's stomach. With an almighty cry, Jack rolled off the desk and pulled the knife from his stomach and the other one from Mr. Reeve's arm. Blood gushed from both their wounds. Jack was now holding a knife in each hand. Mr. Reeve stood and backed away, trying to stop the flow of blood with his hand.

"You're a dead man," said Mr. Reeve. "Killing me won't change that."

"The way I see it, there ain't all that much difference between life and death," said Jack.

Mr. Reeve made a desperate lunge for the door, but Jack was too quick for him. He brought him down with two knives plunged into his back. Mr. Reeve's legs buckled. Jack grabbed his chin and pulled his head back. "Good-bye, Mr. Reeve," he said, and he dragged Reeve's own knife across his throat. More blood, but Jack didn't leave things there. He fell on the twitching body and repeatedly stabbed it until it went still.

Jack stood back to admire his work. Out of his right eye he saw a translucent figure standing next to him. He turned to Mr. Reeve's ghost, enjoying the look of confusion on his face, taking pride in the fresh, bloodless wounds that covered his ghostly body.

"Jack?" said the ghost, its voice tinged with fear. The

sound of knocking came. "That's them coming for you," said Mr. Reeve's ghost.

"No, it ain't," replied Jack, with a wicked grin. "That's them coming for *you*. Go through the door, Reeve. There's nothing left for you in this world."

Mr. Reeve looked at Jack's wound. "I'll be seeing you soon, Jack." The ghost turned and stepped through the Unseen Door.

Jack dropped Mr. Reeve's knife on his body and wiped his own on the side of his coat.

He heard the sound of thundering footsteps. The door swung open, and Inspector Savage stepped inside. Behind him Jack could see a stairwell packed with coppers, all of them baying for blood. His blood. A couple of men at the top gasped as they saw the remains of the body on the ground, but Savage looked Jack squarely in the eyes.

"Jack Toop, I had a feeling you might show up here. I'm arresting you on the charge of three murders . . . that of Mr. Bazeley, who you have left so badly butchered on these premises . . . of Mr. Reeve, who lies before you, and of Inspector Heale of Scotland Yard."

Jack smiled and raised his dagger.

"Put it down, Jack," said Inspector Savage. "The game's over."

"Oh, no, the game is far from over," replied Jack, and ever so calmly he rammed the knife into his own neck.

73
THE FRENCH ANGEL

SAM STOOD OUTSIDE AYSGARTH HOUSE. HE LOOKED up the stairs leading to the door, but his feet remained rooted to the spot. He felt anxious about seeing Clara again. He planned to tell her everything. He wanted to be honest with her. He would explain the real reason he had entered her house before. He would tell her about his job and the errands he ran for the dead. He would tell her anything she wanted to know.

Except, how could he tell her the truth about Emily Wilkins? How could he admit that she had died because of him? Sam had judged his father for his part in a murder. It was only right that he now turn that judgment on himself. Sam wasn't just related to the Kitchen Killer. He was responsible for him.

The sound of an ear-piercing scream from within the house jolted Sam out of his paralyzed state. He rushed up the stairs and pushed the door open.

In front of him the ghost of Emily Wilkins hung in mid-air, slowly revolving. A priest stood before her muttering, with one arm outstretched. "Wretched spirit, you are lingering in a world that is not yours."

"Who are you? What do you want with me?" begged Emily.

"My name is Reverend Fallowfield, and you are a trespasser here," replied the priest.

"Please don't. It hurts!" The girl threw back her head in distress but appeared unable to move any other part of her body. He had her completely in his power.

"Leave her be!" yelled Clara. Her voice came from behind a closed door.

"What is this?" demanded Sam.

The priest turned to him and snarled, "Get out."

"Sam? Is that you?" cried Clara.

"Clara?" shouted Sam.

"Help me," said Emily.

Sam tried to step through the ghost to the door, but to his surprise, he felt her ice-cold hands on his face, blocking his way. Whatever spell Reverend Fallowfield had cast on her, it had made her as solid and as impassible as though she were alive again. Sam stepped back in shock.

"I'm sorry," said Emily. "I have no control."

"You have no business here, boy," said Reverend Fallowfield. He raised a finger and caused the girl to lift her arm, manipulating her like a puppet, in order to keep Sam from the door.

"What are you doing in this house?" demanded Sam.

"I am here to perform God's work," he replied.

"God's work is locking a girl in a room with a dead child as her guard?" replied Sam.

"Whatever it takes." Reverend Fallowfield's eyes twitched in their deep sockets, and it seemed to Sam that the three-pointed birthmark on his head turned a deeper shade of red.

"*Très bon*, Father." The voice came from another ghost that materialized in the hallway. This one was a smartly dressed man with a thin mustache. He spoke with a thick French accent.

"The angel," gasped Reverend Fallowfield, bowing his head.

"*Oui*," replied the ghost. "It is I, Monsieur Vidocq, your guardian angel."

Clara was banging on the other side of the drawing room door to no avail.

Monsieur Vidocq turned to Sam. "I see we have a Talker in our midst. What brings you here?"

"My name is Sam Toop. I am a friend of this family's. This man has locked a girl in that room."

"You are caught up in something far beyond your understanding," said Monsieur Vidocq dismissively. "But if you wish to see the wailing girl behind this door, you may simply follow me. Reverend Fallowfield, let him pass."

The French ghost slipped through the door, and Reverend Fallowfield moved Emily out of Sam's way. From the other side of the door, Clara let out a pained scream.

"What are you doing to her?" demanded Sam.

Sam hurriedly unlocked the door and entered. To his horror, he saw Clara hanging in the air while Monsieur Vidocq floated above, holding her by the hair. She screamed in agony. Sam charged in and grabbed her around the waist, taking the strain from her hair.

"Ah, her knight in shining armor," said Monsieur Vidocq. He released Clara and flew back into the hall, slamming the door shut behind him, locking them both inside the room.

Clara fell into Sam's arms, her face soaked with tears of pain from the torture she had endured. "What's happening?" she asked.

"I don't know," he replied. It was all he could think to say. He had no idea what any of it meant. But it didn't matter. Clara was in his arms. She was safe.

74

THE NEW RESIDENT OF AYSGARTH HOUSE

LAPSEWOOD HAD GROWN INCREASINGLY FRUSTRATED looking for Tanner. On and on, through street and alleyway, Lapsewood searched, his body turned to Ether Dust so he could cover more ground. Eventually, above a steeple in Aldwych he spotted a cloud of black smoke hanging in the air. He watched it as it suddenly swooped down to the street. The hellhound. To get close would be to risk its picking up on his scent, so Lapsewood kept his distance. He followed it to a house in a courtyard off Fleet Street. Lapsewood materialized and looked up at the building. He remembered it from the list. It was the first infected house he and Tanner had found.

Lapsewood thought of the Marquis and wondered what words of encouragement he would have conjured up for this moment. Faced with the possibility of stepping into an infected house, he would deliver a speech about freedom and sacrifice. He thought of poor old Grunt, lying in the gutter, wallowing in self-pity, drunk on spirit ale. He thought of Alice and Nell and Tanner. He thought about all the trusting spirit dogs they had sent into houses. He took a deep breath and entered Aysgarth House.

Stepping through the solid bricks into the hallway, he found, not the hellhound, but Monsieur Vidocq and the ghost of a young, ragged girl suspended in the air, looking utterly petrified. In front of her stood a priest, who turned as Lapsewood entered and sniffed. "I smell you," he muttered. "I can smell your presence."

"Your senses do not betray you, Reverend Fallowfield," said Monsieur Vidocq. "A second demon is among us." With the girl held by one of his straining hands, the priest moved his other toward Lapsewood, who suddenly felt his arms pressed down against his sides as though they were bound by unyielding rope. Reverend Fallowfield squeezed his hand, and Lapsewood felt as if it were crushing his windpipe.

"Don't . . . do . . . this," he gasped.

From another room he could hear two voices crying to be freed. One was male, the other female.

Monsieur Vidocq laughed. "You think you can tell me, Monsieur Eugène Vidocq, the world's greatest detective, what I should or should not do?"

"Colonel Penhaligan is using you," Lapsewood said.

"But of course," replied the French ghost. "He is employing my talents. Who else but Monsieur Vidocq would have found this priest? Who else could have persuaded him to do this necessary work, then provided him with the list with which he could do so? None but I."

"What you're doing is illegal," said Lapsewood.

"What poisonous lies does this demon spit?" demanded Reverend Fallowfield. "The only law I follow is that of God himself."

"That is right," said Monsieur Vidocq. "We are doing what is right."

"Allowing the hellhound to kill Rogue ghosts?" exclaimed Lapsewood. "You can't call that right."

Monsieur Vidocq shrugged. "It was you and your friend Tanner who created the beast," he said. "Fitting, then, is it not, that it has already devoured your friend's soul?"

"Tanner's gone?"

"The hound eats the scraps left over from life," said Monsieur Vidocq. "The hound services the city and keeps it free from unwanted pests like you."

Monsieur Vidocq turned to Ether Dust and swept across the room, rematerializing behind Lapsewood.

"Behold, the hellhound," he whispered in his ear.

From the opposite wall appeared a huge dark head with a long, pointed snout. It was as silent as the night, and its black eyes were fixed on Lapsewood.

"What new devil approaches?" asked Reverend Fallowfield, the fear visible in his eyes and audible in his quavering voice.

"This foul creature will help you destroy every wretched, unwanted soul in this city," said Monsieur Vidocq.

Held by Reverend Fallowfield, Lapsewood was unable to move. Slowly the hound approached until it wrapped its smokelike limbs around him and loomed over him. He struggled helplessly. The hound raised its head and let out a strange howl. Lapsewood heard the sound of a hundred splintered souls screaming in eternal agony. He shut his eyes, knowing that soon he would join those fragments. The demon hound edged forward, tightening around him. Squeezing. Crushing. Its long tongue protruded from its black jaws in anticipation.

Lapsewood shut his eyes.

Then, out of the darkness, he heard a voice speaking three words.

"Li'l Mags, no," it said.

"Tanner?" said Lapsewood, believing the voice to have come from within the creature itself.

"Not him, Li'l Mags. Not him," said Tanner.

Lapsewood felt the hellhound release him. The blackness subsided, and he slumped to the ground. When he stood again, he could see the creature cowering in the corner with Tanner standing in front of him. "Good girl, Li'l Mags," he said. "Good girl."

"You?" exclaimed Monsieur Vidocq angrily.

"Thank you, Tanner," said Lapsewood.

"You're welcome, Words," said Tanner.

"But how?"

Tanner grinned. "When this thing took hold of Li'l Mags's body, it also took some of her soul," he said. "And Li'l Mags, like all dogs, has a good soul. I've been hunting for her since this Frenchie tried to turn me into dog food in the park. I've tried to stop her killing, but she grows wilder with every soul she devours. She can't help it, poor girl."

"Ridiculous," responded Vidocq. "Spirit hounds and anomalies. They do not have souls. Reverend Fallowfield, dispense with these evil spirits in our midst."

"I can only exorcise one at a time," said the priest.

"Then get on with it," snapped Monsieur Vidocq.

Reverend Fallowfield raised his arms and lifted the weeping girl higher into the air. "Forces of the afterworld," he cried. "Draw near, push open the doors that lie between us, and devour this demon."

"I'll now bid you adieu," said Monsieur Vidocq, beginning to turn to Ether Dust.

"Oh, no, you don't," said Tanner. "Li'l Mags, dinnertime."

The hellhound pounced on Monsieur Vidocq and pinned him down.

"Get off me, you mutt," he cried. "I am no Rogue ghost. I am Monsieur Eugène François Vidocq, *the* great . . ." The rest of his words were lost in a terrible scream that grew like an orchestral crescendo of agony and rose up from between the demon hound's black jaws.

The hellhound devoured Monsieur Vidocq in a single bite.

"Draw near and dispense with this lingering spirit," cried Reverend Fallowfield, who was too focused on the torture of Emily Wilkins to notice anything else.

"Help me!" yelled Emily.

"We have to stop him," said Lapsewood.

"Leave it to me," said Tanner. Channeling all of his energy, he picked up a vase and hurled it at Reverend Fallowfield. It collided with his shoulder and smashed on the ground, but the Reverend barely flinched.

"Throw something else," urged Lapsewood.

"There is nothing else," said Tanner.

From the other side of the door, two voices shouted, "Let us out!"

"The Talker," said Tanner. He flew to the door and concentrated on turning the key. However, without Tanner to hold him back, the hellhound was on the move again. It sniffed at Emily's revolving feet.

"Get away!" she screamed.

But the hound opened its mouth and clasped its jaws around her ankles.

"Do not resist me, foul spirit," cried Reverend Fallowfield, feeling the spirit being tugged away from him.

"No, Li'l Mags!" yelled Lapsewood.

The hound's breath was tinged with the stench of tortured souls.

"Please!" screamed Emily.

"Open the gates that lie between this world and the next, and take this demon from us," cried Reverend Fallowfield.

Lapsewood looked up at the magnificent chandelier and realized what he had to do. He turned to Ether Dust and flew up.

Tanner finally managed to turn the key all the way. The door was flung open in time for Sam and Clara to witness Reverend Fallowfield laughing insanely. Sam saw with his right eye black cracks appear all around him, as though the priest were tearing holes in the air itself.

"Begone, foul spirit. Begone!" cried Reverend Fallowfield.

Emily screamed, caught between the jaws of the hellhound and the grip of Reverend Fallowfield. Above them, the huge chandelier rattled.

Reverend Fallowfield's hands shook violently as he yelled, "Let this spirit be banished forevermore!"

An ear-shattering cacophony of agony filled the air as Emily and the hellhound were both torn apart and vanquished into the Void. It was the sound of every half-digested soul inside the hound's belly being exploded into nothingness.

Silence followed. Tanner stared at the space where Reverend Fallowfield had held Li'l Mags and the girl. He tried to understand the horror he had just witnessed. Life after death was one thing. But this was something else. Death after death. He tried telling himself that ghosts couldn't feel pain, but he knew from Emily's agonized screams that her final moments were filled with unutterable agony and violence. As much as he tried to imagine that those poor spirits had moved on to a better place, he knew it was not so.

Reverend Fallowfield lowered his hands, exhausted. "And now for the rest of you," he muttered darkly.

The chandelier rattled. There was a creak. He looked up in time to see it come crashing down on his head.

In the doorway, Sam shielded Clara from the shattering crystal. When he turned to look again, the Reverend was lying flat, underneath a pile of broken glass. Unmoving. He was dead.

With his left eye, Sam could see Reverend Fallowfield's bloody body under the chandelier. With his right, he saw the Reverend's ghost standing next to him, his transparent skin decorated like a pincushion with the thousands of glass shards that had crushed him to death. The Reverend raised his hand and looked straight through it.

"I'm a . . . a . . ." he began.

But it didn't need to be said.

There came a Knocking.

"The Unseen Door," whispered Reverend Fallowfield, his ghostly eyes full of fear. "What lies on the other side?"

"Hopefully whatever you want to," said Lapsewood, rematerializing next to him.

"I'm scared," said Reverend Fallowfield, turning to face him.

"The unknown is a scary place," replied Lapsewood. "But look at your choices."

The ghost of Reverend Fallowfield nodded and solemnly stepped through the Unseen Door.

Clara, who was clinging to Sam, looked up at him. "Is it over?" she asked.

"I think so," he replied.

"Emily's gone, hasn't she?"

Sam nodded and held Clara tightly while she wept quietly.

"Never a dull moment when you're around, is there, Words?" said Tanner.

"Sorry about Li'l Mags," he replied.

"It's better this way. But you know what all this means. If this house's Resident has gone, one of us is stuck here."

"Yes, but which one of us?" asked Lapsewood.

"There's only one way to find out," replied Tanner. They looked at the outside wall.

"Ready?" said Lapsewood.

"Always ready," replied Tanner.

They both stepped forward. Lapsewood passed straight through while Tanner hit his head on Mrs. Tiltman's tasteful wallpaper.

Lapsewood stepped back inside. He placed a hand on Tanner's shoulder. "I'm sorry," he said.

"Don't worry about me," said Tanner. "I can think of worse places to be stuck. I knew a ghost who ended up stuck in a toilet. Imagine that. The rest of eternity surrounded by people doing their business. This will be fine."

75
JACK'S FUNERAL

SAM AND HIS FATHER LEARNED OF JACK'S DEATH from the newspaper. The report on the police's capture of the Kitchen Killer was full of exaggeration and overblown hyperbole, but one thing was clear. Jack Toop was dead. According to the report, he had taken his own life after confessing to the crimes and repenting the atrocities he had committed. Sam found this hard to believe.

Mr. Toop had been quick to consider the practicalities, announcing that he would go and speak to Inspector Savage about the body.

Sam couldn't remember the last time his father had gone to London. He offered to accompany him, but Mr. Toop said it would be better if he went alone and requested that Sam remain and help out Mr. Constable with the shop.

In fact, it was a quiet day at Constable & Toop. Mr. Constable busied himself by updating the accounts ledger, while Sam spent most of the day in the workshop, finding odd jobs to do. Around midday, Mr. Constable suggested they sit down to eat together.

Over lunch, Sam said, "How long do you think it will take?"

"Dealing with the police can be a lengthy process," Mr. Constable replied.

"Father has barely spoken since he heard the news. I can't tell whether he's upset or relieved."

"I would expect it to be both those emotions and many more. Jack was always trouble, but one cannot discount the bond of blood."

Sam felt no connection with his uncle, even though he had more than most, yet he couldn't rid his mind of thoughts of how he could have prevented all those deaths. "Do you really think Jack killed himself?" he asked.

"I can easily believe it," said Mr. Constable. "Jack preferred to take matters into his own hands. And the distinction between the living and the dead was especially blurred for him."

"You mean as it is for me?"

Mr. Constable shook his head solemnly. "I mean that Jack was dead inside long before he turned his knife on himself."

The winter sun was low in the sky when Mr. Toop returned with the body, wrapped in a cloth bag tied up with string. Mr. Constable helped him carry it to the back room. Mr. Toop took a knife and cut open the bag, revealing Jack's body. It was covered in congealed blood and dirt. His face was bruised and lifeless.

"I will clean him up tonight," said Mr. Toop.

"Is there any need?" asked Sam, concerned that such a job would take hours. "After all, we are the only ones who will see him."

"I can't bury him like this," said his father.

Mr. Toop toiled long into the night, and Sam fell asleep waiting to hear his footsteps on the stairs.

The following morning, Sam looked inside the coffin before they nailed down the lid. His father had done a good job. He had cleaned up the wounds, changed Jack's clothes, and combed his hair. It occurred to Sam that this was how he had first seen Jack, lying in a coffin, except this Jack didn't look like the same man at all. He wore no sneer on his lips. There was no fire in his eyes. Somehow this Jack looked more human.

A dense fog hung low over the cemetery. It felt strange to Sam to see his father at a funeral. As they stood beside the grave, he kept having to remind himself to listen to the vicar's words. The service was mercifully brief and impersonal. It would have felt wrong for the vicar to have spoken of Jack's contributions to the world or of the grieving loved ones he left behind.

Before they lowered the coffin into the ground, Mr. Constable requested permission to say a few words while Mr. Toop stared at the ground and said nothing.

"Many will judge Jack Toop for his actions in life," said Mr. Constable. "He was as flawed as all men are flawed men. But now that he is dead, we search for the strength to forgive. The dead deserve our respect. They can do no further harm, and gone is any hope of redemption. If the dead live on in our memories, let us try to remember them well."

"Thank you," said Mr. Toop.

The vicar said a final prayer, and the coffin was lowered into the ground. As they walked away from the grave, Mr. Toop and Mr. Constable kept their heads bowed, but Sam gazed searchingly into the fog. If Jack's ghost had resisted the pull of the Unseen Door, he would certainly be nearby. Sam had never met a ghost who had not attended his own funeral. He was relieved when he saw no sign of him.

Finally Sam could look past the dead who clouded his vision and see the living. Soon he would see Clara again. Walking slowly through the cemetery, he raised a hand to his face to hide his smile.

76

THE ENDLESS CORRIDOR

ALICE BIGGINS WAS LYING ON THE SINGLE BED IN her small room along the Endless Corridor. An unread book lay by her side. Sleep was the thing Alice missed most about being alive. She missed the ability to switch off. In life there was respite. Death was relentless. She wished now she had been more appreciative of afternoon snoozes, oversleeping, and early nights. Sometimes she tried to trick her ghostly body into thinking she was asleep, allowing her mind to drift into a fragmented, dreamlike state, hoping this would make the time pass faster.

When she heard a knocking sound, her first thought was that it was the Unseen Door and that finally her endless existence in the Bureau would be over.

It came again, and she realized it was just the door to her room. She stood up and opened it.

"Lapsewood," she said.

Lapsewood smiled. "Alice," he replied. "May I come in?"

"It's not safe for you here. Penhaligan's got half the Bureau looking for you."

"That's why I asked to come in," he said.

"Of course. Sorry." She moved aside, and Lapsewood closed the door behind him.

Alice had never had a visitor before. Unsure what to do with herself, she sat down on her bed. Lapsewood sat next to her. In his hands was a heavy-looking document bound with string.

"What is that?" she asked.

"My report," he said. "I'd like you to get it to General Colt."

"Why?"

"It has an updated Tenancy List for London. All the houses have ghosts now. It wasn't hard to find volunteers willing to enter infected houses once they knew the conse-quences of leaving them unoccupied."

"You're still working with Rogue ghosts?" said Alice.

Lapsewood sighed. "No. I'm working with ghosts. There's no difference between us and the Rogue ghosts. It's all in my report. It's not just the spirit hounds that are anomalies. We are all anomalies. The only difference between us and them is that we do more paperwork. Ghost status doesn't mean anything. Licenses, forms, permissions—none of it does anything except monitor what's going on. The Bureau just pretends it does to justify its own existence."

"So why do you want to give the report to General Colt?"

"Colt needs to assign a new Outreach Worker. They're the only visitors a lot of these Residents get. But there's more to it. Colt will take this report to one of the Cross-Departmental meetings. Then they'll have no choice but to see my findings. Once they learn what Penhaligan was planning, not even he will be able to wriggle out of it. It may take time, but Penhaligan's days are numbered, Alice. I'd be willing to wager that he won't see his centenary in this place. It's time for a change."

"But if nothing we do makes any difference, what's the point of any of it?"

"Alice, you and I have unfinished business. Aren't you curious to find out what it is?"

"Yes, I suppose . . . but I'd be scared, you know, of stepping into the Void."

"We're all so scared of the unknown, but who says it's something bad that happens when you go through the Unseen Door? Hanging around like this, living these half lives, doing work that doesn't need doing, filling out forms, following procedure, applying for licenses. We're all in limbo."

"So that's what you're going to do, is it?" asked Alice. "Finish your unfinished business?"

"I'm going to try. That's why I'm here." Lapsewood took Alice's hands in his own.

"You're confusing me," she said, looking into his eyes.

"That's because I'm confused," said Lapsewood. He smiled. "After a life and death of dull, predictable certainty, I'm finally confused. Beautifully confused, Alice. And that's how it should be. The world *is* confusing. But I do know one thing." Lapsewood gave Alice's hands a little squeeze. "Once you've delivered the report, I'd like to ask you out, Alice."

"Out? Where?"

"I don't mind. Paris . . . Vienna . . . Blackpool. We can go anywhere. We're free spirits, Alice. I don't mind where I am, as long as I'm with you. You see, I think you're my unfinished business."

"Me?" she exclaimed. "But we never even knew each other in life."

"I'm not explaining myself very well," said Lapsewood. "Love, Alice. I never loved. I *was* never loved. I never fell in love. Not in life. Not in death. Don't rot away in this miserable place. Come with me and see the world. Maybe we'll find our unfinished business, maybe we won't, but at least we'll be together. What do you say?"

Alice Biggins glanced at the drawn curtains in front of the window that looked out onto the Endless Corridor. She turned back to Lapsewood and smiled.

"Yes," she said.

77

HONOR OAK

CLARA STEPPED OFF THE TRAIN AND DREW THE fresh, cold winter air into her lungs. Her mother was ahead of her, talking to her father incessantly about new opportunities and bright beginnings. Clara had stopped listening. She knew what her mother was doing. Mrs. Tiltman needed to fill her head with thoughts about furnishings, wallpaper, and home decor to keep out the horror of a second corpse found in Aysgarth House.

Clara had spent every available minute since that day writing about the curious incidents of Aysgarth House, but the resulting work was too long for an article, and it was such an extraordinary and unbelievable tale that no newspaper or journal would publish it as fact. This didn't matter to Clara. She was no longer working on an article. The only way to do justice to the incredible truth she had learned was to turn it into a form that welcomed such flights of fancy. The only way to make it believable was to transform it into fiction. Clara finally understood what she was writing. It was going to be a novel.

The train pulled away, and Mr. Tiltman busied himself by organizing the team of porters who had been waiting to greet them. Clara looked up at the bridge. As the steam from the train drifted away, it revealed a boy with mournful eyes. She smiled at him and raised a hand.

Sam Toop smiled and waved back.

AUTHOR'S NOTE: THE WRITING OF
CONSTABLE & TOOP

THE IDEA FOR THIS BOOK CAME TO ME WHILE I SAT in a South London coffee shop. I was gazing at the funeral home opposite, and something in its name, *Constable & Toop*, leaped out at me. Once I had written down the name, the skeleton of the story appeared very quickly on the page. I should point out that, beyond sharing the same shop space in Honor Oak, the funeral parlor described in these pages bears no relation to its namesake and inspiration.

The story is set in 1884, the forty-seventh year of Queen Victoria's reign. Mourning was an important part of Victorian culture. The queen herself had worn nothing but black for over two decades, since the death of her beloved husband, Albert. Following her example, mourning rituals became more elaborate, funerals increasingly lavish, and the newly developed cemeteries boasted magnificent monuments to the wealthy dead. Death was a national obsession and, for those in the undertaking business, a lucrative occupation. By the 1880s there had been attempts by the National Funeral and Mourning Reform Association to curb the excesses of mourning, but many of the rituals and associated costs lingered on.

In the world of Victorian fiction, writers penned ghost stories exploring what happened after death. In the world of fact, newspapers pored over the lurid details of murders, turning the victims and murderers into celebrities. The more gruesome the killings, the better. In the autumn of 1888 they would become obsessed with London's most infamous killer, sensationally christening the anonymous murderer roaming the streets of Whitechapel "Jack the Ripper."

Among the books I found especially useful while researching this story were Catharine Arnold's *Necropolis: London and Its Dead*, Charles Dickens Jr.'s *Dictionary of London* (a guide to London published in 1888), and a number of ghost stories written by his father and other great nineteenth-century writers. Lee Jackson's excellent Web site, *The Victorian Dictionary*, was also an invaluable source when it came to recreating historically convincing dialogue.

But my main method of research was to take long walks around London. Once you start looking, you realize that

London is crammed with dates, stories, and history. Reading the plaques and signs and studying the buildings themselves can provide as much information as opening a book on the subject. Soon the entire city was transformed into a huge interactive museum for me to explore, each turn of a corner transporting me to another aspect of its rich history. These walks, intended to flesh out details of the story, actually fed the ever-growing plot.

On a cold January day I wandered into the Drury Lane Theatre and explained to the man on the door that I was looking for an old haunted theater. He informed me that Drury Lane was not only the oldest theater in London but the most haunted in the world. Later that day a tour guide, actor, and writer by the name of David Kerby-Kendall took me on a tour and told me about many of these ghosts, but it was the story of the Man in Gray that instantly grabbed me.

The ghost of Paddy O'Twain was an invention of my own, but the location of his pub came from the discovery of a plaque outside The Tipperary on Fleet Street, detailing the pub's history and giving its original name, The Boar's Head.

St. Paul's of Shadwell has been a favorite church of mine since I used to live in the area. It boasts the graves of seventy-five sea captains and has links with Captain Cook himself. When I went to look around, a pastor by the name of Andrew Sercombe was kind enough to let me in. A list inside revealed the name of the rector in 1884, although I was entirely responsible for Rector Bray's dubious character and for the story of the unfortunate bell ringer.

On buses and trains, in coffee shops and pubs, I wrote this book, while London's history bled into the pages. My daily wanderings took me to many valuable sources of research, including the Museum of London, the Museum of Transport, Bethnal Green Museum of Childhood, and the archive section of Lewisham Library.

Many of the houses, pubs, and streets are of my own invention, but I hope they have the ring of truth to them. I also took a number of liberties with historical details. Although this was a period of rapid suburban growth, I have exaggerated the extent of that development in Honor Oak and the surrounding area. I hope that anyone who notices any of the liberties I have taken will forgive them in the name of fiction.

I also hope that I will be forgiven by those dizzied by the sheer number of characters who worked their way into this story. Following its inception in that Honor Oak coffee shop, as I wandered the streets of London with my notebook, this book grew very rapidly and spread in many unexpected directions, very much like nineteenth-century London itself.

ABOUT THE AUTHOR

GARETH P. JONES IS THE AUTHOR OF THE DRAGON Detective Agency series (Waterstone's Book Prize shortlist), *The Thornthwaite Inheritance*, *Space Crime Conspiracy*, *The Considine Curse* (Blue Peter Book of the Year 2012), and the Ninja Meerkats series. In addition to writing, Gareth produces TV shows and plays a slightly ludicrous number of stringed instruments. He lives in South London with his wife and son.

This book was designed by Maria T. Middleton. The text is set in 12.5-point Mrs Eaves, a typeface created by Zuzana Licko in 1996. Designed as a revivial of the classic Baskerville face, Mrs Eaves was aptly named after Sarah Eaves, wife of the famous eighteenth-century typographer John Baskerville. The display font is Cg Virile.

This book was printed and bound by Worzalla in Stevens Point, Wisconsin. Its production was overseen by Kathy Lovisolo.